What a night. Face-to-face with Buck Bravo again.

And now she'd be expected to eat.

So B.J. faked drinking her wine. She even managed to get a little food down. On the polite conversation front, she nodded and made interested noises when spoken to. And she scrupulously avoided looking directly at Buck. No point in going there, nosiree.

Buck was, in all honesty, the man of the hour. There was talk that he'd get a Pulitzer for his last book. And the tabloids...to read what they wrote about him, you'd think every unattached woman in America longed to claim him for her very own.

Every woman except B.J. She didn't long to claim him. She only longed for him to go away.

And soon he *would* go away. He'd go off and write his story and leave her alone to come to grips with the fact that she was going to have his baby....

Dear Reader,

The editors at Harlequin and Silhouette are thrilled to be able to bring you a brand-new featured author program for 2005! Signature Select aims to single out outstanding stories, contemporary themes and oft-requested classics by some of your favorite series authors and present them to you in a variety of formats bound by truly striking covers.

We want to provide several different types of reading experiences in the new Signature Select program. The Spotlight books offer a single "big read" by a talented series author, the Collections present three novellas on a selected theme in one volume, the Sagas contain sprawling, sometimes multi-generational family tales (often related to a favorite family first introduced in series) and the Miniseries feature requested previously published books, with two or, occasionally, three complete stories in one volume. The Signature Select program offers one book in each of these categories per month, and fans of limited continuity series will also find these continuing stories under the Signature Select umbrella.

In addition, these volumes bring you bonus features...different in every single book! You may learn more about the author in an extended interview, more about the setting or inspiration for the book, more about subjects related to the theme and, often, a bonus short read will be included. Authors and editors have been outdoing themselves in originating creative material for our bonus features— we're sure you'll be surprised and pleased with the results!

The Signature Select program strives to bring you a variety of reading experiences by authors you've come to love, as well as by rising stars you'll be glad you've discovered. Watch for new stories from Janelle Denison, Donna Kauffman, Leslie Kelly, Marie Ferrarella, Suzanne Forster, Stephanie Bond, Christine Rimmer and scores more of the brightest talents in romance fiction!

The excitement continues!

Warm wishes for happy reading,

Marsha Zinberg

Marsha Zinberg
Executive Editor
The Signature Select Program

Signature Select™

SAGA

CHRISTINE RIMMER

BRAVO UNWRAPPED

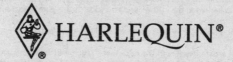

HARLEQUIN®

TORONTO • NEW YORK • LONDON
AMSTERDAM • PARIS • SYDNEY • HAMBURG
STOCKHOLM • ATHENS • TOKYO • MILAN • MADRID
PRAGUE • WARSAW • BUDAPEST • AUCKLAND

ISBN 0-373-28534-5

BRAVO UNWRAPPED

Copyright © 2005 by Christine Rimmer.

www.eHarlequin.com

Printed in U.S.A.

Dear Reader,

Strong women. You gotta love 'em. I do. I like to think
that I *am* a strong woman. And I like to write about strong
heroines, women who know what they want and aren't afraid
to go out and get it.

Such a woman is B. J. Carlyle, the heroine of *Bravo
Unwrapped*. B.J. is brilliant and, okay, she's more than a little
domineering. She loves pricey designer shoes and she's a
New Yorker through and through. She also happens to be
pregnant, *and* she's just decided that she's no good at the
man/woman thing. Her relationships somehow never work
out. She's giving up men.

I know what you're thinking: Not going to happen. You are so
right. Because, of course, there's the father of her baby,
Buck Bravo, the one man she's never been able to forget.

Buck can't forget her, either—and he doesn't even know
there's a baby involved. Buck has decided he's getting
himself another chance with B.J., whether B.J. wants that
chance or not. From New York to California and back again,
Buck is determined to lay claim to the woman he knows is
meant for him.

Happy holidays everyone,

Christine Rimmer

For my dad, who always believed I could do anything I set out to do—and who made sure that I believed it, too.

One

For B. J. Carlyle, features editor at *Alpha* magazine, that fateful day in late October started out in abject wretchedness—and went downhill from there.

B.J. was not someone who hit the snooze button as a rule, but that morning she did. She hit it. And she kept hitting it every five minutes for over an hour. Eventually, she realized it was either get up—or admit she was taking a sick day. B. J. Carlyle did not take sick days.

So she crawled out of bed groaning and headed straight for the bathroom, where she dropped to her knees, banged the seat lid back and threw up. Repeatedly.

By the time she finally stopped gagging and staggered upright, it was much too late for her usual session on the Stairmaster, let alone her blenderized breakfast cocktail of fruit juice and vitamin-packed protein powder.

Okay, she told herself. Fine. Tomorrow for the Stairmaster.

And the protein drink? Skipping it was not a problem, considering that the thought of gulping it down had her queasy stomach threatening to bring her to her knees again.

B.J. ate three saltine crackers and grabbed a quick shower. Precious extra minutes went into her makeup. She troweled on the concealer in a mostly failed effort to hide the ravages incurred by five virtually sleepless nights in a row. Finally, she put on her favorite short black pencil skirt and that cute pink Donna Karan silk blouse with the opera-glove sleeves and the wild spill of ruffles at the neck *and* the black snub-toed Pradas with the four-inch heels. Though she was a tall woman—five-eight in flats—on a day like this, she could use all the extra height she could get. She pulled on a short, snug pink leather blazer over the blouse, grabbed her big black alligator bag and her briefcase, and went out the door without so much as glancing at her message machine.

That little red light was blinking and she knew it. It had been blinking when she came in the night before. She knew who'd called. She'd checked the display.

Buck.

She wasn't talking to him—she wasn't even going to listen to his deep, sexy recorded voice. Uh-uh. Not a chance.

Downstairs, she waited, trying not to tap her toe, while sweet old Melvin, the doorman, got her a cab. Traffic on Broadway was a zoo—no surprise. The cab smelled of garlic and wet shoes. Her cell rang twice. Probably Giles, her right-hand man at *Alpha.* By now, Giles would be wondering where the hell she was.

B.J. ignored the calls. She stared out the side window at the sea of scurrying pedestrians and honking vehicles and told herself she was not going to vomit—garlic and stinky-shoe smell be damned. She was keeping down her three measly crackers and that was that.

At West 58th, she got out of the cab and sucked in a deep breath of lovely exhaust-rich, garlic-free air. She paid the cabbie. She tugged on her blazer and brushed at her skirt. Then she yanked her shoulders back, stuck her chin in the air and strode purposefully toward the black-marble-and-glass building that housed the offices of *Alpha* magazine. B.J.'s father, L.T. Carlyle, owned the building. *Alpha* had the fifteenth floor.

B.J. spent the ride up to the offices trying not to look at her own reflection in the elevator's mirrored walls and ignoring her cell, which was ringing again. She had that Bride of Chucky look around the eyes. Scary. Very scary. And she really should have used a little more blusher....

The doors slid wide and she was facing the *Alpha* reception desk, complete with stunning receptionist Melanie, who had exotic slanted eyes and preternaturally large lips—lips that went with her breasts, as a matter of fact. Melanie automatically beamed her blinding big-lipped smile, as she'd been trained to do whenever the elevator doors opened.

Then she realized it was B.J. "Oh! B.J. You're...late." Melanie stated the obvious with a look of pure bewilderment. B.J., after all, was never late. And beyond the bewilderment, didn't Melanie seem a little...guilty? She had a magazine open in front of her. She flipped it closed, folded her slim French-manicured hands on top of it and blinked three times in rapid succession.

Even with Melanie's tightly clasped hands in the way, B.J. could see enough of the cover to make a positive identification: *TopMale* magazine. Apparently, Melanie felt guilty for checking out *Alpha*'s competition. Did B.J. care what the receptionist read while she was supposed to be working?

Not today, she didn't. "Good morning, Melanie," B.J. announced vehemently, and headed for the hallway to the left of the desk.

Melanie called after her. "Uh. Giles says he needs to talk to you. He's been trying to reach you...."

B.J. stopped, pivoted on her mean black heels, and gave the receptionist her most terrifying smile. "And I'm headed his way as we speak, now aren't I? Or I was, until you stopped me."

"Uh. Well," said Melanie, coloring prettily. "Yeah. Okay. That's right...."

B.J. proceeded down the hall, sprinkling tight greetings at random colleagues as she went, careful not to make eye contact, which would encourage further communication. She was so not up for anything beyond "Hi," right then—not that anyone tried to get her talking. In fact, they all seemed a little...strange, didn't they? A little sheepish, their grins of greeting bordering on smarmy.

Or was she only being paranoid due to sleep deprivation, unremitting nausea and raging hormones?

Hmm. Could be.

Giles had the office next to hers. His door was open. She had to walk past it to get to her own. She was tempted to try that—zip right by, pop into her own office and shut the door. Silently.

Which was absurd. No point in coming to work just to hide in her office.

She stepped boldly into the doorway of Giles's narrow cubicle, which only achieved the designation of "office" because it had actual walls and a door he could shut. "What?" she demanded.

Giles tossed his head as he looked up. His sleek blond hair flew back out of his eyes. "God. I thought you must have *died.*" People assumed that Giles had to be gay, he was so pretty. He let them assume it. Women adored him. They felt *safe* with him, even though they weren't. He loved to gossip and he cared about fashion. His last name was CynSyr, pronounced *sincere*—which he actually was, on occasion. Giles spotted her shoes. "Darling. I love those. All you need is a whip."

"Is there a problem or not?"

"Unfortunately, there is." He peered at her more closely. "Are you…all right?"

She stood straighter and lied—aggressively. "Fabulous."

"Did you, ah, see the new issue of *TopMale,* by any chance?"

She scowled. "What is it with that? Melanie was reading it just now, when I came in."

"You haven't seen it "

"No. Why?"

"Ah—first, the good news." He grabbed the Starbucks cup at his elbow and held it out to her. "Decaf mocha almond. Venti. One packet of Splenda. Just the way you like it." His golden brows drew together and he wrinkled his aquiline nose. "Sorry, but it's luke-warm by now."

She stepped into the room and took the latte from him. "Thanks. You do have your uses."

"I figured you'd need it."

"I do." Assuming she could get it down without hurling. She gestured with the covered cardboard cup. "Okay. Let me have it."

"Disaster, that's all."

Her stomach lurched. She swallowed. Hard. "I'm listening."

"The Wise Brothers just broke up," Giles said. "Their manager called Mike yesterday. They're not going to be available for the Christmas cover story."

The Wise Brothers were the biggest thing to hit popular music since…comparisons failed her. And this was not good. Very, very not good.

B.J. shoved a stack of back issues off Giles's lone extra chair and sank into it, dropping her briefcase to the floor, letting her bag slide off her shoulder. "Tell me you're joking."

Giles did nothing of the kind. "I'm as serious as a cheap tie. Trust me. 'Christmas with the Three Wise Men' is history."

"But…a different slant, maybe? Their new solo careers? Their, uh…"

Giles was shaking his golden head. "They don't want to do it. They are all, and I'm quoting Mike quoting the manager, 'devastated.' They're also all in seclusion, or some such crap. Mike tried all day yesterday to get through to at least one of them. No luck. And we both know that if Mike can't get to them, nobody can." Mike Gallato, one of the best, was *Alpha*'s top contributing editor.

And B. J. Carlyle never gave up a major story without a fight. She shouldered her bag again, grabbed up her briefcase and shot to her feet. "I'll make a few calls."

"Been done. It's hopeless."

"Never use that word around me."

"Yes, Mistress."

"Hah." She started to turn.

Gingerly, from behind her, Giles suggested, "Just… a point or two more."

She whirled back to him. "Speak. Fast."

"Arnie wants a meeting at eleven to discuss your plans." Arnie Dale was the managing editor. In recent years, Arnie pretty much ran things at *Alpha,* though B.J.'s father, who had created *Alpha* on their kitchen table back when B.J. was in diapers, had never relinquished his twin titles of publisher and editor-in-chief.

B.J. prompted, "My plans for…?"

Giles looked at her patiently. "The new Christmas-issue cover feature."

She blew out a gusty breath. "Fine. Meeting at eleven." She looked at her watch. Nine-thirty-two. She needed to get going on those calls. "Anything else?"

"Ah. Yes." Giles wore the strangest expression, suddenly. Pitying? Worried? She couldn't read it. B.J. made an awkward wrap-it-up gesture with the hand that held her briefcase, after which Giles clucked his tongue and tossed his golden locks again. Then, at last, the perfect line of his square jaw hardened. His fine nostrils flared. He yanked open his pencil drawer and whipped out the latest issue of *TopMale* magazine— the one Melanie had been reading so furtively a few minutes before.

"Oh, please," B.J. said. "As if I've got time to read *that* rag with my December cover feature dead at my feet."

Giles stood—or sat, in this case—firm. "Darling. You *need* to read this."

"Just give me the salient points."

Giles only shook his head and shoved the magazine toward her. "I marked the page. Go in your office, sit down, drink your lukewarm latte and then deal with that. And when you do, keep in mind that it's nothing but meaningless drivel written by a dickless ass."

In her office, with the door firmly shut, B.J. set down her bag and briefcase, tossed the November issue of *TopMale* to the side of her desk, hung her jacket on the coat rack in the corner, booted up her computer, and made those calls.

Giles had been right, of course. She got nowhere. The Wise Brothers had called it quits, they weren't talking to anybody and she had no cover story for the issue that would hit the stands in twenty-eight days.

There would definitely be meetings. Several.

Her head pounded and her stomach churned. Still, gamely, she picked up her latte and removed the lid. She sniffed. Waited.

And didn't gag.

Carefully, she sipped.

Oh, yes. Excellent. It was almost cold, but it went down fine.

Sipping some more, she considered. She had a half an hour until the meeting with Arnie. So? E-mail, phone messages—there had been several new ones while she was making all those hopeless calls—or *TopMale?*

She picked up the phone and punched the code for message pick-up.

Big mistake. The first one was from Buck. She heard his voice—so deep, so sexy, so gallingly tempting. "B.J. Give it up. Give me a damn call."

She slammed the phone down. Later for messages. With a heavy sigh, she slid *TopMale*—by a corner—

from the side of her desk to right under her nose. She sneered down at the eye-candy guy on the cover. A winning smile and six-pack abs. Not terribly imaginative, but effective.

TopMale didn't have *Alpha*'s market share, or its cachet. After all, *Alpha* managed to be all things to a wide cross-section of men. From bon vivants to backwoods survivalists to your everyday Joe with a beer in one hand and the remote in the other, they all bought *Alpha*. Still, the upstart *TopMale* did have a solid readership, a readership that kept growing....

B.J. flipped the magazine open to the page Giles had marked for her. She drank her cold latte and began reading.

Manhattan Man-Eater

Well, okay. A reasonably catchy title. Then she read the byline: by Wyatt Epperstall.

The last time she'd seen Wyatt was the day four months ago when she'd told him she *wouldn't* be seeing him anymore.

Her hand began to shake. Cool milk and espresso sloshed on her wrist and stained her pink blouse.

He wouldn't.

He *couldn't*....

Oh, but he had.

You know her when you see her. She's tall and she's smart and she has great legs. Great legs and killer shoes on her narrow, perfect feet. You know the kind of shoes I mean. Shoes with fancy Italian names and price tags to match, shoes with high, pointed heels that have you dreaming of what it might be like if she wore them and took a walk on your chest.

If you're lucky, she might do just that.

She makes the rules. And she makes sure you live by them. That is, until she's through with you—which, believe me, will be sooner than you think.

Okay, big guy. I know what you're muttering right about now. No driven, focused, powerful steamroller career woman for you. You don't go for that type.

Let me tell you. You would. You could. In the dark heart of every man lies a yearning for a dangerous woman he cannot control. She is that woman. She could have you if she wanted you. One glance from those frosty gray-blue eyes and you are her slave.

In bed, she—

B.J. shut her—admittedly—gray-blue eyes. But shutting them didn't do any good. When she opened them again, the damn article was still there—the article about *her* written by her sleazeball ex-boyfriend, Wyatt. Oh, she should have known better than ever to get involved with him.

He'd seemed so...*nice.* So harmless. So sweet, really. At first, anyway. But then the niceness began to get on her nerves. The sweetness got cloying. She found herself doing what she always did with men she'd dated in the past six years: she compared him to—

No. Not the B-word. She wasn't thinking about B— No way. No more. Not today.

And she really, truly had to face it: she was good at a lot of things. Especially her job. But men? Not her forte. Every time she tried with one—which wasn't all that often, no matter what Wyatt Epperstall wanted every *TopMale* subscriber to think…whenever she tried with one, it always ended badly.

Just like it had with Buck.

Oh, God. Buck…

And there. She'd done it. Thought his whole first name, again—twice—not thirty seconds after promising herself she wouldn't.

Note to self: Do not think of B.

Second note to self: No. More. Boyfriends. Ever.

And really, she should never have taken that big sip of latte. Because, for some reason, her swallowing mechanism seemed to be malfunctioning. Her stomach was rising.

B.J. knocked over her chair as she stood. The latte went flying. It hit the floor and splattered—across the floor tiles, up the wall. She glanced frantically around.

Oh, God. What she wouldn't give right now for the corner office—the one her father never used, the one with its own damn bathroom, for pity's sake.

She spotted her wastebasket in the corner. What else could she do? Making hideous gagging noises, she staggered toward it.…

Good thing she had Giles. Once she was through ruining both her blouse and the wastebasket, she buzzed him and he came right in.

He shut the door. "Darling, my God," he said, wincing and wrinkling his patrician nose. Then he considered. "Ditch the blouse. Wear the blazer, buttoned up. It's going to be fine. I'll just crack the window…"

He went out while she changed and came back with one of the maintenance people. She escaped to the ladies' room. When she returned, her office smelled of floral air freshener. The wastebasket had been replaced and the splattered latte mopped up. She gave the maintenance guy a massive tip and he took the blouse, promising he'd have it back, good as new, in a day or two.

"Alrighty." She forced a grateful smile, thinking at the same time that if she never saw that blouse again, it would be more than alrighty with her. The janitor left her alone with her assistant.

Giles looked at her and frowned. "Go home," he said.

"Not on your life—BTW, you are invaluable."

"I am, aren't I?"

"And it's ten-fifty-five. Arnie awaits…."

The meeting was not a success.

They came up with zip. The alternative features simply wouldn't do. Either the slant was wrong or the story wasn't big enough for the cover. There was nothing in the works that could effectively be moved up. Fresh ideas were in short supply.

Arnie told her to "work it out" and get back to him by the end of the day.

After the meeting, there was lunch. B.J. took a pass on that. She ate more crackers from the box she'd stowed in her desk and drank some water and racked her exhausted brain for a solution to the cover-feature dilemma. Racking did nothing. Her brain refused to spit out a single viable idea.

The afternoon brought more meetings. Tense ones. She made frequent trips to the restroom and avoided the eyes of her colleagues. When she wasn't in a meeting or hugging the toilet bowl, she received sniggering and/or sympathetic calls from acquaintances and associates who had seen—one even went so far as to say she had *devoured*—the "Man-Eater" article.

At four-thirty she met with Arnie again—to tell him she'd have something for him by the next day. Arnie was not pleased.

At five, as she and Giles were brainstorming madly, her outside line, set on silent page, began flashing. She glanced at the display. Her father. So *not* the person she wanted to talk to right then. But also not someone she could ignore.

"L.T.," she said to Giles. Her father's name was Langly Titus, but everyone, including B.J., called him L.T.

Giles nodded, got up, and left her alone.

She picked up. "Hello, L.T."

"We need to talk," said her father, and then fell silent. L. T. Carlyle fully understood the power of silence. He would make pronouncements, then wait. And wait some more. First one to speak was the loser. L.T. never lost.

B.J. allowed a full count of ten to elapse before prompting wearily, "About?"

More silence. Then, at last, "First, and of minimal importance, that pissant, Wayne Epstein."

"Wyatt. Wyatt Epperstall," she patiently corrected as her stomach gave a nasty little lurch. So. L.T. had read the "Man-Eater" article. She wasn't surprised. Though he rarely left his world-famous mansion, Castle Carlyle, upstate, L.T. made it his business to know just about everything that was going on in the outside world. He subscribed to every newspaper and magazine known to man, *TopMale* included. And he could read two thousand words a minute.

"Wyatt, schmyatt," grumbled L.T. "A wimpy,

whiny-assed piece of work if ever there was one. Didn't I warn you about him?"

"Yes," she said carefully. "I believe that you did."

L.T. laughed his lusty laugh. "But I have to say, B.J. You make your old dad proud."

"Oh? How's that?" she asked, though she knew she wouldn't like the answer.

She didn't.

He said, "'Manhattan Man-Eater.' That's my girl. Tough, smart and always on top. Takes after her old man, and that is no lie."

"Gee, L.T. I never thought of it that way."

"Do I detect a note of sarcasm? Stand tall. Be proud. Let the Waldos of the world whine and whimper."

"Wyatt. The weasel's name is Wyatt. And I'm sorry. But I don't see it that way. That article just happens to be a total invasion of my privacy."

Her father swore. Eloquently. "B.J. You shame me. You've got to do something about that Puritanical streak."

That was way below the belt. B.J. was no Puritan, far from it. But she wasn't an exhibitionist either. She wanted the details of her private life to remain exactly that: private.

She said nothing. She told herself she was exercising the power of silence on L.T. for a change, though in reality she was simply too frustrated and miserable at that moment to speak. Her head pounded and her stomach kept threatening to eject its contents all over her desk pad.

She hated to admit it, but maybe she should have stayed home today, after all.

L.T. moved right on to the next item on his agenda. "I heard about the Three Wise Men." Again, no surprise. Arnie would have called him. "Too bad, so sad. And I've got it covered."

She sat a little straighter. "Meaning?"

"I'm on top of the problem. I'll tell you all about it. Tonight. Dinner at eight. Be here. We'll put this situation to bed."

"A story?" She sounded ridiculously grateful—and she didn't even care that she did. "You've got my Christmas feature story?"

"I have. And it's good. Very good. Puts those puny Wise Men to shame—if I do say so myself."

"The story. What is it?"

"Tonight."

"L.T., I can't. Not tonight. I'll be here at the office until nine, at least. I have a mountain of work to…" She heard the click, right there in the middle of her sentence. Her father had hung up.

During the limo ride upstate, B.J. tried to work. Her queasy stomach wasn't going for it. She ended up staring out the window, tamping down her frustration and resentment that L.T. just had to step in, that he'd ordered her presence upstate and refused to listen when she tried to tell him she didn't have time for the trip. The loss of the Wise Brothers was *her* problem, *her* challenge to handle as she saw fit.

Or at least, it should have been.

Then again…

I'm a true professional, she reminded herself— which meant she'd take any help she could get. And as autocratic as he could be at times, her father was a genius when it came to knowing—and getting—what was needed for *Alpha.* So if L.T. said he had her cover story, he probably did.

She shouldn't be so put out with him—and she wasn't, not really.

Not any more than she was put out with her life in general in the past five days. Or maybe not so much put out as *freaked* out. Since the stick turned blue, as they say. Since the panel said pregnant.

Six years since she called it quits with…B. She'd moved on. He'd moved on.

And then, seven weeks ago, she'd run into him. Your classic Friday night at that great club in NoHo, the underground one with the incredible sound system. Fabulous music and one too many excellent Manhattans and they'd ended up at his place. She wasn't careful—with B, that had always been her problem: a failure to be careful.

Or one of her problems, anyway. To be painfully frank, there were several.

So she'd slipped up, she'd reasoned, feeling like a drunk off the wagon, a junkie back on the stuff. Once in six years. That wasn't so bad she kept telling herself. Oh, no. Not so bad. Not to worry. She wasn't taking his calls. He was out of her life and she'd make absolutely certain that what had happened in September would never happen again…

And then, just when she'd pretty much succeeded in convincing herself that one tiny slip-up did not a crisis make, she'd realized her period was late.

Very late.

Thus, the disastrous encounter with the pregnancy kit five mornings ago. Now, everything was all messed up all over again.

And speaking of again, she was doing it. Again. Thinking about B, and what had happened with B *and* the result of what had happened with B—all of which was *not* to be thought about. Not tonight. Not…for a while.

The limo rolled up to the iron gates that protected the Carlyle estate. The gates swung silently back. The stately car moved onward, up the long, curving drive that snaked its way through a forest of oak and locust trees, trees somewhat past their fall glory and soon to be winter-bare.

At the crest of the hill, the trees gave ground and there it was: Castle Carlyle, a Gothic monstrosity of gray stone, a Norman conqueror's wet dream of turrets and towers looming proudly against the night sky.

Roderick opened the massive front door for her. Roderick was tall and gaunt and always wore a black suit with a starched white shirt and a bow tie. He'd run the castle since before her father had bought the estate from an eccentric Dutch-born millionaire twenty years back. L.T. liked to joke that Roderick came with the castle.

"Ms. B.J. Lovely to see you," Roderick said with a faint, slightly pained smile. He wasn't very good at smiling. Loyalty and efficiency were his best qualities.

"Roderick," she said with a nod, as he relieved her of her bag and briefcase. "The oak room?" she asked. Roderick inclined his silver-gray head. She told him, "I'll see myself in."

"As you wish."

Her heels echoing on the polished stone floor, B.J. proceeded beneath the series of arches down the length of the cavernous entry hall, past a dizzying array of animal heads mounted along the walls. For about a decade, back when B.J. was growing up, L.T. had amused himself hunting big game all over the world.

Being neither a modest nor a subtle man, L.T. proudly displayed every trophy he took—whether it was a handsome buck with a giant rack, or one of an endless string of gorgeous girlfriends known in the press as his *Alpha* Girls.

The oak room, named for the dark, heavily carved woodwork that adorned every wall, branched off toward the end of the entrance hall. The room boasted a long bar at one end, also ornately carved. L.T., wearing his favorite maroon satin smoking jacket over black slacks, sat in a leather wing chair near the bar, a Scotch at his elbow and one of his trademark Cuban cigars wedged between the fingers of his big, blunt-fingered right hand.

His current *Alpha* Girl, Jessica, had found a perch on the arm of his chair. Jessica was, as usual, looking stunning. Tonight she wore red velvet, her plunging neckline ending just below the diamond sparkling in her navel. As B.J. entered, Jessica threw back her slim golden neck and trilled out a breathless laugh.

L.T. and his *Alpha* Girl weren't alone. On a brocade sofa across a Moorish-style coffee table from the pair sat the one person B.J. did not want to see.

Buck Bravo, in the flesh.

Two

Jessica spotted B.J. first.

"B.J.," said the *Alpha* Girl breathlessly—Jessica did just about everything breathlessly. "How *are* you?"

"About time," said L.T., and puffed on his cigar. He tipped his steel-gray head in Buck's direction. "As I recall, you two have met."

B.J. resisted the urge to say something scathing. L.T. knew very well that she and Buck had once been in love. He also knew that it had ended badly and that Buck was not, by any stretch of an active imagination, B.J.'s favorite person.

Yes, okay. She'd had sex with the man last month. Or nearly two months ago, actually. Sometimes even a smart woman makes mistakes, especially when there are too many Manhattans involved. But no way would L.T. know that. Buck could be ten kinds of unmitigated

SOB, but he wasn't the type to go blabbing about subjects that were nobody's business.

"Hello, Buck," she said and tried not to sneer.

"B.J." He looked at her through those sexy dark eyes of his and, in spite of her determination to remain unaffected, she felt the familiar thrill go pulsing through her.

Dumb. Stupid. Never again.

She ordered her mind off steamy images of her and Buck—in his bed, minus their clothes—and turned to her father. "I thought you ordered me up here to discuss my Christmas cover feature."

L.T. blew out a thick cloud of cigar smoke. "That is exactly what I did."

B.J. sent a sideways glance at the handsome hunk of aggravating temptation sprawled on the crimson sofa—and then spoke to L.T. again. "Buck has a story?"

"Not *a* story," said her father, gesturing grandly with his double corona. "*The* story."

Her pulse picked up—this time for purely professional reasons. Buck, after all, was your quintessential *Alpha* male. He was not only a gold miner, a cowpuncher, a wildcatter and a bull rider. He also just happened to be a top-notch journalist and a bestselling author. *Black Gold,* his gritty exposé of life—and death—on a Texas oil rig, had hit the bookstores in June and quickly climbed all the major lists.

If Buck had a story for her…

Oh, yeah. Just his name on the byline would be a coup. She should have thought of him. And she probably would have—if they didn't have a serious past. If she hadn't been so busy ignoring his phone calls. If she didn't just happen to be pregnant with his baby…

She made herself look directly at him. "Okay. I'm listening."

Buck smiled that charming, infuriating, warm, slow smile of his. The one that had made her fall in love with him in the first place, back in that fateful February, when they were both slaving away in the boiler room of *Alpha*'s circulation department. Back then, B.J., fresh out of Brandeis, was in the early stages of learning her father's company from the ground up. Buck? Straight off a West Texas oil rig, still shaking the red dust off his boots, getting his start in the big city, determined to be a writer, though he had no formal education beyond a high-school diploma.

"Well?" she prompted, when Buck gave her nothing except that killer smile.

Her father chuckled. "Patience, B.J. How about a drink?"

"I'll pass."

L.T. stubbed out his hundred-dollar cigar in the brass dish beside his glass of Scotch. Then he stood and held out his hand to Jessica. With a glowing smile, she took it. He kissed her slim fingers. "Then let's sit down to dinner, shall we?" He gestured at the round table across the room. It was set for four, with a white cloth, gleaming crystal and china rimmed in gold. "Nothing like a good meal to get the creative juices flowing."

What a night. Face-to-face with Buck again. And now she'd be expected to eat. Her father loved nothing so much as a nice, big slab of rare red meat. Ugh. "If you'll excuse me, I'd like to…freshen up a little."

In the lavish black-marble half bath across the main hall, B.J. washed her hands and fluffed her hair and dreaded going back out there and dealing with Buck. But it had to be done and somehow, she would manage it. She would be pleasant. And professional. She'd get the damn story and—at work, at least—things would be fine until the next crisis came along.

She joined the others in the oak room, sliding into the chair between Buck and L.T. with a determined smile on her face. Roderick came in and opened the wine. Colette, one of the maids, appeared and began serving the meal.

B.J. faked drinking her wine. She even managed to get a little food down. On the polite conversation front, she nodded and made interested noises and spoke when spoken to. And she scrupulously avoided looking directly at Buck. No point in going there, nosiree.

Colette had served the main course—rare venison, wilted greens and whipped sweet potatoes—when L.T. finally got down to business.

"Arnie called me this morning and told me the problem. The solution came to me instantly, as it so often does. I thought, *Buck Bravo.* And immediately after, *Of course. Who else?* So I gave Buck a call. And wouldn't you know? Buck was amenable *and* told me he could make himself available.

"The December cover feature—" L.T. raised his glass of cabernet high and then paused to knock back a mouthful "—will *be* Buck."

B.J., who had her own wineglass near her lips at that moment, set it down without even pretending to drink from it. "Buck's the story?"

Her father laughed. "Yes, indeed. Buck Bravo. His life, his past, how he got where he is now."

B.J. turned her full glass by the stem and admitted, "All right. It's good…."

"Good?" crowed her father. "It's a damn sight better than good. It's perfect. Ideal. Terrific. Better than terrific."

Buck cut in. "Well, I wouldn't go that far…"

"I would," L.T. insisted. "Any story the competition would do murder to get is, unequivocally, better than terrific. Right, B.J.?"

"Right," B.J. gave out grudgingly. Buck was, in all honesty, the man of the hour. There was talk that he'd get a Pulitzer nomination for *Black Gold*. The tabloids couldn't get enough of him. To read what they wrote about him, you'd think every unattached woman in America longed only to claim him for her own.

Every woman except B.J. She didn't long to claim him. She only longed for him to go away.

And as soon as they got the details ironed out here, he *would* go away. He'd go off and write his story and leave her alone to come to grips with the fact that she was going to have his baby.

Argh.

Colette cleared off the plates and began serving brandy, dessert and coffee. L.T. lit up another corona and continued to rave—about how Buck's hometown, a tiny mountain hamlet in the mountains of California, was named New Bethlehem Flat. "Bethlehem. Could it get any better? And the Bravo family history? Pure gold—scratch that. Platinum. Platinum all the way…"

Buck's father, the notorious Blake Bravo, the "bad seed" of the Los Angeles Bravos, had faked his own death at the age of twenty-six. Once everyone believed the evil Blake dead, he went on to kidnap his own brother's baby son for a king's ransom in diamonds and to litter the American landscape with illegitimate children—Buck and his three brothers among them.

Blake had died for real a few years ago and the whole story had at last come out. A day late and a few dollars short, as they say. Because Blake Bravo had managed to live on for thirty years *after* everyone believed him dead. He'd gone to his grave without answering for a single one of his many crimes.

L.T. announced, "So it's 'Buck Bravo: Unwrapped.' Could there be a better holiday cover story?"

B.J. silently agreed that there couldn't.

And it was about time she got past her personal issues with Buck and took control of this discussion. "All right, L.T. I'm convinced. It's a great story and we'll go with it."

"Great? It's—"

"I know, I know. It's better than great." She turned her head in Buck's direction and looked at him without actually meeting his eyes. "I'll settle the details with your agent tomorrow, and you'll get going on it right away."

"Agreed."

"I'll need you to pull it together in two weeks, if you can manage that. There is some leeway—just not much."

"I understand."

"I'm thinking I can get Lupe to go with you to California for the pictures." Lupe Martinez was their top contributing photographer. "Is there snow in the Sierras yet?" she pondered aloud. "There had better be. This *is* the Christmas feature, after all."

Buck let out a low chuckle, one that sizzled annoyingly along every one of her nerve endings. "I'll see what I can do about the weather."

"Thank you." B.J. realized it was time to be gracious—and grateful. "I'm…so pleased about this, I truly am."

"Glad to help out."

"I know you'll write us a terrific Christmas feature. I can't wait to read it."

"But I'm not writing it."

B.J. opened her mouth to lay on more compliments—and snapped it shut without speaking. Surely she hadn't heard him right. "Excuse me?"

"I said, I'm not writing it. You are. You're going with me. And you're right. We should leave tomorrow. I'm guessing L.T. will provide one of his jets."

"Happy to help out." Her father beamed, an overbearing Santa in a smoking jacket. "No problem. The jet is yours."

Stunned and appalled at the mere idea of being thrown into constant contact with Buck for days running, B.J. gaped. Openly. Her head swiveled from her father to Buck and back to her father again—and she saw the truth right there in L.T.'s pewter-gray eyes. He had *known* this was coming. How could he do this to her—and not even give her a heads-up in advance?

A thousand volts of pure fury blazed through her. She was certain her hair must be standing on end. Her stomach clenched tight—and then rolled. She looked down at her coffee, at the creamy chocolate dessert with its topping of fresh whipped cream. The few bites of food she'd eaten lurched upward toward her throat.

She gulped—hard. "Excuse me," she said quietly—and then she shoved back her chair and dashed for the bathroom.

"Is she sick or something?" asked the doe-eyed Jessica as B.J. raced toward the door to the entrance hall, pointed heels tap-tap-tapping.

"Yeah. Sick of me," Buck replied with a grim

smile. Things weren't going exactly as he'd hoped. Uh-uh. Not as he'd hoped—but pretty much as he'd expected.

"Maybe it was the venison," said L.T. philosophically. He shrugged and blew a few smoke rings. "Seemed fine to me, though."

"She's upset." Jessica, distressed, stated the obvious. Both men turned to look at her. "Well, she *is,*" Jessica insisted in that breathy way of hers. "I'm sorry, Buck. But, you know, I don't think she likes you."

"No kidding?"

"And I don't get it. Why would you want to make *her* write the story? *You're* the one who writes." Jessica's smooth brow furrowed as if great thoughts troubled her. "Aren't you?"

L.T. chuckled and puffed on his cigar and, for once, didn't comment.

That left Buck to make a noncommittal noise in his throat and take a sip of the excellent brandy and wonder if he was biting off a big wad more than he would ever be able to chew.

Maybe so.

Should he back down, agree to head home to California with only a photographer for company? Write the damn story and turn it in and forget it—forget B.J.?

Hell. Probably.

But then there she came, tap-tap-tapping back to the table in her skinny little skirt and dangerous black shoes, shoulders back and head high. She looked sexy as all get-out—and also ready to start spitting nails.

Buck still wanted her. He wanted her bad. The past year or so he'd come to grips with the fact that maybe he always would.

Back down? Not this time. This time he was taking

it all the way. And if she wanted her damn cover story, she could come and get it—*his* way.

"Are you all right, B.J.?" Jessica asked, doe eyes wider than ever.

B.J. slid into her seat again. "I have been better," she informed L.T.'s girlfriend with a stately nod of her shining blond head. "Thank you for asking." She turned on L.T. again, eyes stormy, mouth set. "In case you might have forgotten, I have a department to run. I can't just go traipsing off to the wilds of California. And really. Where is the sense in this? That Buck's got the byline is half of the story." She threw up both hands. "Oh, this is all just too, too insane. He's going to do a much better job of writing the damn thing than I ever could. That's what he *does*—write."

L.T. waved a hand, dismissing her objections. "Don't worry about the features department. Giles can handle things for a week or two. And the piece shouldn't be a memoir. It needs an objective eye."

B.J. looked at her father as if she'd like nothing better than to grab his cigar from between his fingers and put it out in his face. "Excuse me. An *objective eye?*"

Her father faced her right down. "That's what I said."

"Oh, please. It's better with Buck's name on the byline, don't try to kid me it's not."

L.T. nodded. Regally. "Unfortunately, he's not offering his name on the byline. And we have to work with what we can get."

She whipped around to glare at Buck again. "Come on. Write it yourself."

He only shook his head.

"You…" Evil epithets lurked right behind those lips he couldn't wait to kiss again.

But she held them in. She sat back in her chair, regrouping. Buck could practically *see* her quick mind working. Cornered but still swinging, she tried again. "I can't see any reason to pay you, if you're not doing the writing."

"Fine. Leave my agent out of it."

"We will. And I'll get someone else to write the piece. Someone really good. Mike Gallato should be available, now the Wise Brothers thing fell through. I can call him right now and we can—"

"No," said L.T. "You're going to write it. And you'll do a fine job. It'll be good for you. You need to get out in the field now and then, anyway."

"Listen very carefully," B.J. said in a voice that could have flash-frozen the testicles off a bull. "I'm *not* going to do this." Her eyes were wild, her mouth a thin line. Two bright spots of color rode high on her cheekbones. Other than that, her face was much too pale.

Buck frowned. Had Jessica been right?

Was she sick?

He wanted to ask her for himself if she was okay. But he didn't. B.J. absolutely refused to show weakness, anytime or anywhere. If he asked, he'd get nothing but a snarled denial. No point in going there.

She said, tightly, "Buck. Listen. I assure you. If you don't want to write this yourself, it's going to be no problem finding someone else, someone really…topnotch. Someone much better than I would be."

Again, for a split second, he wavered. But not long enough that she could see it in his eyes. He was going for it. Going the whole way. And, whether she liked it or not, she was going with him.

True, at the moment, she was madder than a peeled rattler at him for roping her into this. But she'd get over it. He'd have as long as he could keep her in California to make her admit that the two of them were far from over. A big job, admittedly. But Buck Bravo was accustomed to life-and-death challenges.

"No," Buck said. "I want *you*, B.J. You come with me to California and write the story. Or the whole thing is off."

L.T. sipped his brandy and waved his cigar. "Sorry, B.J. But it looks like the decision's been made for us."

Three

Trapped and fully aware of the fact, B.J. stewed all the way home in the back of her father's big, black limousine.

Looks like the decision's been made for us, L.T. had said.

"Us," B.J. muttered under her breath as the car hummed across the Henry Hudson Bridge. *Us?* She should have ripped that prize rhino head off the far wall when her father said that, just got up and ripped it off the wall and stabbed him to the heart with that big, fat horn.

For the first time, as she rode through the nighttime streets of uptown Manhattan, she actually considered quitting *Alpha.*

But the magazine—and her dream of running the whole enterprise someday—had been her life. She simply wasn't ready to walk away from it.

Not yet.

Not ever.

And because she wasn't ready to walk out, she was off to California at ten tomorrow morning.

Off to California, with Buck…

Not twelve hours later, B.J., Buck and Lupe Martinez—sleek and exotic as always in her trademark black—took off from Teterboro for Reno.

B.J. kept to herself during the plane ride. She sat at the opposite end of the cabin from Buck and Lupe, put on a pair of headphones and tried to zone out with the help of her trusty iPod. She did her best not to seethe— not too much, anyway. She composed a long series of e-mails to Giles on her laptop, instructions on how to handle the various challenges he'd be facing while she was away, notes on priorities, on whom to deal with immediately and whom he could safely ignore for a while. Between e-mails, she shut her eyes, leaned back and concentrated on letting go of her anger and frustration. Anger meant tension and tension seemed to trigger unpleasant activity in her pregnancy-sensitized stomach.

She did understand that she would have to work through her rage and get past it; it would be pretty difficult to get Buck's story if she refused to talk to him. Besides, who was she kidding? In the next few months she'd be talking to him, anyway—about his upcoming fatherhood.

Though she'd never given a thought to having kids before, now that B.J. found herself pregnant, she'd discovered she actually *wanted* the baby.

Okay, so maybe she wasn't so hot at the male/female relationship thing. She'd accepted the fact that she would probably never marry. This could very well be her one chance to have a baby and she was grabbing it—even though it was bound to wreak serious havoc on her career.

She'd manage, somehow. She had an embarrassingly large trust fund, courtesy of L.T., so money would be no problem. She'd hire nannies. The best that her nice, fat fortune could buy.

And since Buck was the dad, she probably *would* have to deal with him. How much would depend on how large a part he intended to play in her baby's life.

And no, she wasn't telling him the big news yet. No way. She needed to get through this trip with him, get the damn feature written. Until that was done, she refused to complicate the situation with him any further.

In Reno, a rental SUV awaited them. They piled their bags and all of Lupe's equipment in the back and climbed in. Buck took the wheel and Lupe jumped right in behind him, leaving the front passenger seat for B.J.—if she wanted it. She didn't. However, she did need to practice being civil to Buck.

So she hopped in front and sent Buck a quick, bland smile. There. Civil. Sort of. And that was certainly enough cordiality for now. He started up the car and she aimed her gaze straight ahead.

The ride to Buck's hometown took over an hour. B.J. watched the impressive scenery roll past. Especially after they left Nevada's high desert behind, it was gorgeous out there. The bare hills and scrubby trees gave way to tall evergreens and sharp, dramatic stone peaks. Overhead, the sky was a pale wash of clear blue. No snow, except higher up than the road ever took them, on the topmost peaks. They wound down the mountains, into the green, shady depths of canyons and then back up to sub-alpine heights, where the trees grew farther apart, white-barked and twisted-looking, and the gray ground lay littered with silvery rock.

Lupe kept up a steady stream of chatter from the back seat—about the "crystalline" quality of the light, about how she wouldn't mind pulling an Ansel Adams and doing her own series on the Sierras in dramatic black and white.

Buck answered Lupe's occasional questions, but other than that, he didn't say much. B.J. kept quiet, as well. She avoided turning Buck's way. She might be slowly allowing herself to adjust to the reality of this situation, to accept the fact that she was headed for New Bethlehem Flat whether she liked the idea or not. But she still wasn't quite ready yet to have anything resembling an actual conversation with him.

They reached Buck's hometown at a little after four in the afternoon. B.J. got a quick view of a picturesque mountain village as they rounded a curve. And then they were winding their way down into a valley—or really, maybe more like a big canyon. The highway became Main Street, which consisted of a strip of pavement lined with cute old-fashioned buildings, some of clapboard, some of brick, each with a jut of porch providing cover for the rustic wooden sidewalks.

Buck turned right on Commerce Lane. They rattled over a single-lane bridge and there, on the west side of the street, sat a rambling canary-yellow wooden building with a sharply pitched tin roof. The front yard had a slate walk leading up to a wide, welcoming porch—a porch complete with oh-so-inviting white wicker furniture. There was even a white picket fence. The large sign hanging from the porch eaves read

Sierra Star Bed & Breakfast in old-timey script, the letters twined with painted ivy.

Buck swung in and parked at the curb as the front door of the house opened. A tall, slim middle-aged woman with short brown hair emerged. She wore a green corduroy skirt, a cable-knit sweater and practical flat shoes. Strictly L.L. Bean, B.J. thought: no frills, all function.

B.J. recognized the woman from pictures Buck had shown her way back when: Chastity Bravo, mother of Buck and his three younger brothers, Brett, Brand and Bowie. B.J. turned and looked straight at the man in the driver's seat for the first time that day. "Your mother…"

He gave her a nod and she had the strangest urge to smile at him—an urge she quickly quelled. He was getting no smiles from her. Not now. Maybe not ever.

By then, Buck's mother had reached the low white gate that opened onto the narrow cracked sidewalk. She hovered there, her hands on the pickets, waiting for them to emerge from the car.

When they did, Chastity smiled, a slow, warm smile—a smile a lot like Buck's, though not nearly so dangerous. "Welcome to the Sierra Star," she said in a voice as calm and friendly as her smile. "Good to have you home, Buck."

"Hey, Ma." Buck strode around the front of the SUV and fell in behind B.J. and Lupe. When he cleared the gate, he grabbed his mother in his big arms and hugged her, hard. "Good to be home," he said, lifting her right off the walk and rocking back and forth.

She let out a cry of surprise. "Buck, you put me down this instant!"

Now, there was a weird moment: watching Buck hugging his mother. Yes, B.J. had seen the pictures.

She'd known that a mother—and those three brothers—existed. But still…

Odd. Very odd.

Maybe it was just that she was used to a certain idea of him, as a guy all on his own, unattached in every way that mattered.

Once the hugging was over with and he'd set his mother back on the ground, Buck threw an arm around her and they started up the walk together. By then, Lupe had already mounted the steps and stood waiting by the front door.

B.J. hung back, pondering the whole Buck-has-a-mother thing—until he sent her a glance over his shoulder. "B.J. You coming?" She shook herself and followed them to the front door.

Inside, the foyer boasted a pressed-tin ceiling and classic beadboard paneling painted a nice, fresh-looking white. Cheerful rag rugs covered the scuffed hardwood floors. The drawing room off the entrance contained lots of chintz and plaid furniture, an excess of fat pillows and mismatched antiques.

The effect was far from luxurious. Still, B.J. found it kind of comforting. Homey and welcoming. Already the sun had fallen behind the mountains, leaving it kind of gray outside and dim within, but Chastity had turned the lamps on and a cheery fire burned in the stone fireplace.

Buck made the introductions.

"B.J. How nice to finally meet you," Chastity said, leaving B.J. to wonder just how much Buck's mother knew about their disaster of a love affair six years before.

"Uh. Great to meet you, too." She forced a friendly smile. "We should bring in our things…."

So they all headed back outside again. B.J. and Chastity each grabbed a couple of suitcases and trudged back to the house, leaving Buck and Lupe behind to sort out the rest.

"This way…" Chastity led B.J. upstairs to her room, which contained a queen-sized bed, nightstand and dresser and had enough room for a small sitting area. A tall armoire hid the TV. Not far from the head of the bed, French doors led out to a balcony and a gorgeous view: the rushing river behind the house and the ever-green-clad mountains rising skyward to the west.

B.J.—work, as always, foremost in her mind—cast a doubtful glance at the spindly-legged desk in the corner. "Internet access?" she asked hopefully. She didn't see anything resembling a data port. Maybe wireless?

"Not in the room," Chastity confessed. "But if you want to use my computer, you're welcome to. I have the Internet. Don't do much with it, I admit. I don't have time to sit around and wait for those pages to come on the screen. Takes forever and a day—I'm a busy woman, you know." She added the last briskly, with pride.

B.J. got the picture. Not pretty. "You mean you have…dial-up?" She tried not to shudder. Chastity looked at her vacantly. B.J. tried again. "You dial in to hook up?"

"Yes, I think that's it."

So much for zipping off her long, helpful e-mails to Giles. She'd call him. Later.

An ugly thought occurred to her. "What about cell phones? Do they work around here?"

"Now and then." The twin lines between Chastity's brows—lines that cried out for a little Botox—deepened even further. "Well, the truth is, not that often. The canyon walls block the signals." She gestured toward the window and the rim of tree-covered mountains across the river. "People around here who just have to have cell phones take them up there. Reception's pretty good once you get out of the canyon."

B.J. considered the concept: climb a mountain, make a call. "You know what? Maybe not."

Chastity shrugged. "But we do have regular phones." She pointed at the land line on the dinky desk. It was big and bone-colored, an early push-button model. "They work just fine."

"I'm sure I'll manage."

"Come on, then. I'll show you your bathroom."

The bath was down the hall. But at least it was all hers—Chastity told her so. B.J. reminded herself to be grateful for small favors. It had a sink, a toilet and a claw-footed tub with a tall, added-on shower head and a flowered curtain that could be drawn all the way around.

And most important, she wouldn't have to share it with Lupe—or worse, with Buck.

Buck and the photographer came up with the second load of suitcases and equipment. Chastity showed them their rooms. Buck got one next to B.J.'s. Now, why wasn't she surprised?

"Make yourself comfortable," Buck suggested, dark eyes much too knowing. "And then I'll show you around town."

"Wonderful," said B.J., meaning it wasn't, but what could she do? "Give me ten minutes."

He cast a doubtful glance at her open-toed leopard print Manolos. "Got any decent walking shoes?"

"I can walk anywhere in these," she replied, just to

be difficult. Then she relented. "Okay, okay. I'll change into something more clunky and hideous."

"Do that."

He went into his room. She stared at the door he'd shut behind him and thought a series of evil thoughts. Eventually, when glaring at his door failed to make it burst into flames, she gave up and went into her own room.

First things first: time to unpack.

B.J. loved living large. Though she was perfectly capable of traveling light if the situation demanded it, she preferred lots of options when it came to what to wear. For this trip, she'd brought four full-sized suitcases and a couple of smaller ones for her vanity items.

No worries, though. She was extremely efficient. She could pack half her closet in no time—and unpack it again in less than that. Swiftly, she put things away in the drawers and filled the narrow closet. She even trotted down the hall and put her grooming products away in her bathroom.

With two minutes to spare, B.J. pulled on some jeans and a pair of low-heeled knee-high Michael Kors suede boots—not hideous in the least, actually. But a girl has to score her points where she can. There was a tap at the door. B.J. scowled. Buck, no doubt. Ready to give her the guided tour. Oh, the joy. She grabbed her shearling jacket and answered the knock.

And there he was, wearing jeans and boots and a flannel shirt, looking scrumptiously rugged and far too smug. "Ready?"

She opened her mouth to say something snippy— and a blood-curdling scream erupted from the first floor. "What in God's name was that?"

But Buck had already turned and headed for the stairs.

Four

B.J. took off after Buck as another piercing scream echoed up the stairwell.

"I won't!" a woman shouted. "I will not. No way!" Another scream followed, fading right in on top of the words.

A man spoke—roughly, and low enough that B.J. couldn't make out what he said.

The woman screamed again.

"Now, settle down, Glory." That was Chastity's calm, level voice. "Bowie. Back off."

By then, Buck had cleared the stairs and was striding toward the living room. B.J., right behind him, glanced back and saw Lupe coming down after them. Lupe always wore about twenty silver bangle bracelets on each arm. They jingled together as she took the steps two at a time. "What's going on?" she demanded, kohl-lined black eyes wide with surprise.

As if B.J. knew.

In the living room, they found Chastity in front of the fireplace, legs braced apart, fisted hands planted hard on her hips. Behind her crouched a petite, dark-eyed brunette.

"No, Bowie," the brunette cried. "No, no, no!" She peered through the crook in Chastity's left elbow, gripping hunks of Chastity's chunky sweater in either hand, using Buck's mother as a human shield against the strapping, shaggy-haired mountain-man type over by the window.

"Your brother?" B.J. asked Buck out of the corner of her mouth, tipping her head toward the mountain man.

"'Fraid so," said Buck, sounding midway between amused and resigned.

Even without Buck's confirmation, B.J. would have pegged the guy as a Bravo. Beneath a couple of days' worth of beard, he had that telltale cleft in his chin—not to mention that beautifully shaped, way-too-sexy mouth. "Glory," Bowie said, his tone gentle and careful—the look in his eyes anything but. "Come on, honey…" He took a step toward his mother and the little brunette who cowered behind her.

Not wise.

The brunette let out another wake-the-dead shriek.

"Glory," groaned Chastity, putting a hand to her left ear—the one nearest Glory's wide-open mouth. "Cut that out. You're breaking my eardrums."

"Well, I can't help it," Glory wailed. "I just can't." She spoke to Buck's brother again. "Get it through that thick head of yours. I will not marry you. Ever. You don't love me. You only *say* you do because you think you have to."

"No, damn it. That's not true. I do love—"

"You don't." The brunette bit her trembling lip and shook her head. "Oh, Bowie. You'd make a terrible husband." She edged out from behind Chastity. "We both have to face it. You're wild and irresponsible and…and you can't keep a job." With that, she burst into tears and buried her head in her hands.

Bowie, looking about a mile out of his depth and sinking fast, tried again. "Honey. I *do* love you. And I'll get a damn job."

Glory threw back her head and screamed some more.

B.J. winced at the piercing sound. She slid another glance at Buck. "What's this about?"

"Hey. Don't ask me. I just got here myself."

"I don't care who knows," Glory wailed. "I don't care that the whole town'll be talking. It's nothing to me what anyone says. *I* said no. I meant no—and I will never change my mind!"

"That's it," said Bowie. "Damn it, I've had it."

Whimpering, Glory scooted back behind Chastity. "Don't you dare come near me, you big lunk."

Bowie made a sound like an injured moose. Then he pointed a threatening finger at the sobbing brunette. "You will marry me, Glory. By God, I'll get a ring on that finger of yours if it's the last thing I ever do."

"No, you won't."

"Yes, I will."

"No, you—"

"Enough!" shouted Chastity, so loudly that both Bowie and Glory actually shut up. Into the lovely moment of silence, she commanded, "Bowie. Get out."

"But Ma, she—"

"Out. Now."

"Ma, she's gotta—"

"I said, out."

Mother and son glared at each other. Bowie blinked first. Chastity swept out a hand toward the front door. "Now."

Muttering very bad words under his breath and shaking his big golden head, Bowie turned for the foyer. Buck, B.J. and Lupe were blocking the door. In unison, they each took a sliding step to the right, into the room—and out of Bowie's way.

About then, Bowie noticed his brother. He paused in midstride. "Hey. Buck." His dark look brightened. "How the hell you been?"

"Good to see you, little brother."

"Bowie," Chastity warned on a rising inflection.

Bowie scowled again. "Awright, awright." He clapped Buck on the shoulder. "Good to have you home." And he trudged on by and out the front door— slamming it good and hard behind him.

Chastity clucked her tongue. "That boy. He'll be the death of me, I swear." She turned to Glory. "You okay, honey?"

"Oh, Mrs. B." Glory burst into a fresh flood of weeping.

Chastity gathered the girl into her capable arms and spoke over her head to Buck and the two women flanking him. "If we could have a few minutes…"

Buck nodded. "B.J. and I were heading out, anyway."

Lupe cast a nervous glance at the still-sobbing Glory. "I'm going with you—wait. I want to grab a camera…"

B.J. spoke up before Buck could argue. "Good idea." She beamed Lupe a big smile—and sent a defiant look in Buck's direction. "We'll be out on the porch." Lupe took off up the stairs and B.J. followed Buck out.

"You can't avoid me forever," Buck warned, as they waited on the steps for Lupe to join them.

"Probably not." B.J. wrapped her jacket tighter against the late-afternoon chill. "But I'm giving it my best shot."

"We have to talk."

"So you keep telling me."

"If you'd taken just one of my damn calls—"

She waved a hand. "I know, I know. Maybe you wouldn't have found it necessary to manipulate me into coming here."

"I didn't manipulate you."

"Hah."

"I had a story you wanted. To get it, you paid the price I set."

"As I said, you manipulated me into coming here."

"You could have turned down the story…" He sent her one of those looks—intimate, dangerous. "Or maybe not. Maybe you *couldn't* turn it down. After all, anything for *Alpha,* right?"

As if she'd deny it. "That's right. Anything. Even a week in the sticks with you."

"A week?" His breath plumed on the air. "I don't know. This job is likely to take a lot more than a week…."

More than a week? To cover her dismay, she stuck her hands in her pockets and laid on the sarcasm. "Now you've really got me scared."

He moved in closer—too close, really. But she had her pride. Damned if he'd make her step back. He asked, "Did you notice?"

"What?"

"You're actually talking to me."

"Don't let it go to your head."

He loomed closer still, close enough that she could feel his breath across her cheek, marvel at the thickness of his lashes over those damn night-dark eyes of his. "You're not scaring me off." He spoke the threat tenderly. "Not this time."

She held her ground. "Watch me."

"I am. I do."

The door behind them opened and Lupe appeared, a black pea coat flung over her black jeans and short-sleeved black sweater. Her bangles jingled as she held up a Nikon. "Ready."

B.J., deeply grateful for the photographer's timely appearance, flashed her a blinding smile.

Buck muttered, "Fine. Let's go." He led the way across the bridge to Main Street.

As they strolled along the town's major street, Buck played tour guide. He pointed out landmarks: the post office, the school on a rise one street over, the hardware emporium, the town hall, the firehouse. Three gift stores, a beauty shop, two restaurants. He showed them the bars, of which there were also two—one on either side of the street. And the Catholic church on the hill behind the school. Lupe got several shots of the white clapboard building sporting one central spire and nestled so prettily in a copse of autumn-orange maple trees. There was also a Methodist church, Buck told them, farther up Commerce Lane from Chastity's B & B.

Everybody seemed to know him. It was "Buck, how you been?" and "Buck, nice to have you home again," and "Great to see you back in town." Some had even read his book.

One grizzle-haired old fellow perched on a bench outside the grocery store asked him when he was going to write a book about "the Flat," as the locals called it. "Now, there's a book that needs writin'." The old character winked at B.J.

"One of these days, Tony," Buck promised.

"You be sure to come and talk to me before you put down a single word," Tony warned, turning his bald head this way and that, hamming it up for the camera as Lupe snapped shot after shot. "I got all the best stories—and I can tell you where all the bodies are buried…if you know what I mean." He wiggled his bushy white eyebrows.

"Tony, you know you're the first one I'll come see."

The old guy nodded, looking gratified. "I'll hold you to it, see if I don't." He winked again at B.J.—and then at Lupe, too. "I like a pretty woman. Which one of these is yours?"

Buck sent B.J. a far too intimate look. She pretended not to notice.

"Well?" prompted old Tony with a chuckle.

Lupe blew a midnight strand of hair out of her eye and brought her camera into position again. "Leave me out of it. I'm just here to take the pictures."

"Ah," said Tony, turning to size B.J. up. "You, then."

"No. I'm not his—and he's not mine."

"You sound real definite about that," said Tony. "Maybe too definite. So definite I'm wondering who you're tryin' to convince." Tony did some more chuckling.

Buck stepped in and made the introductions. "Tony Dellazola, this is B. J. Carlyle and Lupe Martinez."

"Well, I am pleased to meet you both—so Buck. Tell me. You still livin' in New York City?"

"That's right."

"Never been there, never will. It's not healthy, folks livin' all on top of each other that way. Like rats in a maze. They start chewin' off their own tails."

"Hey." B.J. couldn't let that remark pass. "*I'm* a New Yorker. You couldn't pay me enough to live anywhere else."

"And I like a good-lookin' woman who knows her own mind," declared old Tony. He pulled a toothpick from his shirt pocket, stuck it between his yellowed teeth, leaned back on the bench and asked Lupe, "What d'you need all those pictures for?"

Lupe kept shooting and let Buck answer for her. "We're here to do an article for *Alpha* magazine."

Tony snapped to attention. "What's that? I'm gonna have my picture in *Alpha* magazine?"

"Could be."

Tony thought it over. "Well. I suppose that's okay with me. *Alpha*'s a fine magazine. Classy, you know? And those *Alpha* Girls…each one prettier'n the last, all of 'em wearing a nice, big friendly smile—and not a whole lot more." He gave yet another cackling chuckle and then grew serious again. "You'll send me a free copy so I'll know I was in there?"

"Absolutely," said B.J.

Buck thanked the old guy and they moved on, crossing the street and heading down the other side, back toward the bridge to Chastity's place.

"Quite a character," Lupe remarked once they were out of earshot.

Buck said, "He was sitting on that bench all day every day back when *I* was a kid. I swear, he looks exactly the same today as he did then. He's gotta be ninety by now. Glory's his great-granddaughter."

"Glory." Lupe looked pained. "You mean the screamer?"

Buck ignored Lupe's question. He seemed faintly bemused. "Glory was maybe ten years old when I left town. And now look at her."

"Yeah," said Lupe, "hanging around your mother's B & B, terrorizing the clientele."

Buck shrugged. "No one to terrorize. It's the slow season. For tonight, I think we're the only guests—and whatever she was screaming about, Glory does have a valid reason to be there. She lives downstairs, in an add-on apartment in back. She's the maid."

Lupe shuddered. "Remind me to lock up my valuables when I leave my room."

"Relax," Buck said. "Glory's a good kid. Yeah, she's got a little drama queen in her. Like all the Dellazolas. They're a big, rowdy family and generally, with them, the one who screams the loudest gets the most attention. But they're sweet and harmless, really—and honest as the day is long. Every last one of them."

Back at the Sierra Star, all was quiet. They went in the front door to find the fire still burning cheerily in the fireplace and nobody in the living room or the front hall. Lupe headed for the stairs. B.J., oh-so-casually, fell in behind her, hoping to reach the safety of her room without Buck suggesting another outing—one with just the two of them this time.

She made it halfway up.

"B.J."

With a sigh, she turned and looked down at him. Their eyes met. Zap. There went that disgusting hot little thrill coursing through her.

Really, he was much too attractive—an attractiveness consisting of more than mere good looks. He had a certain…energy about him. An energy that radiated off him and kind of filled up the space around him with excitement, with a sense of expectation.

And why, oh why, was she thinking about how attractive he was? She really had to watch herself or she'd be falling into bed with him all over again.

And she wasn't going to do that. She really, truly wasn't.

He said, "I want to take you to dinner." He glanced beyond her at Lupe, who had paused at the head of the stairs. "Lupe, you're officially *not* invited."

Lupe shrugged. "So I'll check out the club scene."

"Bars, Lupe. They're just bars."

"Leave me my fantasies, at least." She turned for her room.

Buck waited until the photographer disappeared from view before insisting, "Dinner. In an hour. We'll walk over town."

More eating. So not her favorite thing lately. And eating with Buck, as well. That would mean an hour, at least, of sitting across from him, counting his eyelashes, thinking stupid thoughts like how no other man smelled like him, or laughed like him, or looked at her in such a dangerously delicious kind of way.

She was in trouble here.

No doubt about it.

Then again, there *was* the interview. She should concentrate on that. The sooner she got the material she needed, the sooner she could get back into her Manolos and away from Buck and New Bethlehem Flat. "I'll bring my tape recorder."

"One hour. No excuses."

She turned and left him without actually saying yes, though both of them knew she'd be ready. On time.

In her room, using the push-button phone, B.J. called Giles, who was still at his desk, bless his ambitious little heart, though it was well after seven at night in New York.

He listened patiently to her long list of notes and suggestions, then told her that everything was going fine. "Not a crisis in sight."

"That's not normal."

He laughed. She pictured him tossing those thick blond locks of his and felt homesick—for the city, for her office, for her own world where she could so easily avoid dealing with Buck.

"B.J.," Giles chided. "You worry too much."

"Call me. The minute there's any kind of problem, any time you need advice…"

"I will, I will."

"Use this number." She rattled it off. "Cell phones don't work here. And forget the Internet. It's not happening, either."

"Okay, okay."

"If I'm out of the room, you can leave a message. I'll get back to you as soon as I can."

"Makes sense to me. And I mean it. There is zero to worry about."

The call was over too quickly, leaving her standing in her cozy little room at the Sierra Star B & B, staring out the window at the rough, silvered reflection of the moon on the river, wondering what she was doing there—and silently vowing to pull the damn article together fast and get the hell out of New Bethlehem Flat.

Five

Buck took B.J. to the Nugget Steakhouse—on Main Street, wouldn't you know? The Nugget had a main dining room and another room next door, which contained one of the town's two bars.

A stocky waitress in jeans and a polo shirt greeted Buck by name. He gave her that grin that bowled all the women over. "Nadine. How you been?"

"Can't complain." Nadine led them to a booth. "What can I get you to drink?" She handed them each a menu.

Buck ordered a whisky and soda. B.J. asked for water. The waitress hurried off through the door to the bar.

B.J. opened her menu. "What's good?"

"How would I know? I haven't eaten here in over a decade."

The menu was big enough that, held upright, it

blocked him from her view. Which was fine. After all, every time she looked at him, she only wanted to look some more.

He said, "You probably can't go wrong with the filet."

She grunted in answer, staring blankly at the menu, wondering why she'd bothered to ask for his recommendation. It wasn't as if she would be eating or anything.

Morning sickness. Who ever thought of calling it that? Probably some idiot with a disgustingly positive attitude. For B.J., the problem went on all day and all night. If it kept up, she'd be the skinniest pregnant lady in Manhattan. She might die of starvation, and her poor unborn baby with her.

And she just knew he was waiting over there across the table for the moment when she had to stop hiding behind the menu and look at him again.

Might as well get it over with. She shut the menu, set it aside and went ahead and met his eyes.

Wouldn't you know? Compelling as ever.

She glanced away. For something to do as she tried not to look at him, she studied the decor.

The place was aggressively rustic, a virtual sea of knotty pine. Knotty pine crawled up the walls and spread across the ceiling. Their booth and the tables grouped in the center of the room were all made of knotty pine. The ladder-back chairs? Yet more knotty pine. Even the wagon-wheel chandeliers overhead were knotty pine, stained dark enough that it was hard to make out the knots. But B.J. wasn't fooled.

She knew knotty pine when she saw it—and she didn't care for it in the least. B.J. had *history* with knotty pine, history that involved a dead animal, a rifle and a hunting lodge in Idaho.

In October, the year she turned twelve, L.T. had taken her to Idaho to hunt elk. B.J. had always loathed hunting. She didn't want to watch her dinner die, she truly didn't.

But she'd learned to shoot and how to handle herself in the woods just to prove to L.T. that she could. That trip, she'd actually shot an elk. A gorgeous big bull with a massive rack. It was one of those things that just happened. She had the rifle and she knew how to use it and she knew what L.T. expected of her.

In the sub-freezing pre-dawn, she'd crouched behind a big, gray rock and waited there for hours, being quiet and tough and self-reliant, the way L.T. expected her to be. She had it all figured out in her twelve-year-old mind. No elk was even going to come near her, so she wouldn't have to actually shoot anything.

Wrong.

The animal appeared out of nowhere. All at once it was just standing there in the early-morning gloom, looking off toward the snow-capped mountains to the east and the bright rim of light where the sluggish sun was slowly rising. Soundlessly, she shouldered her rifle, got the creature in her sights—and pulled the trigger. A perfect, clean shot. The bull dropped dead where it stood, forelegs crumpling, big brown eyes going glassy, making no sound but a loud thump as it hit the ground.

B.J. emerged from behind her rock and stood over it, still not believing that she'd actually killed the poor thing.

The knotty pine had come into play that night. Their hunting lodge was paneled, like the Nugget Steakhouse, all in pine. L.T. and the other men stayed up late, drinking and laughing and loudly discussing how "little B.J." had got her elk. Little B.J., who had gone to bed early, lay awake in the open sleeping loft upstairs, counting the knots in the paneling, thinking that she really hadn't meant to shoot that bull, and wishing the men would just shut up about it.

"You're too quiet," Buck said.

She blinked and focused on him. "Sorry. Just thinking."

"About?"

Nadine reappeared, saving B.J. the trouble of coming up with an answer. The waitress set their drinks in front of them, along with a bread basket, bread plates and their flatware rolled in white cloth napkins. "You two ready to order?"

"I am," said B.J. She rattled off what she wanted and Buck did the same. Nadine scribbled it all down and hustled off again.

"So," said Buck.

"What?"

"What was on your mind, just then?"

"When?"

He gave her a look—kind of weary and put-upon.

Oh, what the hell? "I was just thinking that I hate knotty pine. Knotty pine is depressing. Every damn knot is like a big, sad, reproachful brown eye—an eye that watches your every move."

"Never thought of it that way."

"This is probably not a good place to be on medication."

"I kind of like it myself." He tipped his head to the side and looked toward the center of the room. Admiring the knots in the tables and chairs? Apparently. The light from the hurricane lamp on their table shone on his dark hair. So silky, his hair.

And thick. Very thick…

"My dad brought us here once," he said, turning to her again, smiling slowly when he caught her eye, causing certain responses, certain small, shivery feelings she instantly denied.

She cleared her throat. "How old were you?"

"Pretty little. Maybe five. It's one of my few memories of him. He was gone so much. He would show up out of nowhere, now and then, for a week or two, and then disappear again. That was the last time he came to town, when he brought us to dinner here. It was before Bowie was born—nine months before, if you know what I mean."

She did. Blake had gotten Chastity pregnant, gone away, and never come back. "What a guy."

Buck said, "That was pretty much his M.O. He'd show up, get my mother pregnant and leave. He'd come back in a year or so, get her pregnant again. Leave again. None of us ever got to know him or anything. He was the stranger who happened to be our father."

Her editor's brain kicked in. *The stranger who happened to be our father.* That might make the cutline under a photo of the notorious Blake. They'd need to dig up an old picture….

And she should be getting this down. Any revelations about Blake Bravo could definitely be usable.

She grabbed her bag, dug out the mini-recorder, turned it on and set it on the table, down toward the hurricane lamp—out of the way, but close enough to pick up everything they said. "So Bowie never even met his father?"

Buck eyed the recorder. "Always on the job, right?"

"That's what I'm here for."

He looked at her. A long look. "I keep hoping for more."

"Well, don't—about Bowie and Blake…"

He said nothing, just looked at her some more.

And if she'd didn't watch it, she'd be looking right back, going ga-ga over his eyelashes and the sexy curve of his mouth. "Talk," she commanded.

He made a low sound—something between a grunt and a chuckle. And at last, he got down to it. "Bowie, as the youngest, never met our father. And Brand, Brett and I never *knew* him. Not really. He hardly ever came around, and we were mostly too little to have a clue who he was." Buck glanced down into his drink and then back up at her. "He had the weirdest, scariest light-colored eyes. Wolf eyes…but I told you that, didn't I? About his eyes. Back when you and I were together?"

She nodded. Back then, he never talked about his family much. Just that his dad had left them when Buck was very young—and about Blake's pale, strange eyes. "Tell me more about the time your dad brought you here, to the Nugget. You were five, you said?"

"Yeah. I was the only one of the kids who got to go. Brett and Brand were…two and three, I guess. Ma left them with my grandmother. It was December. I remember there were tinsel garlands looped on the light fixtures." They both glanced up at the wagon-wheel chandelier over their heads. "And a tree, over there by the door to the street—a fresh tree, strung with those old-style big lights and shiny glass ornaments. I remember passing it as we came in, breathing in the piney smell of it, getting off on the way the lights glowed in the branches. It meant Christmas was coming and that gave my five-year-old heart a thrill."

"You had good Christmases, growing up?"

He nodded. "Ma made a big deal of it. She baked like a champion, played Christmas carols all day and half the night from the morning after Thanksgiving on. She decorated a huge silver-tip fir in the front room. She seriously decked the halls—and every flat surface in sight. The hotel—in those days she called it a hotel—was a damn Christmas wonderland and that is no lie. My brothers and I loved it."

"It sounds fabulous."

"It was." Those dark eyes of his were shining.

Nadine trotted up, bearing a pair of totally retro salads: iceberg lettuce and wedges of tomato drizzled all over with ranch dressing. "Here we go." She plunked them on the table and bustled away again.

B.J. looked down at her plate—and her stomach actually growled. Amazing. For the first time in a week, out of nowhere, she was starving.

"Back to dinner out with psycho-Dad," she prompted as she unrolled her napkin, spread it on her lap, grabbed for her fork and dug in.

It tasted *so* good. She had to make a conscious effort not to groan in delight at the crisp texture of the lettuce, the creamy, perfect consistency of the dressing. She gobbled down several crunchy, delicious bites before it came to her that Buck wasn't talking.

She looked up from devouring her salad to find him watching her—again.

"Hungry?" he asked, annoyingly amused.

She took time to swallow, lick a spot of dressing off her upper lip and wipe her mouth with her napkin, before replying. "Yeah. So?"

"Last night at the Castle, you didn't eat much of anything."

She wisely refrained from comment on that one and instructed instead, "Your father. With lots of detail, please. If I have to write this thing, you have to give me something to work with."

"You can be very bossy, you know that?"

"And you can be a manipulative SOB—or did I mention that already?" She dropped her napkin in her lap and forked up another huge bite of salad.

"Yeah. You mentioned it." He stared at her mouth as he lounged back in his seat, keeping one strong arm resting on the table—to the right of his empty drink and his untouched salad. "You're still steamed because I dragged you into this."

She paused before stuffing that big bite into the mouth he kept staring at. "How did you guess? The story, please."

He picked up his drink, rattled the ice cubes as Nadine rushed by—and finally continued. "We took a booth that night. The one right behind you, I think it was. I remember that Ma and my dad sat together. I sat across from them. I tried to be very, very good. And whenever my father would look at me with those scary eyes of his, I'd get this tightness in my stomach, this feeling that I wouldn't mind so much when he went away again. Little did I know that when he left that time, he was never coming back."

B.J., having polished off her salad, longed to pick up her plate and lick the last of the dressing from it. Somehow, she restrained herself.

And besides, there was still the bread basket. She grabbed it and peeled back the warming towel to reveal four nice, big dinner rolls. Snatching one up, she slathered on the butter and then tore off a hunk and stuck it in her mouth.

God. Bread. Delicious—and Buck was watching her again, grinning that grin of his. She made a move-it-along circular gesture with her free hand.

He took his cue. "Recently—since a few years ago, when it all came out in the papers and I found out who he really was—I've been learning about dear old Dad. Blake kept a home base in Norman, Oklahoma, with a woman named Tammy Rae Sandovich. He had one child with Tammy Rae. A boy, Marsh."

She swallowed. "Your half-brother…"

"One among many. I met Marsh last year. Great guy. Blake used to beat him—and his mother, too. A lot. So in hindsight, with the information I have now, I can't say I regret that dear old Dad didn't show up much, or that he stopped coming around when I was so young."

B.J. felt a faint twinge of something that might have been sympathy—for Buck, for all the left-behind children of the evil Blake. With that twinge came the urge to reach across the table, to cover Buck's hand with her own, to reassure him, the way a friend would. It was an urge she took care to suppress.

Nadine set Buck's second drink in front of him. "Everything okay?"

B.J. swallowed again. "Great," she said, and popped the last of the roll into her mouth.

Nadine beamed at B.J.—and scolded Buck. "Eat your salad. Steaks are on the way."

"I'm getting to it, Nadine."

The waitress clucked her tongue and left them—and Buck reached over and turned off the recorder. Before B.J. could swallow that last chunk of bread and object, he leaned closer and spoke low. "I talked to Ma— about what's up with Bowie and Glory."

Okay, she was curious. She washed the bread down with water. "So, and?"

"Glory's pregnant."

"Pregnant." She set down her glass. She probably should have guessed—and was this too close to home, or what?

"Bowie wants to marry her."

"So he said—more than once. And she said no. Repeatedly. At the top of her lungs, as I recall."

Buck finally picked up his fork. "It doesn't matter what she said. He'll marry her, one way or the other."

"Not if *she* keeps saying no."

"You just don't get it."

"That's right, I don't."

"Bowie's a Bravo."

"And that explains…what?"

"Everything."

"Oh. Well. To you, maybe."

He wore an excessively patient expression. "My brothers and I were raised minus a father. That's not going to happen to our kids."

"Ah." And given her own circumstances, B.J. wasn't sure she liked the sound of this. "Okay. Just to recap here. Bowie's a Bravo. So he *has* to marry Glory—because she's going to have his baby?"

"Yeah."

"As in, one and one equals two?"

"That's right."

"Buck. Hello. Twenty-first century, U.S. of A."

He waved his fork for silence. "Look. A Bravo may make mistakes in life. Big ones. But you can bet your favorite pair of sexy shoes that when there's an innocent kid involved, a Bravo will always find a way to do the right thing."

A stream of perfectly valid arguments scrolled through B.J.'s brain: that sometimes marriage just isn't the right solution, that a child can have a productive, happy life without her parents being married. That some people—herself among them—just aren't *meant* for marriage, that a bad marriage is never a good thing, for the child, or her parents....

She kept those arguments to herself. This was much too dangerous a subject to get into right now.

Chewing on another roll, she watched him as he ate his salad, thinking, *I am now going to turn on the tape recorder and get on with the interview.*

But then again...

Okay. She *had* to ask. "You, too, Buck? You'd marry some woman you didn't care about, didn't...love, just because she was having your baby?"

He speared a tomato wedge. "Bowie does love Glory. He said so."

"Well, yeah. To convince her to do things his way."

"Uh-uh. I don't think so. I think he really does love her."

"And you determined this, how?"

He considered a moment. "Call it an informed opinion. He's my baby brother. I grew up with him. It's my *informed opinion* that he meant what he said. He loves Glory."

There was a moment. They looked at each other and B.J. felt...sparks. Heat. That burning energy, way too sexual, zipping back and forth between them.

Why *this* guy? she thought, as she'd thought a thousand times before. Why, always, in the end: Buck?

Nadine appeared with their steaks. She served them and took their salad plates away.

Buck started in on his T-bone. B.J. sipped her water

and told herself not to go there—after which, she promptly went there. "And anyway, I wasn't asking about Bowie. I was asking about you. If you got a woman pregnant, would you think you *had* to marry her, whether you really *wanted* to or not?"

"Why do you ask?"

"Just curious," she baldly lied.

Those eyes of his seemed to bore holes right through her. And then he lifted one hard shoulder, sketching a shrug. "Honestly, I can't say for certain. It hasn't happened." Then he frowned. "Wait a minute. Are you trying to tell me something?"

"No. No, I'm not." Well, it was the truth. Barely. She *wasn't* trying to tell him. Not now. Not yet…

"I'll say this much."

She gulped. "Yeah?"

"Any kid of mine is going to know his dad and know him well." His steak knife glinted as he sliced his T-bone.

B.J. realized she'd been holding her breath and let it out. Slowly. "Buck?"

He set the knife aside. "Yeah?"

"Why are we doing this?"

He arched a dark brow. "Because it's dinnertime? Because we have to eat—by the way, your filet's getting cold."

Stop, a voice inside her head commanded. Drop it. Now. But her mouth kept right on talking. "No. I don't mean dinner. I mean this whole thing. You and me, here in your hometown. Why did you find it necessary to drag me across the country with you? We both know there's no reason you can't write this damn piece yourself."

"No denying it now," he said wryly. "You *are* talking to me."

"Against my better judgment," she shot back, then

cut the sarcasm enough to ask, "And will you please answer my question?"

He looked at her in a measuring sort of way. The seconds ticked by. At last, he said, "Eat your steak so we can get out of here."

"And then?"

"You'll get your answer."

Buck said nothing after they left the restaurant. In the chilly Sierra darkness, they strolled down the street, around the corner and across the bridge. The stars overhead, no city lights to mute them, shone thick and bright against the black-as-velvet night sky.

At the Sierra Star, the curtains at the front window were still open. Inside, as they mounted the steps, B.J. could see Chastity, sitting alone by the fire, reading a paperback book, an orange tabby cat curled in her lap.

Buck opened the door and ushered B.J. in—still without saying a word. Evidently, he'd decided against explaining why he'd forced her to head for the hills with him.

Fine. She was having second thoughts, anyway, wondering what had possessed her to ask him why in the first place. Whatever his reasoning, she didn't need to hear it.

And it had been a long day. She'd go upstairs, enjoy a soak in her own private claw-footed bathtub and then watch some TV. Maybe jot a few notes for the story. Play a computer game. Read a book.

Whatever.

The keyword here was *disengage*. When it came to Buck, prolonged contact inevitably meant trouble. If she didn't watch herself, she'd start obsessing over how attractive he was, how smart, how funny. In no time she'd be thinking that maybe they could get something going, after all.

It could end up just like that night in September—with her naked on top of him, demanding more. Or beneath him, *begging* for more. Or...

Now, see? See what she was doing? All it took was dinner and a little semi-friendly conversation, and she was back with the vivid images of the two of them doing things they were *never going to do again.* Italics intended.

Chastity looked up from her book. "Did you two have a nice dinner?"

"Great," said Buck.

"We did," B.J. agreed. She brought her hand to her mouth as she faked a yawn. "I'm pretty tired, though. Jet lag, I guess. Goodnight."

"Sleep well," said Chastity with a serene little smile. The cat looked up at Buck's mother and twitched its caramel-colored tail. Chastity petted it as she turned her attention back to her book.

Buck said nothing. Why? What was he thinking? What did his silence mean?

Bad questions. Pointless questions. Keyword: *disengage.* B.J. turned for the stairs.

He fell in behind her. He walked softly. Still, she could feel him at her back all the way up the stairs and down the hall to their side-by-side rooms. She had her key ready. She slid it smoothly into the lock and pushed the door open. Stepping swiftly in, she turned to shut it behind her—to shut *him* out. She almost made it, too.

At the last possible second, he said, "Five minutes."

Disengage, disengage. Without a word, she shut the door the rest of the way and shot the bolt, heard that reassuring click as the lock slid home. She turned with a groan and sagged against the door.

"Shit," she said to the empty room. Five minutes. What did *that* mean?

Six

Once B.J. had shut her door in his face, Buck turned and headed back down the stairs. Chastity glanced up with a questioning smile as he entered the front room.

"Where's the brandy?"

"Try the mirrored sideboard." She gestured toward the door that led to the formal dining room. "Top shelf on the left."

"Thanks, Ma." Buck continued on through to the dining room, got the brandy and two small snifters and retraced his steps back through the front room and up the stairs again.

In his own room, he waited the final two minutes until the five-minute deadline and then exited the French doors onto the balcony. Three steps and he stood at the glass doors that led into B.J.'s room.

She hadn't pulled the curtains. He could see her in

there, sitting on the edge of the bed, slim shoulders drooping, looking…what? Dejected?

Could be. He smiled to himself. B.J. would never let her shoulders droop if she knew someone was looking. She was too tough by a mile. As long as Buck had known her, she'd been that way. Probably because she *had* to be. No choice in the matter, with a father like L.T.

It wasn't easy getting through that toughness, no simple task to peel B. J. Carlyle down to her soft, passionate feminine core. But Buck had this crazy idea he was man enough now to understand that things didn't always have to be easy—especially the important things.

He tapped lightly on one of the panes and watched her slim back snap straight. Slowly, carefully, she turned her head in his direction.

They regarded each other through the glass—a stare-down. Her gorgeous frosty eyes sent a clear message: *Go away.*

He held up the brandy and the two snifters.

She pinched her mouth tight and shook her head. He nodded.

At last, she stood and came toward him.

"Chilly out here," he said, when she pulled open the door.

She stuck her head out far enough to peer around toward his side of the balcony. "I didn't know we shared the balcony," she muttered glumly.

"Let me in. We'll have some brandy." He stepped forward. Reluctantly, she moved back.

"I don't want any brandy." She shut the doors. "Why are you in my room?" He set one glass on the night-stand and poured a nice, stiff drink into the other. He held it out to her. She didn't take it, asking instead, "What part of no do you find confusing?"

He shrugged—elaborately—and drank from the snifter himself. It burned all the way down to his stomach where it spread out to become a warm and satisfying glow. "This is excellent."

"Oh, I'm so glad. I'll ask a second time. Why are you here?"

A small wing chair waited across from the bed. He dropped into it. "You asked me a question back at the restaurant, remember? I'm here to answer it."

"Never mind my question. It wasn't important. And now that that's settled—" she flung out a hand toward the French doors "—you can go."

Other than to set his brandy on the little table by his chair, he didn't move.

"I'm serious," she said. "I don't need to know why you boxed me into coming here."

"I think you do."

"How charming. Now you're telling me what I need."

"Okay, okay. Let me put it this way. *I* need to tell you."

She turned from him, wrapped her arms around herself and stared out at the silver ribbon of river, the shadowed pine-thick hills, the unreadable face of the moon. When she spoke this time, there was no sarcasm. "Buck. Please. It's no good." She looked at him then. "When are you going to accept the truth? That night in September? Never should have happened. I regret it. I honestly do. It was a mistake. A huge one."

A mistake. A huge one…

Okay. That hurt.

Yeah, he'd already known she felt that way. How could he help but know? He'd called and called and she'd never answered, never called him back. Still, to hear her say it right out…it cut. A ragged cut made by a rusty knife.

"A mistake?" he repeated, keeping it light, relaxed, not letting the hurt show. "I don't think so."

He watched her slim throat move as she swallowed. "It was…just something that happened, something that shouldn't have. Because you and me, well, that was over a long, long time ago." He sipped his brandy and didn't say a word. She must have read what he was thinking in his expression, because she insisted, "It *is*, Buck. It's over. Long over. You have to accept that."

He set down the snifter and said what he should have said years ago. "I'm sorry, B.J."

She blinked and put her hand to her throat—and then pretended to misunderstand. "I meant what I just said. It was one of those things. It happened. No more your fault than mine."

He laid it right out for her. "I'm not talking about that night in September. I'm talking about that *other* night—the one six years ago."

She fell back a step. "Buck. Look…"

He went on as if she hadn't spoken. "I'm not the least sorry for what happened in September. As far as I'm concerned, *that* night was long overdue." She whirled for the glass doors again, for the cool, silvery face of the moon. He called her back. "B.J."

With obvious effort, she turned his way again, met his eyes. "Let's just not go there, okay? It was a long time ago and—"

"Don't give me that. Listen. I screwed up six years

ago. I screwed up bad. I didn't believe in you. Not enough—not in you, or in myself."

"Buck—"

"Not that anything I might say is any kind of excuse. I blew it. Blew it all to hell and I know it."

"Buck. It was over. I'd turned you down. You had a perfect right to—"

"If I had a perfect right, then why did you look like I'd stabbed you to the heart when you walked in on us?"

She marched over and dropped to the edge of the bed again. "Please. Will you just go?"

"Not till you hear me out."

She gave him a long look. "Let me get this straight. You speak—and then you go?"

He nodded.

"All right, then." She crossed those slim legs, leaned back on her hands, and stared at him defiantly. "Get it over with."

Now she'd said she would listen, he hardly knew where to start. He took a stab at it. "I never should have let you walk away back then."

"As if you could have stopped me."

He pinned her with a glance. She pressed her lips together and shrugged, but she did keep her sweet mouth shut.

He clarified, "The point is, I didn't even *try* to stop you. You want to talk mistakes? Well, that was the real one. That I let you walk out of my life without a fight. I despise myself for that. That won't happen again. This time, things are going to be different."

"Buck. Get with reality. There is no 'this time.'"

"Yeah, there is."

The light in her eyes threatened dire consequences. "Oh, you are so asking for it, you know that?"

"I am. And I do."

She gave up the defiant pose and jumped to her feet. "Okay. Get this. If you insist on dredging up all that old stuff, I'm done being fair about it."

He looked her slowly up and down. She was, and always had been, real easy to look at. "Good. Because you being fair about it? That's all just crap and we both know it."

She took a step toward the chair where he sat. "Your turn to listen."

"Fair enough."

"Okay, then. This is how I really feel. What you did was scum-sucking low. What you did proved that you're nothing but a dog, Buck. You asked me to marry you. I said I wasn't ready—not get lost, not *never*. Just not now. I said not now and you said we were through. Then you went right out and got drunk and picked up a stranger, an innocent bystander, and took her home. I came to find you, to try to work things out. And there you were, boinking some brunette. It was, to say the least, a pivotal moment. It was the moment I realized you weren't worth my time, let alone my pitiful, ridiculous broken heart."

He waited to see if she'd say more. When she didn't, he nodded. "You're right. I wasn't worth it. And I'm sorry."

"It's a little damn late to say you're sorry."

"It's a lot late. I'm saying it anyway."

"Why?"

"Better late than never?"

"That's no answer."

"Best I can do."

She made a face. Not a happy one. "Just go now. Please."

"I will. Soon."

"Promises, promises."

He rose from the chair. "There's still that question of yours. Remember? The one about why I made you come with me on this trip in the first place."

"I told you. It doesn't matter. It never mattered. I shouldn't have asked."

"But you did ask. And it does matter." He dared another step.

It was a step more than she could accept. "Don't come any closer."

"Scared?"

She made a rough, scoffing sound. "Of you? Not in the least."

He didn't believe her. She *was* scared—that tonight would turn out like that night seven weeks ago. He put up both hands, palms out. "Hands off. I swear it."

"Oh, terrific. Like your word means a thing to me."

He took a step back, a gesture of good faith. "I said hands off. And I meant what I said."

She peered at him, narrow-eyed and wary. Then, at last, she gave in. "Okay," she said grimly. "Tell me all about it—about why you manipulated things so I ended up here with you in this dinky, bend-in-the-road, blink-your-eyes-and-you-miss-it hometown of yours. Tell me about it and then you can leave."

"It's so damn simple."

"Good to know, Buck."

"I want another chance with you."

To that, she said, in a tone as flat as it was final, "No way."

He gave her a pained smile. "Well. That was simple and direct."

"That's right. And now that we understand each

other, will you please write the damn article yourself
and let me go back to New York?"

Not on your life. "Here's the deal…"

"No deal."

"Maybe you're right."

"Will wonders never cease? The man admits I'm
right."

"The more you interrupt, the longer I'll be standing
here in your room."

"Excellent point. Consider my lip officially zipped."

"Yeah, but for how long?" He waited, figuring she'd
just *have* to come back with some smart remark. She
only looked at him, widening her eyes. When several
seconds went by and her mouth remained shut, he said,
"You're listening?"

She nodded, keeping her lips pressed tightly
together.

"All right. If I can't have another chance with you,
at least I want some time with you. I realize it's
probably hopeless. I can be a real SOB and I know that
I can." She was smirking. He instructed patiently,
"Don't give me that look." She batted her eyelashes
and shook her head. He grunted. "And then, beyond
me, there's you."

"Um?"

"Not exactly the soul of submissive femininity, now
are you?"

She bounced her head from side-to-side, a
movement that clearly communicated, *No, I'm not,
and I'm proud of it.*

He laid out his terms. "Two weeks, that's what I
want. Two weeks, you and me, here in my hometown.
Two weeks, where you're not avoiding me—meaning
that when I want you with me, you're there. When I

say we're going somewhere, you go. Two weeks to find out if there could be any hope for us, together. Two weeks to see if there could *be* an 'us.' You give me that, those two measly weeks, and I'll write the damn article. You'll not only get my story, you'll get my name on the byline." By then, her face was beet-red—from holding in a raft of objections, he had no doubt. "You may speak," he said.

"Two weeks?" The words exploded from that tempting mouth of hers. "You don't need two weeks...."

"Not for the article, maybe. But for you and me, definitely. For you and me, I probably need a decade, at least. But I figure two weeks is all I'm likely to get."

That sexy mouth pinched up again. "What do I have to do? Put it on a billboard in Times Square, take out an ad in the *Village Voice?* How can I get it through to you? There *is* no you and me. There hasn't been for years. You really need to accept that, Buck."

"And I will. In two weeks. If things don't improve between us, I'll give it up. You'll finally be rid of me. Once and for all."

She shook her head as she sank to the edge of the bed again. "This is mad, bad and crazy. You have to know that."

"Two weeks. And *I* write the article."

"I have to *work,* you know? I can't just—"

"Two weeks."

Something happened in her eyes. Something...accepting. Or at least, acquiescing. His hopes soared. She said, "I'll speak with your agent tomorrow."

Bingo. He had her. "Fair enough."

And *then* she said, "No sex. That would have to be understood."

Scratch the bingo. And so much for his hopes soaring. Now, if he was hoping for anything, it was only that he hadn't heard her right. "Why do we have to make a deal about sex? Can't you just say no on a per-incident basis? Are you *that* afraid that you might end up in bed with me?"

"Well, to that I would have to say, yes."

"So why is it a problem, then?"

"Take my word. It just is."

"Let's look at it logically."

"Logically? Are you kidding?"

"You want it. I want it. We're both free to want it. From each other. What's wrong with that?"

"Everything—and this is not a point up for discussion. This is, quite simply, a deal-breaker. No sex. And no tricks involving sex, or the deal is off."

"Tricks?" He put on his most reproachful expression. "B.J. You wound me. Deeply."

"Hah. I get at least eight hours a night in my own room—alone. Understand me? Yes, I agree to be with you, right here in Podunk, U.S.A. But not for twenty-four hours a day. I'm not…sleeping in your room or anything. Are we clear?"

"Sleeping in my room. Why didn't I think of that?"

"No tricks. I mean it, Buck. Or the deal is off."

Now he was the one turning to look out the French doors. The damn moon looked back him, giving him nothing—just like the infuriating woman sitting behind him, straight-backed, on the bed.

Look at it this way, he thought.

He'd come this far. Yeah, he wanted her in his bed, where he was more than reasonably certain she'd always belonged. But then again…

She *was* giving him the two weeks. During that

time, she would go with him wherever he decided to take her. She would *be* with him whenever he wanted her to be—except in bed.

It wasn't perfect. But it could have been a hell of a lot worse.

And who was to say she wouldn't change her mind on the issue of sex? Some rules, after all, begged to be broken.

He faced her. "All right. Two weeks. No sex. My byline."

She sat up even straighter and muttered curtly, "Agreed."

Seven

After making her deal with Buck and finally ushering him out through the French doors to his own side of the balcony, B.J. grabbed her robe and headed down the hall to her bathroom.

A box of drug-store bath beads waited on the white wicker stand next to the tub. Just what she needed. *Calgon, take me away.* Please.

She sprinkled the beads liberally into the tub, turned on the water, locked the door, got undressed and sank gratefully into the hot, slippery, foaming bath.

It was fabulous. She soaked for an hour, her head pillowed on a towel, staring at the white beadboard ceiling, wondering what she'd gotten herself into, back there in her room, with Buck.

Okay, he'd slipped under her defenses by apologizing like that. She hadn't realized how much it would mean to her, that he could say flat out, "I'm sorry," that he could stand there and take it while she told him exactly what she thought of what he'd done six years ago.

It meant a lot. It kind of…cleared away the old garbage between them. At least, to a point, it did—and no, that didn't mean she planned to try again with him. She did not.

Just because Buck was a better man than she'd thought he was didn't make *her* a better woman. She had to remember Wyatt the weasel—and the others before him. She was the Manhattan man-eater, after all. Genetically unsuited for the male/female relationship game.

Which was why she'd insisted on the lovemaking clause. When Buck put his hands on her, her brain had the most alarming tendency to leak out her ears. There could be no brain leaks. Oh, no. With Buck, she needed all her wits about her all of the time.

They'd get through the two weeks, maybe even get to…understand each other a little better. And when they returned to Manhattan, they'd be going their separate ways.

Pretty much.

Except for the baby.

The baby. A second, more important reason—beyond the feature article she needed—for her to reconcile herself to fourteen days in the piney woods with Buck.

She hadn't forgotten what he'd told her at dinner: that bit about being a Bravo and a Bravo always doing the right thing…

Message received. It was looking far too likely that, where the baby was concerned, she would have to come to some kind of working relationship with him.

Maybe in the next two weeks, she'd get a clearer idea of the best way to do that. Maybe they would grow… closer. In a purely friendly kind of way.

"Hah." The mocking sound escaped her at the very thought of being "purely friendly" with Buck. "So never going to happen," she announced to the bead-board above, and then she slid down in the tub until the water closed over her head.

She came up a moment later, blinking and sputtering, a taunting voice in the back of her mind whispering wickedly, *You'll never keep your hands off that man for two whole weeks and you know damn well that you won't.*

Bright and early the next morning, as she sprinted over the rag rugs in her bare feet and a silk sleep shirt, racing to make it to the facilities before she horked up what was left of last night's steak dinner, B.J. discovered the worst thing about having her bathroom down the hall: the distance from the toilet.

She did make it, though. Barely.

One morning down. Thirteen to go. Oh, the joy.

B.J. brushed her teeth, pulled herself together and went on downstairs.

The dining room was done up in classic B & B Victorian: dark wood floor and paneling, cabbage-rose wallpaper above the plate rails. On one wall loomed a heavily carved mirrored sideboard. There were four small tables, all decked out in varying china patterns with depression-glass accessories. A larger table, set in the same charming mish-mash of styles as the others, waited by the room's bow window. B.J., Buck and Lupe took that one.

Chastity did the cooking and Glory served. The girl bustled around, setting out the muffin basket and pouring coffee from a silver pot, her shining brown hair tied back, a blue bib apron over her jeans and light sweater. B.J. had to make an effort not to stare at her. This Glory seemed like a completely different person from the bug-eyed, screaming, wild-woman of the day before.

"Coffee?" Glory bent close and asked the question in B.J.'s ear.

She almost said decaf. But right then just the smell of the stuff made B.J.'s stomach lurch. "Ah...no, thanks." B.J. craned back to meet Glory's warm brown eyes. Glory smiled. She had dimples: a pair of cute little dents to either side of her plump mouth. "Do you have apple juice?"

"Comin' right up."

The girl hustled away and B.J. stared after her, still marveling at the difference: Glory Dellazola, then and now. She turned back to the table—and there was Buck. Watching *her.* B.J. gave him a shrug and a smile and he smiled back and...

Well, other than that irritating shiver of excitement that danced along the surface of her skin, it was okay. Nice. Cordial. They'd be best friends in no time.

Yeah, right.

Since there were no other guests, Chastity and Glory joined them at the table by the window.

Bowie came in late. He'd shaved his scruffy beard and combed his long, thick blond hair. He seemed kind of sweet, really. Big, handsome in a raw-boned sort of way—and embarrassed.

"Sorry about yesterday," he muttered, when Buck formally introduced him to B.J.

"No problem," B.J. told him. What else was there to say?

Bowie took the empty seat next to Glory—for about half a second. His rear end hit the chair and Glory leapt to her feet.

"I'll get you a plate," she said, looking everywhere but at Bowie. Then she took off.

When she returned, she shoved a full plate under his nose, picked up her own plate—and relocated to the other side of the table. Bowie glared at her across the needlepoint tablecloth and depression-glass condiment bowls.

She grabbed her fork and ate, head down, never once looking up to meet Bowie's angry eyes.

"Well," said Chastity, far too brightly, in a transparent attempt to take the focus off Bowie and his pregnant girlfriend. "What's up for today?"

Buck sipped his coffee. "For starters, I thought we'd have another look around town."

B.J. saw her chance and went for it. "Oh. Well, since you're writing the article yourself now, you won't need me for that. I think I'll just—"

"B.J." Buck set down his cup. "We'll need you."

They didn't. No way they needed her. Buck could take Lupe and wander up and down Main Street, soaking up the atmosphere of the old hometown without B.J. along. And B.J. could do…other things. "But really, I—"

"You're going." He gave her a piercing look. It had *Remember the deal we made* written all over it.

She considered saying something snide.

But they *had* made a deal. She picked up her apple juice and toasted him with it.

B.J. called Buck's agent before they left. The agent, who said she'd already heard from Buck, named a figure. A very reasonable one. B.J. agreed to it. The agent said goodbye.

B.J. stood there with the phone in her hand. Whatever happened to the fine art of negotiation? Hours of it would have been nice. She could have told Buck, *Sorry. No can do. Business, you understand....*

But no. The deal was a wrap. Time to head on downstairs for a morning of looking at clapboard tin-roofed buildings and waving at people Buck had known as a child.

Wait. What about L.T.? True, she remained thoroughly annoyed with him. If she never spoke to him again it would be much too soon.

And yet...

L.T. should know about the contract. He could call the business office and get things rolling—okay, it was a weak excuse to stall a little longer. But at that moment, she'd take what she could get. She dialed the Castle.

Roderick answered. He asked her to please wait. A moment later, L.T. came on the line.

"What's up?" her father growled into her ear.

"Good morning to you, too. Buck's decided to write the piece for us."

"Excellent."

She couldn't resist. "We now have a memoir. No more *objective eye*. Aren't you upset?"

"Screw that. His name on the byline's better."

"Exactly." She told him what they were paying and asked him to put the contract through.

"No problem. How'd you do it?"

She hadn't, of course. Buck had. But no way she'd tell L.T. that. "You don't want to know—and I'll be here for two weeks."

"What the hell? You don't need to be there at all, now you're not doing the writing. I'll send the jet for you. Get back here and get back to work."

"Ah. So you need me." She would have felt warm and fuzzy all over—if such a thing were possible in connection with L.T.

He didn't admit he needed her—he never did. "You're damn well not needed *there,* now, are you?"

"No. But to get Buck to do the writing, I had to promise him I would stay here for two weeks while he steeps himself in all things 'hometown.'"

There was a silence on the line. She could *hear* her father's big brain working. Eventually, he said, "He's still got a thing for you, hasn't he?" Before she could come up with a suitably vague answer, he went right on. "I suspected as much—you sleeping with him again?"

"This is so not a convo we need to have." There was a knock at the door. "Look. Gotta go now."

"B.J., you have a real good time," her father said.

"I don't think I like your tone," she replied, and hung up, thus, for once, getting the last word on L.T. She was smiling in enjoyment of the historic moment as she strode to the door.

It was Buck. Big surprise. He had one muscular arm braced on the door frame, and he lounged there, watching her through those smoldering, sexy dark eyes. Lupe stood in the hallway behind him, wearing her pea coat, a camera swinging from each shoulder.

"Ready?" Buck asked.

"Oh, I suppose."

B.J. grabbed her jacket and they were off to see New Bethlehem Flat. Again.

It was a gorgeous fall day out, brisk and cool, not a cloud in the pale-blue sky.

Buck took them west on Main, past the grocery store where the ancient Tony Dellazola already manned his post on the bench outside. The old guy, deep in conversation with another character about his age, spared them a wave as they went by. They turned left at yet another gift store, wandered through a parking area, passed between the gas station and a pizza parlor, and crossed another bridge.

Once they reached the other side, Buck had more landmarks to point out: the clinic where his brother, Brett, worked; yet another white clapboard house with a tin roof—and a shingle out front that read Cook and Bravo, Attorneys at Law.

"Brand's office," Buck said. "He works with Ma's brother, my uncle Clovis."

There were county offices—the Flat, as it turned out, was the county seat—and a cute little courthouse with a miniature gold dome. Lupe snapped away and B.J. said nothing as she pondered the usual: Was there a point to this, and what she was doing here?

They met more of the locals, including a trio of sweet-faced elderly ladies: Sidney Potter, Margaret Rose and Velma Wiggins. The three, red-nosed in quilted parkas, chided Buck for not coming home to see his dear mother often enough, and then invited him to a pancake breakfast in the town hall before church tomorrow, which was Sunday.

Buck said he'd be there, shooting B.J. a look that said *she'd* be there, too.

The joy, truly, was never-ending.

About eleven-thirty, they headed back to the B & B— at last. They found Chastity in the drawing room, taping paper decorations to the front windows: black cats, witches' hats and dentally challenged jack-o'-lanterns.

Buck grinned at the sight. "Hey. That's right. Tomorrow night's Halloween."

"The thrill of it all," B.J. grumbled and watched in envy as Lupe went on up the stairs without having to ask Buck for permission.

"Lighten up," Buck instructed. "When are you carving the pumpkins, Ma?"

"After lunch."

"B.J. and I will help."

Speak for yourself, she thought, but didn't say. "I'm going upstairs for a minute or two—if that's all right with you?" My lord, my master, my least favorite tour guide…

He gave her a wave, turned his back on her and started digging through the open cardboard box of decorations. "Will you look at this?" He held up a black coffee mug with a white cobweb painted on it.

His mother, still at the front window, glanced over her shoulder and murmured fondly, "My Halloween mug."

Buck dug around in the box again. "And this…"

B.J. didn't stay to see what other touching memento of days gone by he'd discovered, but fled before he could change his mind and call her back.

Upstairs, the door to her room stood open, a maid's cart in front of it. Oh, great. Five minutes to herself and nowhere private to go.

But how long did it take to pick up a room? Maybe Glory was almost done. B.J. slid between the door and the maid's cart and poked her head in.

Glory sat on the bed, shoulders slumped, shining brown head hung low. The bed was made. A quick glance around the room told B.J. that the room was clean and ready for her use.

Well, except that the maid was still in it.

B.J. cleared her throat. Glory started and looked up. "Oh!"

"All finished?"

"Uh. Yeah…yeah, I am. I, uh…" She hung her head again, clearly lost and feeling miserable.

B.J. looked at her pretty down-turned profile, and sympathy—all warm and gooey and totally unacceptable—welled up inside her. Not smart, ever, to get involved in the problems of the help.

Still, B.J. did understand exactly what the girl was going through. After all, B.J., too, was pregnant and planning to go it on her own.

Pregnant by a Bravo, just like Glory.

Since it wasn't the *same* Bravo, that probably didn't amount to any real connection between the two of them. Still, for some strange reason, it *felt* as if it did.

Against her better judgment, B.J. entered the room, shut the door and went to sit beside Glory on the bed. B.J.'s arm, pretty much of its own accord, reached out and gathered the girl close. With a heavy sigh, Glory leaned her dark head on B.J.'s shoulder.

B.J. realized it felt…kind of good. Just to sit there, to feel the other woman's warmth at her side. Kind of friendly. Companionable. Something, for once, without aloneness in it. Without aloneness and also without desire.

For most of her life, B.J. had felt alone. It wasn't a bad feeling, really, and it went hand-in-hand with self-reliance and inner strength, two qualities B.J. was proud to claim. Yes, sometimes, more than *alone,* she felt lonely, which wasn't so great. But she bore her loneliness without complaining, as she'd been brought up to do.

During her time with Buck—that incredible, magical six months, six years ago—she had not felt alone. But there *had* been desire, then. Desire that was hot and wild and insistent and a world away from right now, sitting here, with Glory Dellazola. Now, the lack of aloneness had a peaceful, restful kind of quality about it.

Very odd.

B.J. looked at the vulnerable crown of Glory's head and wondered at herself. Why, this was kind of a… bondy moment, wasn't it?

She'd never been the type to get bondy with other women. It wasn't that she didn't *like* other women. Women were fine. But she simply had no talent for the ways with which they communicated with each other.

B.J.'s mother had died when she was two. L.T. had never remarried. Instead of a wife, he'd had his *Alpha* Girls. An endless, stunning string of them. The kindhearted ones—and the ones who'd hoped in vain to get L.T.'s ring on their fingers—would try to take L.T.'s little girl under their wings.

Wings.

Yes.

Birds…

That was, really, how B.J. saw other women and their complex, cooing, flighty ways of relating to each other. Other women were like birds—another species altogether. B.J. didn't really *get* them, didn't understand what made them tick.

Not that she understood men, either. But then, she wasn't a man, so no one expected her to fully comprehend *them*.

Glory looked up at her. "What's that perfume you're wearing?"

"I have it made."

"Perfume made just for you?"

"That's right."

"I love it."

"Well, thanks."

"And your shoes—yeah, it's true. I peeked at your shoes. That's kind of disgusting, huh?"

"Don't worry about it."

Glory sighed. "Your shoes are incredible."

"I'm flattered you like them."

"You're rich, aren't you?" Glory didn't wait for an answer. She laid her head back on B.J.'s shoulder and went on talking. "I'd like that. To be rich. To be one-hundred-percent totally in charge of my own life. To do what I want when I want and never worry about how I was going to pay for it. To go to college… You went to college, right?" Glory paused long enough for B.J. to make a sound in the affirmative. "And you have a great job at a big-time magazine and an apartment in New York City…." It was a high-floor, corner two-bedroom, one-and a half-bath, on lower Fifth Avenue in a top prewar full-service building, to be specific. But B.J. saw no reason to rub it in or anything. Glory lifted her head again and met B.J.'s eyes. "Bowie told my father that I'm pregnant."

"Oh, no."

"Yeah. He couldn't get me to say yes, so he told my Dad so that my Dad would get me to say yes. I'm furious at Bowie for that."

"And well you should be."

"He had no right…."

"I so agree."

"My Dad told my Mom. And my Mom told my sisters and my sisters told…just about everyone else. And now the whole town knows and everyone in my family is after me, to do like Bowie says and marry him."

B.J. rubbed Glory's shoulder and suggested gently, "I kind of gathered, from what you said the other day, that you knew this would happen."

"Yeah. I did. And I knew I'd hate it, too. And I do. My great-grandpa Tony thinks I'm a slut."

The old guy on the bench? How *could* he? Outraged, B.J. demanded, "He *called* you that?"

"No. He didn't have to. I could see it in his eyes. I can see it *everyone's* eyes."

"Not mine."

A sad little giggle escaped Glory. "Well, no. But you're from New York City. They do things differently there—plus, you're not Catholic, are you?"

"Well, no…"

"I am. So's my whole family. You know how Catholics are, don't you?"

B.J. had a pretty good idea. "No birth control. No abortions. Abstinence. Priests."

"Yeah. All that. And all that means that when you're a Catholic, you're supposed to get married *before* you get pregnant. But if you *do* get pregnant first, you should *get* married as soon as possible—to the father of your baby, if you can. And then, once you've married him, you're supposed to *stay* married, forever. Like a life sentence—which is fine, as long as you're smart enough to pick the right person to be sentenced with."

"You don't think Bowie's the right person?"

"Well, he does *feel* like the right person…"

"Meaning you love him."

"Yeah. But, well, love is great and all that. But I have older sisters, you know?"

"You mentioned that, yes."

"Six of them. And two brothers. Nine of us alto-gether—but back to my sisters. The oldest is Trista. The second-oldest is Clarice. Trista's thirty now and Clarice is twenty-eight. When they were about my age—which is twenty—they married wild guys like Bowie. It was love and passion and forever and all that. Tris and Risi are both still married. Also, they're miserable. Tris has three kids and Risi has two. Their husbands stay out all night and neither one of those guys has a job at this particular moment. Maybe I don't have a college education, but I can add two and two and come up with four, if you know what I mean. A leopard doesn't change its spots—and a wild guy with no job? Well, when all the hot passion and heavy breathing wears off, that guy is wild as ever and most likely still unemployed."

B.J. agreed with her. But she didn't say so. No reason to belabor what was already crystal clear—and Glory was looking at her strangely. "What?"

"Are you in love with Buck?"

Ouch. Direct hit. "No."

Glory leaned closer. "You hesitated. I saw you."

B.J. hardly knew what to say. She sputtered out, "Uh. Buck and I have…history. And issues."

"That sounds bad."

"I can't believe I'm talking to you about this."

Glory giggled. "You're not. Not much, anyway. I'm the one doing all the talking. I think the world of Buck."

"Oh, really?"

"Yeah. Buck's pretty special. He's kind of the exception that proves the rule, if you think about it. I mean, he was crazy-wild as a kid. Do you know that the night of his high-school graduation, he got drunk and went skinny-dipping under the Logan Bridge? That's the bridge behind the Pizza Parlor. He got hungry after his swim, so he went on up to the Pizza Parlor—without bothering to put his clothes back on first."

Now, there was an image. Buck in the Pizza Parlor, naked and soaking wet, ordering himself a slice and a jumbo soft drink to go with it. "No, he never mentioned that."

"There's lots of wild things he did, before he headed off to Texas, supposedly to work in the oil fields. No one believed he was actually going to work—in the oil fields or anywhere else—when he left town. Because while he was here, he never could hold a job. He couldn't even *get* one by the time he left. No one would hire him after he almost burned down the grocery store taking a smoke break in the back."

"You're kidding."

"I'm not. He never told you?"

"No."

"He was so hopeless. But so cute, you know, like all the Bravo boys? So…sexy, in that dangerous, what-will-he-do-next kind of way. Half the girls in town had a crush on him. And then, when he left, no one ever expected he'd amount to anything. But look at him now. He's pretty famous, isn't he?"

"Yes, he is."

"And he lives in New York City and writes stuff for good money. He's written a whole book, even. It's not a regular job—but it *is* a job. Sometimes, when I think of Buck, it gives me hope that Bowie might change, after all. You know?"

B.J. said softly, "Yeah. I can see that."

Glory hung her head again and heaved a gusty sigh. "Well, I should probably get back to work, I guess...."

"You sure you're all right?"

"Yeah. As all right as I can be, considering I'm a pregnant unmarried Catholic with a hopeless unemployed wild man for a boyfriend and I live in a small town where everyone spends all their free time gossiping about everyone else." Glory stood and turned to look down at B.J. "Thanks for listening...."

"Anytime." Had she actually said that?

"It's good...to have someone to talk to, sometimes. Someone not involved in your problem in any way. You know?"

B.J. imagined it *would* be good. Maybe. She nodded.

Glory beamed, all dimples and shining amber-brown eyes. "Well. Okay. Back to work." And she turned and left B.J. sitting alone on the bed, marveling.

No doubt about it now. B.J. had just done the bondy thing with another woman. It hadn't been half bad, either—and she'd learned a thing or two about Buck.

Not that it really mattered, what she learned about Buck. Uh-uh. What she'd learned about Buck *didn't* matter.

Not in the least...

Eight

That afternoon, out on the enclosed back porch, Buck, Chastity, Glory and B.J. carved pumpkins. Twenty of them. Enough to line either side of the slate walk out front, from the white picket fence up the steps to the front door.

Bowie showed up not long after the carving began and pitched in, too. Lupe made herself scarce for the event. Lucky Lupe. She was there to shoot a Christmas feature. For Halloween and pumpkin-carving, her presence was not required.

B.J. didn't need to be there, either. Except that *her* only job for the next two weeks was to be where Buck wanted her, when he wanted her there. Buck wanted her on the back porch carving pumpkins—and so, here she was.

How could this have happened?

The night before, when she'd agreed to his terms,

she hadn't truly realized the extent to which he would get to run her life. Oh, she could so easily become bitter....

Then again, B.J. thought, as she bravely dug her bare hand into the seedy, slimy center of her second pumpkin of the afternoon, the situation could be worse. With five people slaving away at the task, it would only take a couple of hours.

And Buck looked so happy. He reminisced as he hacked away at one hapless jack-o'-lantern after another. It was, "Remember the year we..." and "I'll never forget that time when..."

B.J. found herself watching him, feeling something that could only be called fondness. And then he would look up and meet her eyes. They would share a smile....

Okay, all right. This was risky behavior. He could get the wrong idea altogether.

But then she would picture him—a wild teenager, naked in the Pizza Parlor, drunk as the proverbial skunk. And she'd wonder why he'd never told her about that when they were lovers, wonder why he'd never told her what a wild kid he'd been....

And then Glory would catch her eye and give her the smile of a true co-conspirator. B.J. would grin back, warm all over with that new sensation of woman-to-woman bondy-ness.

It was nice. A good time.

Well, except for Bowie. The guy had a terminal case of the sulks. And he didn't seem to care much for Glory and B.J. sharing looks. The first time they grinned at each other, he scowled—B.J. saw him do it out of the corner of her eye. The second time, he grunted. A disgusted sound.

The third time, Bowie threw down his carving knife—splat—into a mound of fresh-scooped pumpkin guts. "Okay, Glory. What the hell's going on? You won't give *me* the time of day, but all of a sudden you and Buck's girl are best friends?"

"What?" Glory stabbed her knife into the side of her pumpkin. It quivered there and then went still. "Now, you don't want me to have any *friends?*"

"Ahem," B.J. ventured gingerly, thinking she really ought to clarify. "I am not Buck's girl."

"She might be, soon, though," Buck put in, teasingly.

B.J. opened her mouth to set Buck straight, but before she could get the words out, Bowie started shouting. "Stay out of this, Miss New York Frickin' City. It's got nothin' to do with you."

"Hey!" cried Chastity.

"Bowie." Buck wasn't teasing now. "Cut that out."

Glory waded in, brown eyes blazing. "Yeah. You leave her alone, you big jerk."

Bowie lunged to his feet and loomed over Glory. "Oh, so now I'm a jerk, am I?"

"Yeah. Yeah, you are. A big, mean, sulky, blabber-mouthed, *unemployed* jerk."

"Why, you little—"

"Bowie!" Buck and Chastity shouted in unison.

That shut Bowie up—for a second or two, during which he fisted his hands at his sides, stepped back and then forward, as if he didn't quite know what to do with himself. At last he spoke again, more quietly this time. "I did the right thing. You know I did."

"Wrong," cried Glory. "Wrong, wrong, wrong."

"Everybody was going to know eventually, anyway."

"That's no excuse and you know it's not."

"Why won't you just—?"

She waved him off with a pumpkin-gooey hand. "Leave me alone. I mean it. I'm through with you."

"But you can't—"

"Yeah, I can. Just you watch me."

"How can you—?"

"I'll say it again. I'll say it a hundred times. I'm through with you, Bowie. Just leave me alone."

Bowie stared down at her. He looked sick. B.J. almost felt sorry for him. Finally, he growled, "Carve the damn pumpkins yourself," and stormed out the porch door.

Everybody winced as he slammed it behind him. He pounded down the back steps.

"Where's he going?" B.J. asked, once the porch stopped shaking.

"Don't know," Glory muttered. "But one thing I'm sure of. He's not going to work—being as how he doesn't have a job."

"Ah," B.J. said, for lack of anything better. She concentrated on her pumpkin again.

An uneasy silence reigned until Chastity said gently, "You shouldn't get him going."

"I know." Glory yanked the knife out of her pumpkin. It made a hollow, sucking sound as it came free. "But I've had it with him. Look at how he behaves—and you *know* what he did."

"I know, I know." Chastity was shaking her head.

"I don't," said Buck, frowning in puzzlement. "What did he do?" Chastity and Glory both stared at him—and then at each other. Neither replied. Buck prompted, "Well?"

Chastity said, "Why don't we just let it go for now?"

Glory leaned closer to Buck and whispered, "Ask B.J. later. She knows all about it."

Once they'd finished with the pumpkins and cleaned up the mess they'd made, Buck decided to get B.J. out of there.

"Come on," he said. "We're going for a ride."

She gave him a look that brimmed with suspicion. "Isn't that what they say in the Mafia? Then they drive you to a deserted cornfield, strangle you and stick a dead canary in your mouth."

He went for ingenuousness. "No cornfields around here."

To which she replied, "I am not reassured."

Still, she ran upstairs and got her jacket and followed him out to the rented SUV. He drove them to a certain place along the highway, pulled to the shoulder and turned off the engine.

She looked over at the sharp drop-off a few feet away from her passenger window. "I'm really getting worried now."

"There used to be a trail leading down to the river from here."

"Do I have any kind of choice in this?"

He let his silence speak for him.

She rolled her eyes. "Oh, fine. Let's go."

So they got out and he led her to the edge of the bank. "See the trail?"

"Unfortunately, yes."

They went down, batting aside fir branches and dogwood bushes as they stumbled along. At last, they emerged onto a shadowed rocky promontory at the river's edge.

"Oh," she said, stuffing her hands in her jacket

pockets against the afternoon chill. "I get it. You're going to drown me."

To that remark, he only suggested pleasantly, "Have a seat."

She sent him one of her how-did-I-get-myself-into-this? looks, but she did sit on the rock. He dropped down beside her. For a few minutes, they just sat there, staring out over the water. Quiet together.

It was nice, really, Buck thought. Just the two of them, here, in this spot he remembered so well. When she shifted beside him and pulled her jacket closer around her against the cold autumn wind, he turned from the view of the opposite bank and studied her profile: strong jaw, full mouth. She'd gotten her nose from her father. A commanding nose. It was red at the tip from the cold.

She asked, still not looking at him, "What, by the way, are we doing here?"

"This was once my favorite swimming hole." He pointed at the shallow rapids upstream. "You can cross there, carrying your stuff, if you're careful and steady on your feet. I used to. I'd take a towel. And maybe a worn-out old pack containing my shirt, my shoes—and a beer or two boosted from Ma's fridge when she wasn't looking."

"Shame on you."

"Yeah, I was bad. I'm not denying it. I'd come here and cross to the sandy side. I'd swim, I'd guzzle my two warm beers and take a nap in the sun. I'd dream about what a big shot I was going to be someday, about how everyone in town who ever called me a loser would one day be kissing my ass...."

She turned to him then, tipping her blond head to the side, resting it on her drawn-up knees. Her hair, loose and curling slightly, fell along her denim-covered thighs and brushed the tops of her knee-high suede boots. He wanted to touch it—her hair.

He wanted to touch *all* of her. Slowly. With great care. He leaned back on his hands so they couldn't reach for her.

She said, "Glory told me that on your graduation night, you went in the Pizza Parlor naked."

He studied her some more, now she was facing him: that mouth, those eyes like blue smoke. "What else did Glory tell you?"

"That you almost burned down the grocery store having a cigarette."

"Did she tell you what *kind* of cigarette?"

She tried not to smile—he saw her mouth twitch. "No, she didn't mention that. But she did say you couldn't keep a job."

"Sad but true." He waited, wondering what she'd have to say about his wild and mostly wasted youth. But she didn't speak, only lifted her head and looked out over the water again. He asked, "So what did Bowie do that has Glory more pissed off at him than ever?"

"I don't know, not for sure…."

"Take a stab at it."

She picked up a pebble and threw it out into the water. It hardly made a splash. "Well, he did tell her father that she's pregnant."

Damn. Bowie. All torn up inside and making one wrong move after another. "You're sure?"

"Yeah. Or at least, that's what Glory said he did."

"Not smart of him."

A slight frown took form between her smooth brows. "Sometimes you do surprise me."

"Because?"

"Well, after what you said last night—about how Bowie would marry her no matter what, since she's having his baby—I would have guessed that you'd be just fine with him going to her father."

"Maybe I would be fine with it—if Bowie's talking to her father had a chance in hell of doing any good. But it doesn't. Bowie knows she's not the type to be pushed around, by her boyfriend *or* by her father. Plus, Bowie had to realize her father wouldn't keep quiet about it."

She actually smiled at him then, that wonderful mouth blooming wide. "Yeah. Glory said that her father told her mother and her mother told—"

"All six of her sisters."

"Who promptly told everyone else."

Buck grunted. "I just can't figure what gave Bowie the wild idea that Little Tony could *make* Glory marry him."

"Little Tony?"

"Lots of Tonys in the Dellazola family. Old Tony— that's the guy on the bench. Tony, Jr.—Old Tony's son, Glory's grandfather. And Little Tony."

"Glory's dad."

"See? You're catchin' on. And let's not leave out Anthony, Glory's brother—and Anthony's son, baby Tony."

She shook her head at the idea of all those Tonys and then said, "Well, Bowie's a desperate man, I guess."

He moved a fraction closer to her.

She sat very still. The wind took several strands of her hair and blew them across her mouth. She smoothed the strands behind her ear and looked at him warily. "We should go back now."

"Back where?"

"Oh, come on. Where else? The B & B…"

"You don't like it here, in the shade on this freezing rock, across from the deserted beach on which I drank a large number of stolen beers during my troubled, misspent youth?" The strands of hair blew across her mouth again. She reached up. He caught her wrist.

"Buck…" It was a warning.

One that he didn't heed. "Let me."

Several seconds went by. He held onto her wrist, felt the cool, silky texture of her skin, thought about how he had missed the hell out of her for six damn years and, the whole time, kept telling himself he didn't. Six whole years, during which he'd pretended that he couldn't care less if he ever saw her face again.

But then there was that night in September.

And he finally realized he was through pretending.

She whispered, "Watch it," and pulled her hand free of his grip.

What she didn't do was guide those strands of hair out of her mouth.

He asked, "May I?"

She swallowed. Her nod was almost imperceptible.

He took his time about it, leaning closer, sucking in the scent of her, brushing the pads of his fingers against her upper lip and across the satiny skin of her cheek. "There."

She drew in a tiny gasp of a breath and her eyes were softer, smokier than ever, the way they got when he kissed her, when he did to her all the things she'd made him promise he wouldn't. "No sex, remember?" She whispered the reminder.

"I remember." Sadly enough. "But don't worry. This isn't sex."

"It's what leads up to sex."

"Not necessarily."

"Whatever. It's too close for comfort."

"Did I promise you comfort?"

"No, Buck. You didn't."

He told the naked truth. "I want to kiss you."

She swallowed, caught a corner of her lower lip between her pretty teeth. "Bad idea…"

"No. Not so. Good idea. Excellent, even…" He leaned even closer, until he could feel her breath across his mouth. "You want to kiss me, too. You know you do."

"Damn you, Buck…."

It wasn't a no. So he went for it. He leaned that quarter-inch closer and covered her mouth with his.

Nine

B.J. sighed.

Good, Buck thought. He wanted her sighing. He tasted her lips—the softness, the sweetness. He kissed her with care, with tenderness. With barely leashed desire.

Much too soon—within seconds—she pulled away. He looked down at her kiss-pink lips, her flushed cheeks. Her eyes were softer than ever now. Those eyes betrayed her. They begged him to kiss her some more.

But then she said in a husky whisper, "I mean it. I want to go back now."

He rose and held down his hand to her. She let him help her to her feet.

That night, B.J. and Buck met his two middle brothers at the Nugget for dinner. A couple of big, good-looking bachelors, Brett and Brand each possessed an actual sense of humor—unlike the morose and temperamental Bowie.

"We were the boring Bravo brothers," Brand, the lawyer, told B.J. Brand had gold hair a shade darker than Bowie's and hazel eyes.

"Meaning we worked hard in high school and then went on to get our degrees and do our internships," Brett explained. He had darker hair than Brand's, though not as dark as Buck's. "And we now have—wait for it—real jobs."

"Bowie and Buck are the wild ones," Brand said. "As you've probably noticed, Buck has succeeded in shocking the hell out of everyone in town by turning out okay, after all."

"Gee, thanks," said Buck.

"The jury's still out on Bowie," Brett added, sounding rueful.

"Signs are not favorable." Brand looked somber.

Buck said, "Give the kid time. He'll work through all this crap."

His brothers only looked at him, their expressions frankly skeptical. Buck shrugged and asked Brand how he liked being in partnership with their uncle Clovis.

"It's all right," said Brand. "I have the office pretty much to myself. Uncle Clo is all but retired now...."

B.J. let the brothers talk. She was busy with her salad, anyway. Raging hunger had struck out of nowhere again, same as last night. Her salad was incredible. The best she'd ever tasted.

Brett lifted an eyebrow at her. "This girl can really pack it away."

Beside her, Buck chuckled. B.J. only grunted and went on shoveling in the food. When her steak came, she ate it all. And two dinner rolls slathered with butter. And her baked potato with sour cream and chives, as well—oh, and the salty, crumbly bacon bits. To die for. She ate every last yummy one, pressing her fork on them to get the last few off the plate after the potato was gone.

She'd be running down the hall in her silk sleep shirt tomorrow morning, on her way to give the toilet a big hug. But that was tomorrow. Right now, while she could, if it wasn't nailed down, she was eating it.

It was all gone much too soon. Nadine cleared off their plates and served coffee to the men, herb tea to B.J.

Brett said, "I hear you work at *Alpha* magazine."

B.J. nodded. She was still chomping her final piece of bread. She swallowed it and caught Nadine before she got away again. "About the rice pudding?"

Nadine nodded. "Lots of cinnamon and raisins. You want some?"

"Oh, yes. Please."

Nadine glanced around at the Bravo boys. "Anyone else?"

The men all shook their heads. The waitress trotted off.

Brand said, "I understand that L. T. Carlyle's your dad?"

"That's right." B.J. dunked her teabag in the little metal teapot and wished that Nadine would hurry up with that pudding.

"L. T. Carlyle," said Brett in a musing tone. "A living legend, and that is no lie."

Buck said, "B.J.'s the features editor at *Alpha*. One of these days—and it's not going to be all that long, trust me—she'll be running the whole enterprise." He sounded so…proud.

B.J. forgot all about the rice pudding as she felt her face start to color.

Omigod. The horror. She was actually blushing with pleasure.

She had to face it. The guy was getting to her. They were barely twenty-four hours into her two weeks of virtual slavery to his every whim—and she *blushed* when he said something nice about her?

And what about that kiss? a disapproving voice in her head inquired.

What kiss?

You know what kiss.

The kiss she'd been trying not to think about since it had happened—out there on that icy rock by the river in the afternoon.

But that hardly counts, she tried to reason. It was only a little, tiny, brushing breath of a kiss....

Stop, the disapproving inner voice commanded. *No more excuses. You've done what you've done and a kiss is a kiss, no matter how brief.*

She had to quit kidding herself. Her situation was nothing short of dire. A slippery slope and she was on her way down.

He'd have her in one of those bondage collars before you knew it. In a bondage collar, on a lead. He'd be trotting her up Main Street. It would be, *Sit, B.J. Stay.*

She took great care not to look at him, to concentrate instead on dunking her teabag until it sank. If she looked at him, she just knew she'd grin like an idiot and drool like a fool.

"*Alpha*'s great," Brand was saying. "In-depth articles. I like that."

"And don't forget the *Alpha* Girls," said Brett.

B.J. sighed. "Nobody forgets the *Alpha* Girls."

Hey. That hadn't sounded half-bad, now, had it? Cool and collected and totally unconcerned.

And her blush was definitely fading.

On second thought, she shouldn't let herself over-react. Altogether, she was handling herself fine. Doing splendidly, really.

Nadine appeared with her pudding. B.J. dug in. Oh, it was good! For a minute or two, she didn't hear a word any of the Bravos said, she was so busy having an orgasm in her mouth.

Then Brett said, "*TopMale*'s not bad, either."

B.J. sat very still, a bite of pudding halfway to her mouth. Had Brett read the man-eater article? Did he *know?*

But then Brand said, "Oh, come on. *Alpha* sets the standard. It's been that way for twenty years."

Outside the restaurant, B.J. and Buck said goodbye to his brothers. Then, just as the night before, they headed down Main side-by-side on their way to Commerce Lane and the bridge that would take them to the Sierra Star.

Buck said nothing until they'd walked between the rows of unlit pumpkins and up the steps to the front porch. Then he caught her hand.

She stiffened. But she didn't pull away.

Truthfully, it felt so…

Well, there was no other word for it: *right.* It felt right, to have his hand clasping hers. Exciting. And yet companionable, too—slippery slope, be damned.

"B.J.?" He pulled her over to one of the wicker settees and tugged her down beside him.

Careful, she thought. No idiot grins. And absolutely no drooling. "What now?"

His white teeth flashed in the darkness. "You're so tough."

His teasing gave her the excuse she needed to pull her hand from his. "Believe it."

"Don't worry," he said. "Brett knows nothing…"

She felt her cheeks flame—and not from pleasure, this time. At least, in the dark, he couldn't see her shame.

What to say now?

Play dumb. Maybe he'll take the hint and drop the subject. "About?"

"That obnoxious article by your ex-boyfriend."

Deny everything, cried a desperate voice in her head. But somehow, she couldn't. She looked out toward the rows of pumpkins marching away from them down the walk and heard herself say in a very small voice, "I really know how to pick 'em, don't I?"

He touched her chin. She let him guide her face around until she was looking at him. "Hey, you picked me. Once."

She pushed his hand away. "And look how beautifully that turned out."

"We had some good times, you know we did." He sounded so hopeful. His dark eyes gleamed.

And he was right. They'd had some very, very good times. Sundays in bed sharing *The Times,* afternoons in the park strolling the trails by the carousel, talking late into the night about any- and everything…

And the sex. That had been spectacular. Unforgettable. The best of her life.

And why was she thinking about sex? "What was the question?"

"I said, we had some good times."

She heard herself make a low noise of agreement—after all, he was right.

He declared, "And it's not your fault that Wayne Epperstall is a weasely little bastard."

"Wyatt."

"What?"

"His name is Wyatt—and yes, he is a weasel. He's even got a slight overbite. I thought it made him look sweet and sensitive when I first met him. I thought he *was* sweet and sensitive, if you must know."

"You thought wrong."

"Yeah—and I guess this means I can't kid myself any longer. You did read the damn article, didn't you?"

"That's right. I read it. And after I read it, I considered having a long, up-close and personal talk with what's-his-name."

"Wyatt."

"Yeah. Him. I considered beating the everlovin' crap out of Wyatt. But then I thought again. I decided he wasn't worth the effort." He took her hand once more. She let him have it. Yes, it showed weakness. But at that moment, she just didn't care. He turned her hand over and stroked her palm and she let him do that, too. It felt really, really good—much better than it should have. Electric. Warm. Wonderful. He added, "But I'm open to suggestion. Say the word. I'll rearrange his overbite for you."

She sent him a look from under her lashes. "If I wanted his teeth broken, I'd do it myself."

"That's the spirit—and take it from me. Though it's possible that someone in the Flat could have read that article, it's not possible that anyone could know it's about you."

"Half of Manhattan knows."

"This isn't Manhattan."

"No argument there."

"And the good news is, by the time you get back to the city, everyone will be talking about something else. Wyatt and his spiteful article will be seriously old news."

She slanted him another glance. "Are you trying to make me feel happy I came here?"

"Do you think you *could* feel happy about it?"

No way she would cop to that one. "Let's go in. Okay?"

"Whatever you want."

So completely not true. But since she felt downright affectionate toward him at that moment, she let the remark pass without a word of argument.

"Dear, you haven't touched your breakfast," said Sidney Potter.

B.J., seated next to Buck at one of several folding tables in the dining room of the town hall, looked down at her paper plate. It held two rubbery flapjacks drowned in syrup, a glob of dry scrambled eggs and a matched pair of greasy sausages.

Her stomach did a nasty little roll at the sight.

Swiftly, B.J. looked up and forced a big smile for Sidney, who stood across the table wearing rubber gloves and a chef's apron and carrying a wet rag.

"I'm a light eater as a rule," B.J. explained. "And I had a huge dinner last night." A lot of which she'd lost earlier that morning, but Sidney didn't need to know that.

"Breakfast is the most important meal," Sidney declared with a firm nod of her wiry gray head and a sharp snap of her rag.

"Oh, Sidney. That's so true." B.J. nodded right back, and wished the sweet old lady would go wipe some tables off.

"Eat, eat," said Sidney.

So B.J. picked up her plastic fork and looked down at her plate again.

No. She couldn't do it. And it wasn't a good idea to continue focusing on the congealing puddles of syrup, the soggy-looking…

She glanced up again—fast—and sucked in a big breath through her nose.

Sidney Potter's eagle eyes were waiting. "Dear. You look a tad peaked. Are you feeling well?"

"Just fine." B.J. glanced brightly around. "Nice turnout." The citizens of New Bethlehem Flat had shown up in full force for the Annual Methodist Ladies Auxiliary Pancake Breakfast. The rows of folding tables were half-full. People got in line, got their food, grabbed a seat, ate and then cleared out to make room for the next wave of happy pancake eaters.

Sidney smiled her beatific smile. "Yes, we get a great turnout every year. We're always so pleased—Buck?"

Buck, seated to B.J.'s right, was having no trouble getting *his* food down. He swallowed a mouthful of pancake, took a gulp of coffee and lifted an eyebrow at Sidney to show he was listening.

"I do hope you and B.J. will come on over to the service at ten."

"We just might do that, Mrs. Potter," Buck said with a wink and went back to his pancakes.

"Now, that would be lovely—and I'd best get to work, now hadn't I?" Sidney clucked her tongue in a good-natured way and turned to the next table over where empty plates waited to be carried to the trash bins. B.J., still scrupulously avoiding eye contact with her plate, watched Sidney work her way down the table, clearing and wiping as she went.

Across the room, Glory sat with a big group, Old Tony among them. Judging by certain physical similarities—lots of dark hair, dimples and brown eyes—B.J. pegged them as the Dellazola clan. Glory, looking a little glum, brightened when B.J. caught her eye. The girl waved. Old Tony looked over and gave B.J. a nod.

And right then, Bowie, carrying his tray of flapjacks, eggs and sausage, reached the Dellazola table. The men, their expressions severe, nodded at him. One of the women slid over to make a space between herself and Glory.

Glory shot upright, grabbed her tray, and headed for the trash cans lined up along the kitchen wall. One of the men—her father, Little Tony, B.J. guessed— shouted after her.

"Glory, you get back here!"

Glory pretended not to hear. B.J. watched her dump the remains of her breakfast, drop her tray with a clatter onto the steel counter, and march right out of the hall.

Buck muttered, "Poor Bowie. Can't catch a break— you okay?"

"Of course." She glanced over at him—and found him looking at her full plate.

He met her eyes. "Mrs. Potter's right. You do look kind of pale. And you haven't touched your breakfast. As a matter of fact, I don't think you've eaten breakfast since we got to California."

She thought, *That's right, Buck. The truth is, I'm having your baby.* She said, "I'm fine. Just not hungry."

"Sure?"

"Positive. So. Where are you dragging me off to today?"

There was a moment, a scary one. She was certain

he would insist on more discussion of the serious weirdness of her eating habits lately. Her stomach lurched and her heart did, too.

But no. He let it go. "I thought we'd do a little hiking."

Relief flooded through her. She tried not to show it—which wasn't all that difficult, considering what he'd just said. "Hiking. I hate hiking. Far too much sweating involved."

"You used to sweat on that Stairmaster of yours every morning."

"I still do. And I hate *it,* too. I only do it for my health—and to look halfway decent in my Chloé jeans."

"B.J. You're going."

"I know, I know."

They hiked up two mountains that day—just B.J. and Buck. Lupe decided to take another pass. At the top, they stood and looked down at the picturesque town tucked into its canyon below.

That was what you did when you hiked. You sweated and struggled to the top. And at the top, you looked down. B.J. had done a lot of hiking with L.T. during her childhood. She hadn't much enjoyed it then and she didn't care for it now.

But she kept her bargain with Buck. She went. She sweated. She looked down at New Bethlehem Flat and nodded when Buck said how gorgeous it was.

She also let him hold her hand. Once. When they got to the top of the second peak.

It was a moment of weakness, that was all. Nothing serious. He reached over and his warm, firm hand closed around hers and…

Well, for a second or two there, she didn't want to let go.

So she didn't.

Only for a minute or two…or five.

No worries. A slight lapse, nothing more…

That night was Halloween. They lit the rows of pumpkins on the walk and sat in the drawing room with Chastity, waiting for the trick-or-treaters. When the kids came, they took turns answering the door.

At a little after ten, B.J. and Buck went out together to blow out the candles in the pumpkins. He tried to get her to linger on the porch with him, tried to lead her away from the porch light, into the shadows and the comfort of a wicker settee.

She declined and went on up to bed, feeling pleased with herself and certain she wasn't weakening toward him, after all.

Nope. Not in the least.

The next day, Monday, Lupe announced she was returning to New York. Her agent had booked her a couple of fashion shoots. Since the Bravo project would be going on into the following week, Lupe said she would take care of the two New York jobs and return next Monday to finish up the shots for Buck's story.

B.J. wanted to demand that Lupe stay. But her reasons were purely personal. Without Lupe, it was Buck and B.J., alone together, way too much of the time.

Then again, it was *already* her and Buck, alone, most of the time. Lupe had taken all the shots of New Bethlehem Flat they could possibly need and, though she didn't say it right out, B.J. knew the photographer had to be weary of tagging along while B.J. fulfilled her agreement with Buck.

"Maybe we'll get lucky and it'll snow next week," Lupe said. "Think about it. We're going to need some seasonal-looking shots. What I've got so far just doesn't say Christmas." B.J. promised they'd come up with something and Lupe took off, leaving B.J. firmly resolved to be more guarded with Buck—on the physical contact front, especially.

As a result of her vigilance, Monday and Tuesday passed with minimal incidents.

Okay, there was another kiss. A little one, Monday night, on the porch after they got home from dinner.

Well, maybe a little more than *little*. She'd sucked his tongue inside her mouth before she realized what she was doing.

But she'd pushed it right out again and pulled away. It ought to count for something, that she hadn't let it go too far. And Tuesday, well, he held her hand once— and another time he put his arm around her.

Though she tried to tell herself nothing was happening, these lapses were unsettling. Mostly because she enjoyed them far too much: the heat of his big body pressing close to hers, the thrill of his touch.

All that.

Bad, bad, bad.

B.J. lay in bed awake late into Tuesday night, giving herself lectures, promising the ceiling that she'd never hold his hand again, that his arm would never again hook itself around her shoulder. Eventually, she did drop off.

Then came the dreams—graphic ones.

Dreams in which there was nakedness, panting and a whole lot of sweating. Dreams in which Buck's hand did a lot more than reach for hers. Dreams with long, wet kisses in them. Dreams where she took him inside her, so big and hard and deep.

Naughty dreams. Incredible dreams…

She woke at seven, furious at her own libido—and, as usual, about to hurl.

With a small cry of misery and abject frustration, she shoved back the covers and leapt to her feet. This would be a close one.

She took off— racing to the door, throwing it open, sprinting down the hall. Luckily, she'd left her bathroom door slightly ajar the night before.

She shoved it wide and threw herself at the toilet bowl. Dropping hard to her knees, she banged back the seat.

The yarking commenced.

It went on longer than usual, until her stomach was so empty, it ached. Pregnancy. Not for sissies.

At last, when there was absolutely nothing left in there, she flushed and flipped down the lid, dragging herself upright and over to the sink a foot or so away.

Elbows braced hard on the sink rim, she rinsed her mouth and sloshed water on her face. At last, with a groan, she lifted her gaze to the mirror above the basin.

And saw Glory standing in the doorway behind her.

B.J. wiped her mouth with the back of her hand. "Uh. Hi." She straightened and turned.

Idiot, she silently scolded herself. She should have shut the damn door as she went flying by it—but then again, there just hadn't been time. If she'd paused even a fraction of a second, she wouldn't have made it to the toilet. It had been that close.

Calm, she thought. *Easy.* So she was feeling a little under the weather this morning. It didn't have to *mean* anything. A twenty-four-hour bug. So what? No big deal. She pressed her hand against her stomach. "Feeling a little…sick, I guess. That's all."

Glory blinked. "Holy Mary, Mother of God," she said in a voice full of awe and understanding. "You're pregnant, too."

Ten

"What?" B.J. tried not to sound as appalled as she felt. No one was supposed to know. Not now. Not yet. B.J. shook herself and launched into a denial. "Glory, no. No, I'm—"

"Oh, I should have known." Glory came rushing in, shoving the door shut behind her. B.J. shrank back. Glory kept coming. "I mean, I knew there was *something*." B.J.'s knees started to give way. Rather than collapse to the floor, she stepped to the side and dropped to the toilet seat. Glory patted her shoulder and kept right on talking. "The way you looked that first morning when I offered you coffee—that I-am-losing-my-cookies-right-this-instant expression. Oh, I know that feeling so well. And you still look kind of green. What can I do?"

"I, um—"

"Wait. I know what." Glory turned, snatched a washcloth from the stack on the lower shelf of the bath stand. She ran water on it, wrung it out, and came at B.J. with it.

B.J. craned back. "What are you doing?"

"It's just a cool, wet cloth. I always like the feel of one, after I…well, you know—oh, come on. You'll like it."

B.J. let out a weary sigh. "All right, fine." She gestured for Glory to get on with it. The girl began patting her face with the cool cloth. It did feel good—soothing.

But then Glory started in again. "It's Buck's, isn't it? Oh, don't answer. There's no need to answer. I just know that it is. Does he *know?*" Glory stepped back and hit her own forehead with the heel of her hand. "Oh, of course he doesn't." She moved in again, patting with her wet cloth. "He's much too…relaxed about everything. He's having a fine old time."

"Uh. He is?"

"Oh, yes. A great time, in his hometown, with the woman he loves."

Love? B.J. thought that was going a little too far. "Glory. *Love* is…maybe not the word."

"Yes, it is. Of course, it is—and I'm right, aren't I?"

"About?"

"He doesn't know, does he?" Glory stepped back again. "You don't even have to answer. I don't for a second believe that he knows." She offered B.J. the cloth. B.J. shook her head. Glory sat on the edge of the tub. "Right?"

B.J. gaped at Glory, absolutely certain that whatever she said next was only going to get her deeper into trouble. "Oh, God." She groaned and covered her face with her hands.

"B.J.?"

What a mess. B.J.'s head swam and her stomach churned. She let out a tiny cry, braced her elbows on her knees and lowered her head between her thighs. She took slow, careful breaths.

"B.J.? What can I do? Say something. Please?"

"Shut up."

"Okay. All right…"

And the bathroom, at last, was silent—except for B.J.'s careful breathing and a tiny moan of sympathy from Glory.

B.J.'s stomach settled down a little. She dared to sit up straight again.

"Better?" Glory asked. She looked so sweet and hopeful. Still sucking in air through her nose, B.J. gave a nod. "It gets better, it really does," Glory promised. "I'm almost three months now." With a soft, happy smile, she patted her stomach, which still seemed flat unless you looked really close. She glanced up. "You?"

Deny it, B.J. thought. *Tell her she's got it all wrong.* But when she opened her mouth, "Eight weeks" popped out. And then, after she said it, after she admitted it, she found, astonishingly, that she was *glad* she had.

Glory beamed at her. "Think of it. Our babies will be cousins."

They would, wouldn't they? Amazing. "Listen, Glory…"

"Sure. What?"

"I don't want Buck to know. Not yet."

Glory's slim throat moved as she gulped. "Okay."

"I don't want *anyone* to know."

"Hey. It's your decision. And you don't have to worry about me. I know how to keep a secret—unlike *some* people I could mention."

"Thank you."

"Anything. Really." Glory's dark eyes were soft with sympathy, with total understanding. Gingerly, she spoke again. "I just have to ask…"

"Go for it."

"Well, what are you going to *do?*"

"Have a baby."

"Well, yeah, okay. By yourself?"

"That's right."

Twin lines formed between Glory's smooth brows. "You *will* tell Buck? Eventually, I mean."

"Of course."

"Whew."

B.J. found she was vaguely offended. "You thought I wouldn't?"

"Well, I don't know. For a second there, you had me worried. I mean, I do believe that a father has a right to know—no matter how much of a butthead he might end up being about it when he finds out." Glory sighed, deeply. B.J. knew she was thinking of Bowie.

B.J. said, "I do realize that Buck has a right to know. And in a month or two, I'll tell him."

"Good—and then, of course, he'll want to marry you."

"Too bad. Not happening."

"Why not?"

"What do you mean, why not? Sometimes getting married is no solution to anything. Look at you and Bowie…."

"That's different."

"No, it's not."

"Sure, it is. You're crazy for Buck. I can see it in your eyes when you look at him. You're crazy for him—"

"You said that already. Once is more than enough."
Was it that obvious? Oh, God.

"—and Buck's crazy about you."

"So? Same with you and Bowie."

"Uh-uh. I don't think so."

"Glory, you said yourself that you're in love with Bowie—and we both know that Bowie's nuts for you."

Glory made a low sound, one heavy with doubt and irony. "Sometimes I think that Bowie's nuts, period. Not Buck, though. Buck's...normal."

"Oh, come on. Bowie's normal." B.J. paused to give that more thought. "I think..."

"Exactly." Glory grunted. "Lately, no one's sure what Bowie is."

"But you are sure you're not going to marry him."

"Yes, I am."

"Just as I'm sure I won't marry Buck."

"But why not? Buck's smart and handsome and funny. And he makes a living—and you're rich, anyway. You two will never have money problems."

"Glory, money isn't everything."

Glory waved her washcloth. "Rich people always say that."

"I just don't think it can work between us."

"Because?"

"Buck and I go way back. It didn't work between us then."

"Why didn't it work?"

"You are so nosy."

"Yeah, I am. I really am. Tell me."

B.J. gave her *the look,* the one that sent all the underlings at *Alpha* scurrying off in terror.

The look didn't work on Glory. She only demanded, again, "Tell me."

B.J. relented enough to explain, "It's a long, sad story. Just take my word for it. It didn't work in a really big way."

"How long ago was that?"

"Six years."

Glory waved her washcloth again. "Six years is practically forever. You've both grown up a lot, right? You two need to try again."

"I wish it were that simple."

"Maybe it is simple. Maybe you're just…complicating it, you know?"

"I don't think so."

"But *why* don't you think so?"

Oddly enough, B.J. found she didn't mind telling Glory. "Well, the truth is…" She leaned closer to Glory. Glory took her cue and leaned in toward B.J. B.J. lowered her voice. "This man-woman thing?"

Glory whispered back, "What about it?"

"I'm no good at it. It never works out for me."

Glory sat up straight. "Oh, puh-lease. Look at you. You're gorgeous. You're fun. You're brilliant."

B.J. couldn't help brightening just a little at such high praise. "I do like the way you think."

Glory added, "And did I mention, you're also rich?"

"You did—not that having money necessarily equals a decent love life."

"I'm only saying that if it hasn't worked out for you with a man yet, it will eventually, you can take my word on it. You've got everything going for you and there's bound to be a man who'll appreciate you for how really terrific you are. I personally happen to think that man is Buck."

B.J. sighed and shook her head. "Just…please. Keep the news to yourself."

"Oh, absolutely. I will not tell a soul."

And out in the hallway, as Glory vowed to keep silent, a stunned Buck stepped back from the bathroom door.

Eleven

Buck wasn't the eavesdropping type.

But he'd heard B.J.'s bedroom door bang back, and her footsteps pounding down the hall—the same sounds he'd heard every morning since they'd arrived in the Flat. He'd lain there in bed for a minute or two, debating whether or not to just get up and go ask her what the hell was going on with her.

If she happened to be dying of some obscure disorder that had her wolfing food down at night and tossing it up the next morning, well, he'd really like to know.

Then again, since he was trying to keep it low-key and low-pressure with her, trying to get her to meet him halfway, he had a gut-twisting feeling that confronting her about anything—up to and including whether or not she had some bizarre eating disorder—could mean losing serious ground with her.

Buck couldn't afford to lose ground. Every inch of it was too damn hard to gain in the first place.

In the end, he'd gotten up, yanked on some pants and a shirt and gone out to the hall—just in time to hear Glory say those impossible words:

You're pregnant, too.

After which Bowie's girl had shut the bathroom door—with both her and B.J. on the far side of it.

Buck had moved toward that closed door in what could only be called a daze. He'd stood right where he was standing now, thinking that he had to know—he damn well *had* to know.

Should he have barged in demanding answers?

He'd considered it. A few years ago he would have done exactly that—no considering about it.

But he was a little older now and maybe age did bring wisdom—or caution, anyway. He knew B.J. and he knew that barging in on her at such a moment could have her clamming up tight on him—or going the other, uglier direction, the one where they ended up shouting at each other; lots of noise and carrying-on, no answers.

So he'd opted for the low road known as eavesdropping. He'd put his ear against the door and heard it all. B.J. was pregnant, it was his baby—and she would tell him in a month or two, just not right now.

And, by the way, she would *never* marry him.

A long series of down-and-dirty swear words scrolled through his mind. He thought, *The hell she won't marry me.*

So. What to do next?

Why even ask? He *knew* what to do. He was a Bravo. B.J. was having his baby and that changed everything. There could be no more fooling around, no more taking it slow, no more gritting his teeth and keeping hands off, waiting for her to give it up and admit there was still something important going on between them. It was time for action and that meant his ring on her finger and her tall, slim, sexy body in his bed.

Oh, yeah. It was time, all right. Time to get the truth out in the open between them, time for her to stop hiding the ball. She'd been lying to him by omission for too damn long now.

And speaking of lies, what about that first night here, in the Flat?

That night, they'd discussed Bowie and Glory. And at one point or another, from something she'd said, he'd started wondering if maybe their night in September could have had the classic consequences—wondering if what he now knew for a fact just might be possible.

He'd been direct. Honest. Straight-ahead. He'd asked her right out if that might be so.

She'd flatly denied it.

She'd lied about the baby, lied right to his face, damned if she hadn't.

Tight fury coiled in his belly, a snake ready to strike. Buck reached for the door handle—and changed his mind. He raised his fist to knock—and then let it drop to his side.

He took another step back. He stared at the door that stood between him and the woman he wanted, the woman who also happened to be having his baby.

And hell if he didn't find himself thinking of Bowie. The damn fool.

Bowie made demands right and left. He chased Glory all over town, bullying her, begging her, putting her father—and as a result, her whole family—in the middle of what should have been just between the two of them.

So far, Bowie had gotten zip for his trouble. His he-man, drag-'em-off-to-the-cave-by-the-hair, no-holds-barred approach simply wasn't working. Rather than bringing Bowie and Glory closer, Bowie's methods were pushing them apart.

There had to be a better way than Bowie's to go about getting a woman to say yes.

Though his blood pounded too hard through his veins and a voice in his head called for action, right now, though his hands itched to break down that door, grab his woman and never let go…

Buck held back.

There had to be a better way…

Shaking his head, Buck turned and quietly retraced his steps to his bedroom.

Once inside, he gently shut the door.

In the bathroom, Glory rose from her seat at the edge of the tub. "Listen. Any time you need to talk, you come looking for me. I might not have any answers, but I do understand and I'm willing to listen.…"

"Thanks. I appreciate that." B.J. said the words and realized how much she meant them. It *was* good to finally have someone to talk to about all she was going through, someone who understood from personal experience exactly how she felt. B.J. actually grinned. "You know, I almost feel hungry. I might even have a little toast with my apple juice this morning."

"Hungry is good." Glory showed some dimples. "Sometimes, in those first weeks, I would have oatmeal."

B.J.'s poor, abused stomach actually growled. "I don't believe it. Oatmeal sounds good."

"I'll tell Mrs. B. to make you some."

"Thanks—and Glory?"

"Yeah?"

"It goes both ways. If you need to talk, knock on my door. I'm up for it."

"I knew you'd say that. After all, what are friends for?"

Forty-five minutes later, as she left her room on the way down to breakfast, B.J. found herself hesitating at Buck's door, thinking that maybe she'd knock, invite him to walk down to breakfast with her.

Knocking on Buck's door...

That would be a first. She'd never once sought him out in the whole time they'd been here. She'd kept their agreement and made herself available to him, never more than that.

No reason to change now.

She started to turn...

But wait a minute. Why not knock?

Dumb question. Knocking, after all, would amount to initiating contact and initiating contact might give him the wrong idea. It could get him thinking that she enjoyed his company, that she had begun to consider letting him back into her life.

She hadn't.

Had she?

Of course not.

And really, it didn't have to mean a thing, that they walked down to breakfast together. After all, their rooms were side by side. It was perfectly natural that she might knock on his door and—

Oh, why was she making such a big deal of this?

She lifted her hand, knocked smartly, and waited, her heart beating just a little harder than it should.

He didn't answer.

She knocked again, leaned close to the door, asked tentatively, "Buck?"

Nothing. She put her hand on the doorknob. It turned. And before she even really thought about it, she was pushing the door inward onto a room very much like her own: identical layout, similar heavy, dark furniture. Morning light spilled through the French doors and a laptop waited on the minuscule desk in the corner.

The bed was neatly made and the cargoes and sweater he'd worn yesterday lay folded across a nearby chair. She could just make out the faint scent of that aftershave he always wore.

No sign of the man himself.

For a moment she simply stood there, in the open doorway, her hand clutching the knob, breathing in the scent of him, taking in the room where he slept.

Then she caught herself.

He's getting to you, you know he is....

"No!" The denial grated in her ear. She'd actually said it out loud.

With a furtive glance to either end of the hallway to make certain no one had seen her peering in Buck's room, talking to herself, B.J. pulled the door firmly shut, yanked her shoulders back and strode purposefully toward the stairs.

There were four guests in the dining room when she got down there, all of them strangers. B.J. smiled politely at the others and took one of the small tables near the door to the central hall. A minute or two later, Glory appeared with her breakfast.

"Here we go." Glory set down the food with a flourish just as a heavy-set older guy in overalls went by in the hallway, coming from the direction of the kitchen. He carried a red metal tool box. Glory must have noticed that B.J. had spotted him. "The handyman," she explained. "One of the upstairs sink drains is stopped up."

"Ah." B.J. glanced down at her breakfast. "Looks good."

"Told you so. And you are looking great this morning." Meaning a lot better than she had earlier, following her daily worship at the altar of the porcelain god. Astounding what a shower, a blow-dry and some makeup could do.

"Why thank you. Have you seen Buck?"

"He was here when I got downstairs, but he left maybe a half an hour ago."

"Left the house, you mean?"

"Yeah, I think so."

Odd. "Do you know where he went?"

Glory shook her head. "I can ask Mrs. B…"

"No. That's okay."

"Sure?"

"Positive."

Very strange. He'd actually left the house without her. Why?

Seriously stupid question.

What did she care why? He was gone and that was a good thing. For once, she'd have a little time to herself during the day. She might even get an hour or two where she didn't constantly have to be on guard against his considerable charm and her own wacko hormones.

Oh, yeah. An hour or two on her own would be great. Wonderful. Fabulous.

One of the guests signaled Glory and she hustled off to refill a muffin basket. B.J. ate her breakfast and then went back upstairs. She called Giles, but he was in a meeting. She considered calling L.T.—but why ask for aggravation?

She booted up her laptop and jotted a few notes to herself about some upcoming features. She answered several e-mails that had lain abandoned in her in-box for five days now, sending them off only to watch them get stuck in her out-box, where they were destined to remain until she returned to civilization and an actual Internet connection.

An hour passed. Two.

B.J. jotted more notes. She looked in the mirror over the desk. Hmm. She really should have made time to get her roots done before heading for the hills.

Not that it mattered. Who in the Flat was going to care if her roots were a tad browner than they ought to be?

Not a soul.

She rewrote her bio. Then she started working the bio into an actual résumé.

Now, what was *that* about?

Wishful thinking? Obviously. Because, no matter how rough it got, no matter what L.T. tried next, she was never leaving *Alpha*.

Was she?

What a question.

Of course not. She could not believe the thought had even crossed her mind.

A knock at the door.

Buck! At last. She smoothed her hair and went to answer.

It was Glory. "Housekeeping," B.J.'s newfound

friend announced, all shining eyes and dimpled smile. "Want your room cleaned?"

Where the hell was Buck? Not that she cared. "Uh. Great idea." She was getting a little stir-crazy here, alone in her room, anyway. "I'll get out."

"You don't have to. I can work around you, easy."

"I think I will, though. I'll get out and get some air—by the way, have you seen Buck?"

"Not since breakfast, but you can check with—"

"Chastity. Got it." B.J. reached for her small shoulder bag and snagged her jacket off the straight-backed chair by the door. "Thanks."

Glory grabbed her arm, moved in close and whispered, "Missing him?"

"Hah."

Glory laughed. "I think you are."

"Later." B.J. fled for the stairs.

She found Chastity in the kitchen mixing up muffin batter and talking with the handyman, who looked very comfortable sitting at the round oak table, sipping coffee.

Chastity set aside her bowl of batter to introduce them. "Mr. Panopopoulis, this is B.J."

The handyman set down his cup. "What'd I say? Call me Alyosha. Please."

"Alyosha," Chastity repeated. Was Buck's mother blushing?

The handyman pushed himself to his feet. "Nice to meet you, B.J. I go back to work, now. Chastity, thank you very much for the delicious coffee."

"Anytime…Alyosha."

The two of them grinned at each other. That went on for at least thirty seconds. Finally, the handyman bent to get his tool kit from the floor by his chair. "Ah. Well. See you later, huh?"

"Yes." Chastity went on grinning as the handyman left them through the hallway door. A moment later, they heard the back door open and close.

Chastity smoothed her apron and picked up her bowl of muffin batter. "Now," she said, suddenly all cheery and brisk. "What can I do for you, B.J.?"

"Just wondering if you might have some idea where Buck went."

Chastity's spoon scraped the inside of the bowl as she stirred. She frowned, her spoon going still for a moment. "He didn't say anything to me about where he was headed. Sorry."

"I can't believe he'd just take off like this, I truly can't." B.J. blew out a frustrated breath—and then realized she was sounding way too much as though she missed the man. She backpedaled madly, "Uh, not that it really matters. It doesn't. Not in the least." A hint of a smile flitted across Chastity's mouth. "What's so funny?" B.J. demanded, sounding surly and knowing it.

"Oh, nothing. Did he take that SUV you came here in?"

Good question. "I'll check."

B.J. went back through the dining room to the drawing room and the big window there. A glance through the glass showed her that the SUV still waited where they'd left it, at the curb beyond the white picket fence.

She returned to the kitchen. "The SUV's still out there on the street."

Chastity dropped pastel-colored bake-cup papers into a muffin tin. "You've looked around the house?"

"Well, upstairs. Downstairs. Yeah. I'd say I've looked around the house."

"Then he must be over town somewhere."

"Like where?"

Chastity cast her an indulgent glance. "Over at Bowie's? With Brand or Brett? On the bench by the grocery store, chewing the fat with Old Tony? Down by the river, skipping rocks? Your guess is as good as mine."

"You don't think he...fell down a ravine or something, do you?"

Chastity stopped fiddling with the muffin papers. She wiped her hands on her apron, turned and braced a hip against the side of the counter. "You're worried about him."

Denials rose to her lips. She swallowed and confessed the hideous truth. "Well, yeah. I guess...yeah, I am."

"That's nice to know."

"It is?"

Chastity folded her arms across her middle. "You've seemed a little bit...what? Reluctant with him..." She frowned. "Yes. Reluctant and even hostile. At times I've gotten the feeling you don't even want to be here."

What to say to that? Strangely, B.J. felt the urge to confide in Chastity.

What was *that* about? Twice in one day she'd felt what could only be called *close* to another woman. Oh, really. Once was more than enough. "It's...kind of complicated, between Buck and me."

"But you do care for him?"

"I..."

Chastity smoothed her apron some more. "Forgive me for sticking my nose in. I couldn't help asking."

"It's okay. Honestly. I just don't want to go into it all right this minute."

Chastity turned back to her muffins. "I understand. It's your business, yours and Buck's."

"Thanks," B.J. said, not knowing what else to say.

"Don't worry about him." Buck's mother took two soup spoons from a drawer. "He's just wandered off by himself for a bit. He used to take off all the time as a boy." She began scooping up thick globs of batter with one spoon, using the second to guide the batter into the baking cups. "When he wasn't making trouble, he'd hike into the woods or head down to the river. Sometimes he'd take a book to read, sometimes not." She paused, looked toward the window over the sink and the mountains beyond. "He was…half hellraiser, half dreamer, as a boy. I worried myself sick when he was raising hell. But when he wandered off to do his dreaming? Uh-uh. I knew that was good for him." She chuckled to herself. "When he got a little older, he used to steal beer from my refrigerator to take with him when he disappeared."

"He told me that." B.J. felt absurdly proud. It seemed a detail he wouldn't have told just anyone.

"I'd ground him when he got home," Chastity said. "I can't say the grounding did all that much good…." She stuck her spoons in the batter bowl. "The main thing is, he always came home safe." She turned and moved close enough to pat B.J. on the arm. "He'll be back soon enough, just you wait and see."

Waiting. One of B.J.'s least favorite activities.

She went for a walk, crossing the bridge and strolling up and down Main Street, waving at people when they waved at her—which was often.

Already, the townsfolk knew her by name. It was "Hi, B.J. How's it going?" all up and down Main. When she got to the grocery store, Old Tony tried to wave her over.

He patted the space beside him on the bench. "What're you up to, young lady?"

She didn't linger. She was a little irked with Old Tony, frankly, and had been ever since that remark Glory had made about how her great-grandfather thought Glory was a slut.

Was B.J. judging the old guy too harshly?

Probably.

But now she had an actual woman friend, B.J. had her loyalties to consider.

She waved back at Old Tony and called, "I'm taking a walk."

"Am I still gonna be in *Alpha?*"

"It's very possible. I will let you know." She waved again and went on her way, past the Pizza Parlor, across that other bridge, around by the county courthouse, and back the way she'd come.

The whole time, a part of her kept anticipating the moment when she'd run into Buck. Didn't happen. And when she returned to the Sierra Star, he was still gone.

What next?

She literally had nothing to do. In New York, that never happened.

Read, maybe? She chose a mystery from the book-shelves in the drawing room.

Upstairs, she kicked off her boots, stretched out on the bed, settled an afghan over her legs and tried to get into her book—with minimal success. She kept thinking of Buck, worrying about him a little, even though Chastity had assured her there was no need. She worried anyway, and wondered where he could have gone and why he hadn't bothered to tell her he'd decided to take off.

At some point, she must have dropped into a doze. She came sharply awake.

What was that?

"Huh?" Frowning at the ceiling, she put it together. Someone was tapping on the balcony door. She bolted to a sitting position, glanced over and...

Surprise, surprise. Buck. Big as life and home safe, just as Chastity had predicted.

All her vague, unformed fears for him evaporated, leaving sheer irritation. He signaled for her to open the door.

She threw off the afghan, jumped off the bed and yanked back the door. "Where the hell have you been?"

He looked her up and down, slowly. She felt his gaze burn a sizzling path all along her body. "Hiking in the woods. And down by the river. Thinking."

"Thinking," she echoed in utter disgust.

"That's right. I want to talk to you. Can I come in?"

Huffing, she stepped aside. He came into the room. She shut the door behind him and then turned to confront him. "All right. You're in. Start talking."

Of course, he said nothing. And he stood much too close, smelling of that tempting aftershave of his, and of fresh air and clean sweat. His hair was kind of wind-chopped, his cheeks ruddy.

Her stomach tightened—and not with morning sickness. Uh-uh. This was a low-down kind of tightening, followed instantly by a warming, loosening sensation—no, more than warming.

This was heat, plain and simple. She wanted to grab

him, close and hard, just plaster herself all along the
front of his big, strong body, to hold him tight and lift
her mouth up for his kiss.

Bad idea. She shook herself—and planted her
stocking feet wider apart, assuming an offensive
stance. "You know, if you want to take off, you could
just tell me you're going. Have a tiny little smidgen of
consideration, maybe. Or is that too much to ask?"

His eyes were so soft. His mouth looked way too
kissable. He said, ruefully, "B.J." She whirled away
from him with a cry and stared blindly out at the mountains, at the frothing ribbon of river gleaming in the
thin midday sun. He said her name again, "B.J."

She waved a hand sharply back over her shoulder,
a signal that she didn't care how many times he said
her name, she was not facing him—and not listening
to him. Then she wrapped both arms good and tight
around her. "Oh, I know." She pushed the words out
through clenched teeth. "I know. I'm spending two
weeks at your beck and call. That's our deal, a deal I
agreed to." She found she was shivering, though she
wasn't really cold. "But still, there's no reason you
can't just tell me when you decide to get the hell out.
There's no reason you can't just say you're going off
by yourself and I'm on my own for a while.

"But no. Instead, you…vanish. Poof. Just like that,
leaving me to wonder what's going on, to, um, worry
if you're all right, if you're…hurt or something—"

"B.J." He said it so gently that time. And he took
her elbow. She pressed her arms all the tighter against
herself, even tried to jerk away. But he didn't let go.
And after a moment or two, she accepted the scary
truth that she didn't *want* him to let go.

With some reluctance, she allowed him to guide

her around to him. He took her other arm, too. She couldn't bring herself to look at him. She stared down at his boots and her own stocking feet. "What? Just…what?"

"Come on. Forget my boots. Look up at me…"

Unwillingly, she lifted her head. Damn those eyes of his. They were softer than ever. "Okay. I'm looking up. What?"

"Let's call off the deal."

If he hadn't been holding onto her arms, she might have staggered. "I…call it off?"

"Yeah. Don't worry. I'll hold up my end, write the feature. But you're off the hook. You can go back to New York as soon as L.T. can send the jet for you. What do you say?"

"Um. Buck?"

"Yeah?"

"No. No, I don't want to go."

Twelve

Buck knew he must have heard her wrong. "What did you just say?"

She looked stricken, eyes wide, face pale but for those two telltale spots of bright color high on her cheeks. "I don't want to go." She whispered the words, as if her throat was too tight to say them out loud. "I want to stay here, with you. For the rest of the two weeks, the way we agreed…"

She didn't want to go….

She'd said that. It was real.

And not in the least what he'd expected.

He'd stewed for hours, forging along the narrow, twisting trails of his childhood, up and down hillsides, under the cold shadows of the pines, trying to figure out what to do, how to go on from here.

In the end, he'd decided he wouldn't make demands, he wouldn't bully or shout or tell her how it had to be.

He also wouldn't go on playing this sweet, silly game with her. He would call it off, tell her she was free to go back to New York. He'd assumed she would jump at the chance to get free of him.

And as soon as he'd released her from the deal they'd made, he'd thought they would talk. About the baby. About where to go from here. Not for a nanosecond had he expected her to tell him she wanted to stay.

But she had.

And that meant he was getting somewhere with her, after all, didn't it? That meant the deal they'd made was working. The impossible was happening.

B.J. was ready to give him—give *them*—another chance.

"Buck?" She looked up at him, those eyes that could be sky-blue or stormy, full of light. Full of something that might have been hope.

He had to swallow before he could speak. "Yeah?"

"Did you hear what I said?"

"I heard you."

"I don't believe I said that."

He almost smiled. "Neither do I."

"But the crazy thing is…"

"What? Tell me."

"I actually meant it. I don't want to go. No one expects me back for nine more days. And I want to see where this takes us, you know?"

"I think so."

"Do you want me to go?"

"Not if you want to stay."

"I said I did."

"Yeah. Yeah, you did…"

"Buck?"

"Yeah?"

"I think you should kiss me."

She was *asking* for kisses, now? "Great idea…"

She lifted her sweet mouth and he took it, gathering her in. Her lips parted. He speared his tongue inside and he tasted her.

Oh, yeah. It had been way too long since he'd held her, willing, in his arms….

She sighed into his mouth. He tightened his hold on her, pulling her closer. It was good. Nothing better. B.J., here, in his arms. Where she'd always belonged.

Slow, he thought, *easy…*

No need to rush, no need to push.

She sighed again, melting against him, all pliant sweetness. So much woman. All he'd ever wanted. All he longed for, all he needed…

The bed was behind him. One step, two, three…

His calves hit the edge. He took her hips and lifted her. She let out another urgent, willing cry as he guided her legs around him. Slowly, he lowered them both, till he sat on the edge of the bed with her in his lap, facing him, gripping him between her long, slim thighs. She groaned and wrapped her arms around his neck, pulling him tighter, tipping herself into him, so he could feel the heat and softness of her, even through all their clothes.

Her kiss deepened. She moaned some more, the sound a purring low in her chest. The heady scent of her claimed all his senses. His blood burned through his veins. He took her sweater and slid it up. She raised her arms. Off it went.

Her bra, he dispensed of with a flick of his thumb. He guided the straps down her arms. She did the rest; the bra was gone. He took her full, soft breasts in his hands, felt the nipples, hard and hungry, poking into his palms.

By then, he was the one groaning—deep, rough groans—as he kissed his way down her arched throat, licking as he went. He tracked the slope of one breast until he reached a nipple and caught it in his mouth. He suckled and she bucked against him, moaning out his name.

He brought a hand between them, slid his palm over her mound, cupped her heat—and lifted. She gathered those incredible legs under her and went to her knees, offering access. Still drawing on her sweet, round breast, he undid the snap above her zipper—and he took that zipper down.

That brought a sharp gasp from her. She cradled his head close, fingers splayed in his hair. Her eager moans urged him on.

He palmed her again, outside her clothing, steadying her, and then he slid his hand upward, slipping it beneath the satin barrier of the naughty little thong she wore. Her response was a hungry cry of encouragement. He touched her, fingers sliding into that slick, hot groove, finding the bud where her pleasure was greatest, lifting his head from her breast, seeking her mouth once more.

She gave it. He stabbed his tongue inside and she sucked on it, eagerly, her head bent down to him, as she moved to his touch.

In moments, she hit the peak. Her whole long, slim body quivered and she cried out against his mouth, breaking their kiss, throwing her head back, grabbing his wrist to still his hand.

He felt the pulsing, the sweet, slick spill of greater wetness, her body drawn tight with it, straining in release.

And then, with a slow, deep sigh, she crumpled against him.

He fell back across the bed, taking her with him, so she landed on top of him, her head on his heart.

Again, more softly, she sighed, and he smiled a slow smile at the ceiling as he stroked her hair, wrapping the strands around his fingers—fingers that were wet from her, slick and musky with her scent.

She cuddled closer, catching his other hand, twining their fingers together, and brushing a kiss on his knuckles. "Umm," she said, a sound of pure contentment.

He pressed his lips to the crown of her head and breathed in the clean citrus smell of her shampoo. "Yeah," he said softly, and felt no need to say more.

For a time, they lay there, holding each other. Buck was fully erect and aching for release—or his body was, anyway. But in his mind and heart, he knew an immense satisfaction, just to be there, with B.J., to feel the weight of her against his body, to cradle her golden head on his chest.

But then she murmured, "Too many clothes," and shoved at his sweater, sliding it up.

He helped her to get it over his head and off. Once it was gone, she sat up and looked down at him, eyes softly shining, fly wide open, full breasts and slim belly gloriously bare. He saw that she wore a navel ring now, a tiny hoop of gleaming metal.

"That's new." He reached up to brush it with a finger. "Silver. Very nice…"

"Platinum," she corrected. And then she bent close and laid a trail of nipping kisses, from his left nipple, across to the right. She bit that one, lightly.

"Hey!"

She laughed, a low, oh-so-sexy sound, and rocked her hips, rubbing against him.

He grabbed her, stilling her. She braced up on her arms and looked down at him.

"Watch it," he warned.

She licked her lips, slowly. Deliberately. "Boots next," she said.

"Go for it." He laced his hands behind his head and watched her as she slid down his body and off the bed. She took his boots, one and then the other. They hit the floor with heavy thunking sounds.

Then she crawled back up to straddle him again. He caught her face between his hands, spearing his fingers up into her hair.

He had to ask, one more time. "You're sure?" She swallowed, nodded, showing that shy, self-conscious side she rarely revealed. He whispered, "I only want you to be certain…."

The shyness vanished. She made a show of clucking her tongue. "Buck. Scruples, all of a sudden?" And she moved on him again, taunting him with another slow roll of her hips. He shut his eyes, let out a groan—and heard her say low and so tenderly, "Yes. I'm certain."

He wanted the rest of her clothes off—and his as well. But he didn't move. He was thinking of the condom he'd been carrying with him every moment since they'd boarded her father's jet at Teterboro. He had it with him now.

He was as ready as a man can be. He'd made a point of that, of being ready. Half the time in the past five days, he'd doubted this moment would ever come. But he'd known that if it did, he wasn't going to blow it due to lack of preparedness.

He considered whether to mention it—that condom. Whether to ask her if they needed it; whether maybe to lead her into a discussion of the secret she was keeping.

But this was all so new and so very sweet. Her eagerness. Her admission that she wanted this time with him.

He couldn't take the chance of ruining it.

She *would* tell him. In her own time. And he *could* wait for that.

It would be a pleasure, the waiting. No sweat. As long as she looked at him through hungry eyes, that mouth of hers soft and wet and ready for him, he could wait forever, damned if it couldn't.

"Buck? What's wrong?"

"Not a thing." He pulled her face down to him. Their lips met. They both moaned. He urged her over, onto her side, and he went with her, so they faced each other.

They finished undressing as they kissed, laughing a little, straining to keep their mouths fused, tongues sparring and sliding. He tugged his wallet from his pocket, and got the condom free, kissing her the whole time.

Her hands were busy, too. She shoved down her jeans and slithered out of her little purple thong. She unbuttoned and unzipped his pants, helped him tug them down, his boxers with them.

Finally, they were both naked except for their socks. He reached for her. But she was quicker, pushing him to his back again. Claiming the top position, she kissed her way down the center of his chest…

He groaned and tried not to shout out loud at the agonizing pleasure of her soft fingers closing around him. She licked him like a lollipop, long, slow teasing strokes, from the base to the flare and all around the nerve-rich head, scraping her teeth against him so lightly, making him moan some more, dipping her tongue in the ultra-sensitive groove, until he felt he would burst his skin, he was so hard and ready.

She took him in then, deep into her mouth, lowering onto him by slow degrees, sucking him steadily, working her tongue on him, driving him mad as she slowly moved up, her tongue swirling at the peak—and then sliding down once more…

In the end, when he knew he would lose it if he let her keep on, he tangled his hands in her hair and pulled her up to him. Kissing her deeply, he felt beside him for the condom, which he'd dropped while she drove him wild with that mouth of hers. His fingers closed around it.

And then her hand was there, taking it from him, quickly unwrapping it, sliding it down on him with practiced ease. Their eyes met. He wondered, in a vague and shattered kind of way, what she might be thinking, as she told this subtle, sexy little lie—as she slid on protection with those knowing hands of hers, when it was already too late for that.

But a moment later, he didn't care anymore—about the secret she thought she was keeping from him, about the future, about anything but her soft heat closing around him, milking him, her silky hair rubbing his chest, her tender moans and her hands, stroking.

There was only the scent and the feel of her, the weight of her upon him, her body claiming him, the two of them moving in perfect time, hard and fast, then slow and liquid.

Somehow he held on long enough to feel her coming around him, to know the velvety, intense contractions of her inner muscles as her pleasure crested. He held on that long—and no more.

Then he gave it up to her, pushing to the hilt inside her, as she threw back her head and cried out his name.

Thirteen

"Isn't it convenient how our rooms are connected by that balcony?" B.J. teased softly. She lay on top of him, feeling utterly wonderful, using his big chest for a pillow. Idly, she traced a spiraling circle on the hard, warm flesh of his shoulder.

Buck laughed. She felt the sound, low and deep and lovely, against her ear. "You didn't think sharing the balcony was so damn convenient at first."

"Ah. But now I see how wrong I was."

"The great B. J. Carlyle, admitting she was wrong?" His arms tightened around her. "Never happens."

"Remember this moment," she instructed huskily. "Treasure it."

"Oh, I will."

She snuggled in closer. "So…what's on the agenda for tonight?"

He rubbed her back with long, lazy strokes. "We

could drive down to Nevada City for dinner. It's an hour and a half ride, but they've got more than one good restaurant there."

"Dinner somewhere other than the knotty-pine palace? I don't know. I've gotten pretty much addicted to those iceberg-lettuce salads."

"I noticed."

"Hah."

"And tomorrow, we could run off to Vegas."

Her mouth went desert-dry. "Uh… Vegas?"

Something happened in his eyes, the seductive warmth cooling—for a second or two. But then he laughed. "Scared?"

"I, um, well…"

"Don't worry. It wasn't a proposal—at least, not of marriage."

"Oh. Well. Fine, then."

He tucked a lock of hair behind her ear. "The idea of getting married terrifies you, doesn't it?"

She answered honestly. "I just don't think I'm the marrying kind…."

"And who is?" He asked it so gently.

"Oh, I don't know—nice women, I guess. Cooperative women. Women not brought up by L. T. Carlyle and a bevy of big-breasted *Alpha* Girls."

"You're nice."

She scoffed, "Hardly."

"You are, though sometimes you try your best not to be. And you do cooperate. On occasion…"

"I'm not cooperative enough for marriage—and can we talk about something else, please?"

His expression reproached her. But in the end, he let the scary talk of marriage go and explained why he'd suggested a trip to Las Vegas. "I have two half-brothers in Vegas."

"More sons of the notorious Blake?"

He nodded. "One brother, Aaron, was born in a small Nevada town not far from Lake Tahoe. Aaron has two other half-brothers, Cade and Will. Their mother, Caitlin, is quite a character."

"Yet another in Blake's endless string of lonely wives?"

"You got it—though Caitlin Bravo hasn't been all that lonely since Blake disappeared from her life. She likes men. And they like her."

"And your other Las Vegas half-brother?"

"Fletcher comes from Dallas by way of Atlantic City. Fletcher and Aaron are both in the casino business—high up in the casino business. Aaron's CEO of High Sierra, and Fletcher runs Impresario." B.J. made a sound of admiration. High Sierra and the recently opened Impresario were two of the hottest supercasinos on the Strip. Buck added, "A company called Silver Standard Resorts owned High Sierra at one time. Not anymore. Now, High Sierra and Impresario are owned by the Bravo Group, for which both Aaron and Fletcher work—and *in* which they're both part-owners."

"The Bravo Group being…?"

"A resort/casino partnership created about three years ago and heavily invested in by a Bravo cousin, the famous and fabulously wealthy Jonas Bravo of the L.A. Bravos." Buck caught her head between his strong hands. He kissed her. Slowly. Wetly. When he released her, he whispered, "Don't be scared. I promise, I'm not pushing you anywhere you don't want to go. Not anymore and never again. From now on, if you want out, you just say the word."

She looked into those beautiful deep, dark eyes of his and confessed, "I don't want out."

"Good."

"But, uh, can we just…wing it, you think? See where this goes?"

One corner of that fine, oh-so-kissable mouth of his lifted. "Okay. We'll just bumble along. Follow this road wherever it takes us."

"Bumble along…"

"Yeah."

"Don't laugh, but I kind of like the sound of that."

He traced her brows with a feather-light touch. "Okay, then. Nevada City for dinner?"

"It's a date. And Vegas tomorrow. I'd like to meet your powerhouse half-brothers."

"I'll see if that can be arranged—though we'll need to be back by Friday evening."

"What's going on Friday evening?"

"The Ladies Auxiliary Potluck Supper, no less."

"Oooh. Can't miss that. Margaret, Sidney and Velma would never forgive us."

"You got that right and then Saturday, there's the annual New Bethlehem Flat Harvest Ball."

"I so cannot wait."

"I'll bet." He took her shoulders in those big hands of his.

"What?"

"Move over. Let me sit up."

"Oh, but I like it here, with you as my mattress…"

"Scoot."

Reluctantly, she slid to the side. He sat and swung his legs over the edge of the bed, turning his back to her as he got rid of the condom—the one that would have protected her from pregnancy.

If she hadn't been pregnant already…

Guilt tightened her stomach, a fist of shame, squeezing. She should tell him….

But things were going so well now. The impossible was happening. B.J. actually looked forward to the nine days they had left in California. And really, why rush it? The baby wasn't due for months and months. She had plenty of time.

He turned to her again, and stretched out beside her. He didn't speak. He didn't have to. She saw in his eyes what he was thinking. And if somehow she'd managed to miss the gleam in his eyes, all she had to do was look down….

My, oh, my. She glanced up from the jutting evidence that he wanted her all over again. Those dark, sexy eyes were waiting…

"Oh, Buck…"

He reached for her. She went into his big arms, a heated thrill shivering all through her. He tucked her close, gently, cherishingly, and his mouth covered hers…

Heaven.

She slid her hands up to wrap around his neck—and he caught her wrists.

He straddled her and he brought her wrists out, away from their bodies. He pushed her slowly onto her back, sliding her arms up, high, over her head. She looked into those drowning-dark eyes above her and she knew she was lost and happy to be so. He raised her wrists higher, his hands sliding up the backs of her hands, cupping and turning them, then guiding her fingers to hook on the top rim of the carved headboard.

"Hold on," he whispered, and nipped her earlobe

between his strong, white teeth. She could feel him, the weight of him, down there, pressing, the warmth and heaviness, the promise, the need…

She moaned.

"Do that again."

She did.

"Don't let go."

"Oh, I won't. I swear. I won't…" B.J. held on, squirming, groaning, as he kissed a leisurely, arousing path down her body.

Oh, the incredible things he could do with that mouth of his. He settled himself between her legs, easing beneath her thighs, hooking them over his broad, hard shoulders with practiced ease.

"Oh, Buck…" She dug her heels into the bed as he parted her and she felt his tongue in a wet, rough glide, finding her point of greatest pleasure, flicking it, drawing it in to tease with his teeth…

Her mind flew away, leaving only pure sensation. She murmured between gasps of delight, "Oh, Buck, oh, yes…"

His teeth nipped and his knowing tongue worked its magic. She was so wet and so eager, clutching the headboard, groaning and trying not to shout out loud.

A couple of minutes, max, and she hit the crest. He held her, his palms flat on her belly, pressing her into the mattress as he drew on her, there, at the absolute center of her pleasure.

"Buck, oh Buck…" The pulsing claimed her, spreading out, a flash of liquid fire, spilling in a wild tumble through her veins.

As her climax spiked, he slipped out from under the hold of her straining thighs and swept up her body, sliding right into her, burying himself deep.

She did cry out, then. And at that moment, she didn't care in the least who might have heard her.

He pressed up into her, tighter, all the way.

"Oh," she cried. "Oh, yes. So right…"

Flares of light and heat exploded through her. The tip of him touched that certain place deep in the heart of her, that place no other man ever seemed to quite reach…

She called his name once more. He answered on a guttural moan.

And then she felt him, felt the throb as he came inside her. His coming—the intimate, hot, twitching spurt of it—sent her over the edge all over again.

She let go of the headboard to wrap her hungry arms around him, clutching his broad back, holding on for dear life. The heat and the wonder raced out from the core of her, burning a path of purest erotic ecstasy along every nerve. He cried out, too, then, and went achingly still, pressing hard up to the heart of her, straining with the power of his release.

Finally, with a heavy, surrendering sigh, his big body went limp on top of her. He tucked his dark head into the curve of her shoulder—for a moment and a moment only. Then he wrapped his arms around her and rolled, giving her the top position, relieving her of his weight.

And after that, they just lay there, in the thin sunlight of early afternoon, the sweat drying on their bodies, holding each other close.

It didn't occur to her until two hours later, in the passenger seat of the rented SUV, riding the twisting highway into Nevada City, that they'd forgotten to use a condom that second time.

She wondered that he hadn't mentioned the slip-up. They'd always been so careful about protection up till now. Six years ago, she'd been on the pill, so there was never a whole lot to worry about then. But it wasn't good for a woman to stay on the pill forever. She'd gone off it in the intervening years, when she was between boyfriends. After she broke up with Wyatt-the-weasel, she'd gone off it again.

So she and Buck had used condoms that fateful September night—at least one of which must have failed....

They reached the bottom of a forested canyon and rolled across a two-lane bridge. She gazed out her side window, watching the river foaming and tumbling over huge pale boulders, flowing under the bridge beneath them.

B.J. turned from the river to look at him.

He caught her glance. "What?"

"Oh, nothing."

"Sure?"

"Um-hmm."

She turned her gaze to the twisting road ahead again, feeling grateful and happy for the wonder of what had passed between them in her bed a few hours ago. And not only for that.

Also, for the days of pleasure ahead of them—and yes, for the fact that he hadn't said anything about that condom they'd failed to use.

Maybe he would never mention it. Maybe he figured it was too late now, that if she got pregnant, they'd deal with that when it happened.

And, since she already *was* pregnant, they *would* deal with it. Soon—and there it was again.

That twinge in her stomach. Guilt. Squeezing.

Too bad. She *was* going to tell him. She truly was.
Soon.
Just not right now…

Fourteen

Nevada City was a gorgeous little gold-rush town. Classic clapboard Victorians lined its steep, twisting streets, many of them painted bright colors and adorned with gingerbread trim. Strolling hand-in-hand, your classic pair of dreamy-eyed lovers, B.J. and Buck checked out the shops on Broad Street and Commercial.

They ate at a place called Citronee, where the service was excellent and the food had B.J. groaning in delight. She didn't even miss the iceberg lettuce and hunks of beefsteak tomato of which she'd lately grown so fond.

Buck teased her that she'd get fat if she didn't watch it. She only grunted and dug into her organic mesclun salad with pear-lime citronée dressing, feta-cheese crumbles and hazelnuts.

Yes, there was bread. Lovely, hot bread. She had two pieces. Why not? She deserved them.

And for the main course? Sautéed Muscovy duck breast, but of course, "I need to keep my strength up after what you've been doing to me." She winked at him saucily and sliced off a mouth-watering bite of savory duck.

Umm. Heavenly.

Dinner. Almost as good as sex with Buck.

And she was one lucky woman. She got both. A nice dinner. Great sex.

Did it get any better?

No way. Better simply wasn't possible.

Night had turned the sky to an indigo blanket scattered thickly with stars when they headed back to the Flat. B.J. felt drowsy and took a little nap on the way.

She woke to the touch of Buck's lips on her cheek. The SUV wasn't moving. She yawned and squinted against the light from the streetlamp a few feet from Chastity's white picket fence. "We're here."

He made a soft sound in the affirmative. She turned her head his way. Their lips met and they shared a deep, wet kiss.

"Umm. Very nice," she said when they finally came up for air.

"Yeah." He rested his forehead against hers. "We should go in…"

She had a naughty stroke of pure inspiration. "You ever do it in an SUV?"

He answered with another question. "Is that an invitation?"

She considered. "Well, I don't know. That streetlight's pretty bright…"

He nuzzled her ear, caught her earlobe and worried it lightly between his teeth. She shivered—and not with cold. And he whispered, "Velma Wiggins lives three houses up the street. She's been known to go out for a stroll in the evening...."

"That does it." She pushed at his chest. "Later for my unfulfilled fantasies of having sex with you in an SUV."

There were guests in the drawing room. Buck and B.J. murmured greetings and went on upstairs. He drew her into his arms in the upper hall and kissed her, guiding her backward to the door of his room.

There, he paused to push her coat off her shoulders. It dropped to the floor with a soft whoosh—along with her bag. She broke the kiss. "Time to get behind a closed door. It will never do to shock your mother's paying guests." She bent to scoop up the bag and the coat.

"This way." He grabbed her free hand, pushed open the door to his room and pulled her in there with him. "Better?"

"Much." She put down her coat and bag as he went to flick on a lamp. He returned to her. Tipping her chin up with a coaxing hand, he kissed her—a gentle, teasing, oh-so-arousing kiss.

When he lifted his mouth, she found herself confessing, "I knocked on your door this morning." Still lightly holding her shoulders, he moved back a step. She knew he wanted her to meet his eyes. But at that moment, she couldn't. She looked down at the rag rug under their feet, feeling...what? Embarrassed? Oh, probably. She whispered, "You were already gone."

He tipped her chin up again, so she had to look at him. "If I'd known you were going to knock, I would have made a point of being here."

She gave him a crooked smile. "It gets worse."

He looked puzzled at her choice of words. "Worse?"

"Your door wasn't locked…"

"So?"

"I opened it and looked in here."

"Horrible," he teased.

She didn't smile. "I could smell you…smell your aftershave. I saw your clothes on the chair, your laptop on that skinny-legged desk over there…"

He brushed a soft kiss across her lips. "B.J., it's okay. You have my permission to come in my room any time the mood strikes. Feel free to look around, sniff my aftershave. Anytime. Go for it—and you still don't look happy."

She admitted, "I was…missing you. I didn't want to miss you, but I did."

He drew her close, wrapped those warm, strong arms around her and tucked her head against his shoulder. "It's okay." He kissed her temple, stroked her hair. "Okay, to miss me…"

"Oh, I'm not so sure about that." She pushed against his chest so she could look at him again and she admitted, "L.T. says I have a Puritan streak. Maybe I do. I know I don't like it when the man I'm with gets intimate with someone else."

He understood then. "You mean that night six years ago."

She gave another push at his chest. He took the hint that time and let her go. She went around him, to his bed, and sat carefully on the edge of it. "I suppose this is stupid—to bring this up again. We already talked about it. You said you were sorry. And I did believe you…"

He spoke, softly. "There's no one else, B.J. I swear it. There isn't now. And there wasn't then. Not really. Not in any way that mattered."

She ran her hand, palm flat, over the bedspread, smoothing wrinkles that weren't even there. "That night, at your apartment. That other woman…I guess I shouldn't have used that key you gave me, should have knocked instead of barging right in on you. It was…so awful. One of those what-is-wrong-with-this-picture moments. You were on top of her and I could see—"

"B.J."

"Yeah?"

"Spare me the details, okay? I get the point."

"Okay. But I mean it when I say it was…a truly bad moment."

"I know."

"I've always wondered…" Her throat clutched on her. So ridiculous, after all this time, how much a flash of ugly memory still had the power to stop her dead—the power to wound, and wound so deeply.

"Ask," he said, the sound low and rough, as if that moment had hurt—*still* hurt—him, as well.

She looked right at him then. "That woman. Who was she?"

He hung his head. "I don't know."

"She really was a total stranger?"

"I think she said her name was Sarah. I hooked up with her at that Irish bar around the corner from my place." He'd lived in Chelsea then. In a studio walk-up with an efficiency kitchen along one wall, a bathtub that doubled as the base for the dinner table and a Pullman bed.

That bed was opposite the door…

B.J. shut her eyes to block out the memory of Buck's betrayal. She tried to turn her mind to happier thoughts—and found herself remembering that the place had had waterbugs the size of Chihuahuas. In the good times, they used to joke about putting a leash on one and walking it over to Union Square.

Back then, he could barely afford that tiny, tacky apartment. He worked two jobs—at *Alpha* and at night in a restaurant uptown—to keep up with his lease. They'd mostly lived at her apartment. It was bigger and cleaner, considerably so. Not as nice as her current co-op, but a palace compared to that studio.

She said, "You took me by surprise when you asked me to marry you. The last thing I thought you'd ever do was propose. All those times I asked you to move in with me, you never would."

"Too much pride," he said. "I wanted *you* to move in with *me*. I wanted to have a place of my own that was…I don't know, worthy of you, I guess. I wanted to take care of you."

She swallowed. "Take care of me?"

"That's right." He came toward her then, hesitantly. She signaled her willingness to have him near by scooting sideways a little, making a place for him. He settled beside her on the edge of the bed. "Pretty damn pitiful, huh? Me, wanting to take care of *you?* Considering you were—and are—as self-reliant as they come. And I could barely take care of *myself.*"

"Pitiful?" She met his eyes, couldn't quite hold the connection, and looked away. "I wouldn't say that. But I have to admit, it knocked me right over when you pulled that ring out of your pocket." She stared out at the moonlit dark beyond the French doors, at the endless layers of stars.

He grunted. "I got that ring at a pawn shop. All-Metro Pawn, it was called. The guy behind the counter swore the diamond was a full carat. Even from a pawnbroker, it cost two weeks' worth of commission checks from *Alpha*. And then, after it was all over between us, I took it back where I got it. Guy gave me half what I paid for it."

She allowed herself a long, sorrowful sigh and looked at him again. "A bad business, all around."

He broke the eye contact that time. "Not all of it. There were a lot of good times, too."

She felt the ghost of a smile as it tugged at her mouth. "That place of yours was something."

"Something to get away from."

"What about those waterbugs?"

"Never seen any that big, before or since."

There was a silence. Into it, she confessed, so softly, "I *had* turned you down. Much as I hate to admit it, I do realize you did have every right to go and be with someone else…."

"Uh-uh." He was shaking his head. "You were mine, then. Even if you wouldn't say yes to my ring. You were mine and I was yours. I knew it." He took her hand from her lap, pressed it to his chest. "I knew it here."

She felt the steady beating of his strong heart. "Oh, Buck…"

"The whole time we were together, I felt about a thousand miles beneath you. You were so smart and on top of it, way out of my league. I knew what I was and it wasn't much. And that just got clearer the more important you became to me. Every morning, when I looked in the mirror to shave, I saw a nobody from a small town, a hick with big dreams and no money.

"I tried not to let it all get to me. For a while, I think I succeeded pretty well. But in the end, I couldn't take it anymore, feeling so much *less* than you. I asked you to marry me when I knew you would say no—and then, when you *did* say no, I stomped off in a rage and betrayed you with someone else. I went out and found that other woman and I used her. Because I not only knew you were right to turn me down—I also needed a way to prove to myself that it was really over, that I had lost you. I didn't dream you'd come back to try and work things out. But you did come back—which meant I got exactly what I'd been telling myself I needed. After that, there was no doubt about how *over* the two of us were."

"You *wanted* it to end, between us?"

"No. Never. But I sure as hell hated feeling like I wasn't man enough for you. I hated it so much, I went right out and proved that it was true—I *wasn't* man enough for you."

He released her hand and dropped back across the bed. A few seconds later, she fell back beside him. They lay there, legs bent at the knees, feet still firmly planted on the floor, staring upward, not touching.

He rolled his head to look at her. "You were so right, to say no to me. I was too young. And real stupid. I had too much to prove to the world—and to myself. But you know what?"

"Tell me."

He gave her that grin, then, the one that made all the women go ga-ga. "I like to think that now, I'm not only older, I'm a hell of a lot smarter, too…"

She teased, "Uh-oh. I'm getting worried…"

"You should be." He rolled and grabbed for her. She squirmed away. But he was fast. He'd always been fast. Damn him. "Gotcha," he crowed when he caught her. His tempting lips were barely an inch from hers.

She advised, "Don't get all full of yourself. I *let* you catch me."

He gathered her closer and whispered, "Now, that's what I like to hear."

And then he kissed her.

Several hours later, B.J. woke in Buck's bed with a burning desire for a glass of cold milk and an Oreo cookie—or five. Really, this food thing was getting out of hand.

She checked the bedside clock. Past one in the morning. Then she rolled her head the other way to look at the sleeping man beside her.

He lay face up. At some point after she dropped off, he must have gotten up and turned off the lamp. The room was thick with nighttime shadows. But she could see him clearly enough. His skin looked silvery in the starlight and the shadow of his morning beard already darkened his cheeks.

He looked so peaceful when he was sleeping. Almost harmless.

Hah.

She thought of the things he'd done to her—and with her—before they fell asleep. No, she didn't blush. When it came to sex, B. J. Carlyle never blushed.

But she did have to hold back a long, melting sigh.

And she still wanted that Oreo. Maybe Chastity would have some down in the kitchen.

Guests weren't allowed in the kitchen area—but B.J. wasn't *that* kind of guest. Not really. She was Buck's guest and that made her a *family* guest and…

Oh, hell. Even if she wasn't supposed to go in the kitchen, she didn't care. She wanted those Oreos. She could *taste* the silky coldness of that tall glass of milk.

And really, she had to get up anyway and get back to her own room. Until she got around to mentioning the fact that she was pregnant, there could be no waking up in the morning with Buck. Mornings were for bolting down the hall, late as usual for her regular appointment with the toilet bowl. Buck didn't need to be a witness to that.

Carefully, she inched over until she could ease out of the bed and onto her feet, one hand weighting the blankets, to keep any pesky draft from waking him. She tiptoed over to the chair where she'd thrown her clothes and quickly began putting them on. She was almost dressed, sitting in the chair to pull on her socks, when he spoke sleepily from the bed.

"Wha's up?"

She whispered, "Go back to sleep. I need an Oreo."

"Oreo?"

"I'll be back...." She wouldn't. But he didn't have to know until morning—hopefully after she'd done the daily hurl.

"Wan' me to come?"

"No. Go back to sleep."

He made a muffled, sighing sound, turned over and lay still. Good. She finished putting on her socks and shoes, grabbed her coat and bag and got the heck outta there—on tiptoe, very quietly.

In the hall, Chastity kept the lights in the wall sconces turned on low, so B.J. didn't have stumble around in the dark. She stopped in at her own room first, to drop off her coat and bag, then she headed downstairs.

In the lower hall, she turned for the back of the house. The kitchen door was right across from the one to Glory's rooms. B.J. put her hand on the kitchen doorknob—and heard muffled sobbing coming from the other side.

Poor Glory.

B.J. turned the knob and pushed the door inward. "Hey," she said softly, "Need a shoulder to…?"

It wasn't Glory.

Buck's mother sat at the table, clutching a wadded-up tissue in one hand and the phone in the other. Tears streamed down her cheeks.

Fifteen

"Oops. Sorry." B.J. started to duck back out the kitchen door.

Chastity waved her soggy tissue and mouthed, "Wait." She sniffed and spoke into the phone. "Caitlin. All right. I *will* think about it, I promise. Right now, I have to go… Yes. Buck's girlfriend…"

Buck's *girlfriend?* Wait a minute…

B.J. automatically opened her mouth to deliver a correction—and shut it before saying a word.

After all, she'd just crawled out of Buck's bed following a night of extremely satisfying lovemaking. And she fully expected to spend tomorrow night in his bed, too. This was more than a hook-up, a lot more. At least for the next several days, B.J. realized, if someone called her Buck's girlfriend, she'd be in no position to argue the point.

"Bye." Chastity punched the off button, tossed her

used tissue on the table atop a drifting white pile of them, yanked a fresh one from the box at her elbow— and set the phone down. "What's up?" She dabbed at her eyes.

"I, um, got a little hungry and I thought maybe…"

Chastity signaled her forward. "Come on in. Shut the door. No need to wake the whole house."

B.J. stepped over the threshold and closed the door behind her. "I didn't mean to interrupt anything."

"You didn't, don't worry." Chastity honked into her tissue and then wiped her nose. "What can I get you?"

"You wouldn't happen to have some Oreos around here, would you?"

Another tissue hit the pile. "You know, I just might." Chastity pushed herself to her feet.

B.J. protested, "You don't have to wait on me. Let me—"

"Sit. I'm happy to get you whatever you'd like." So B.J. took a chair and watched as Chastity bustled about, washing her hands, pulling open a cupboard and producing a fresh, crisp bag of Oreos. She transferred several of the dark-chocolate goodies to a small plate and set them on the table in front of B.J. "Let me guess. A big glass of cold milk."

"You're a mind-reader."

"That I am." Chastity poured the milk and provided a napkin.

B.J. dug in. "Um. Perfect."

Chastity retied the sash on her celadon-green chenille robe and took her chair again. She watched, wearing a tiny smile and a faraway look in her still-moist eyes, as B.J. polished off three cookies in quick succession and drank half of her milk. "I like a woman with an appetite."

"I've got that, all right." B.J. spoke around a mouthful of cookie. She ate another and another after that. By then, with the edge off her hunger, she found she couldn't resist asking, "Was that Caitlin Bravo on the phone?"

Chastity sat back. "Buck mentioned Caitlin?"

"Yeah—her and her three sons. I think we're leaving for Las Vegas tomorrow, where I'll get to meet her oldest, Aaron."

"Well. In answer to your question, yes. That was Aaron's mother on the phone just now. Caitlin's my best friend."

"I see," said B.J., kind of taking that in.

Chastity sniffed. "You're surprised—that I would be friends with one of Blake's other wives?"

"Well. Yeah. I guess I am…"

"We met a couple of years ago, Caitlin and me—after the truth about Blake came out in the papers, along with the news that he was finally, truly dead. Caitlin raised her boys barely a hundred miles from here, in New Venice, Nevada."

Mind-boggling. "Blake Bravo must have had one giant pair of *cojones* on him, to keep two separate families that close together."

Chastity chuckled under her breath. "He certainly did. But he was careful, in his own diabolical way. He and Caitlin were together before he faked his own death. Once he supposedly died, she never saw him again. I met him later. I had no idea at first that he was *the* Blake Bravo—not for years, if you want the truth." She began gathering up her pile of tissues.

"I just don't get it. What goes through the mind of a man like that?"

"We'll never know and, truthfully, I don't think I *want* to know."

B.J. sipped her milk. "So. You and Caitlin finally met up…"

"That's right. When our sons found each other, she called me and said she'd like to meet me. I was nervous about that, about us getting together. But she was insistent. I ended up inviting her here. She stayed overnight." Chastity rose and put the tissues in the trash under the sink. Firmly, she shut the sink cabinet door and straightened. "We talked that whole night, never even went to bed. It felt as though I'd known her my whole life. And you know, maybe that's not so surprising. After all, we do have a lot in common. Blake Bravo took both of us for quite a ride—and gave each of us our beautiful boys." She leaned back against the counter and patted her hair, though it looked painfully tidy already. "I never for a minute expected that we would get on so well. We *are* very different. Caitlin's quite the seductive one. Men flock to her."

"So I've heard."

"She's a fine person." The twin lines between Chastity's brows deepened even more with her warning frown.

"That wasn't a criticism. Honestly." B.J. peeled apart an Oreo and licked the sweet, white center.

Chastity pursed up her mouth. "Well, people do judge her. Her men friends come and go—and they tend to be much younger than she is."

"Are they all over eighteen?"

"Of course. But some are as young as their middle twenties. Caitlin's in her late fifties now."

"You should meet my father. He's sixty. The current love of his life is twenty-three."

Chastity made a humphing sound. "It's funny, isn't it? When a man takes a lover young enough to be his daughter, people may talk, but it's mostly about what a big stud the old guy is. Let a woman try that, though…"

"Exactly. And as far as I'm concerned, what goes on between single consenting adults is just not my business." B.J. licked off the rest of the white icing, then popped the cookie in her mouth.

"More milk?"

B.J. beamed Buck's mom a grateful smile. "Please." Chastity provided a refill and then returned to her seat. "Thanks." B.J. gulped another sip, set down the glass and leaned across the table, pitching her voice to a level suitable for sharing secrets. "And speaking of things that are none of my business…"

Chastity sighed, but it was a good-natured kind of sigh. "Yes?"

"What made you cry just now?"

Buck's mom waved a hand. "Oh, well. I'm a little confused, that's all."

"About?"

"It's…man trouble, I guess you could say."

Man trouble. Chastity? More intriguing by the minute. "And you called Caitlin for advice?"

"I know it's late, but Caitlin runs a combination restaurant, bar and gaming parlor over there in New Venice. She's up at all hours—and, as I mentioned, she does know a lot about men." Chastity tapped her fingertips on the table. "I think I'd like a nice cup of tea. How about you?"

"I'll pass." B.J. chose another Oreo.

Chastity rose and set the kettle on to boil, then got down a china teapot, a tea ball and a cozy. She took a canister of tea from a cupboard. B.J., enjoying herself immensely, watched the older woman as she bustled about. It was nice, sitting there in Chastity's warm kitchen in the middle of the night, eating Oreos and getting more dirt on the notorious Blake Bravo and his wives.

Plus, with a little more careful coaxing, B.J. just knew she could get Buck's mom to come clean on that "man trouble" remark of a minute ago.

"The truth is," Chastity said with a quick, rueful glance over her shoulder at B.J., "I loved Blake Bravo. I loved him more than anyone will ever know. He was all I ever wanted—and I know what you're thinking."

"Well. The man *was* a kidnapper, a murderer and a bigamist several times over."

Chastity spooned tea leaves into the tea ball. "I was so young when I met him, barely eighteen, starry-eyed and innocent. We ran off to Vegas together and got married the first weekend we met. Of course, I hadn't a clue then that he already had more than one wife. If someone had dared to try and tell me he was already married—several times over—I would have cursed them for a liar and spit on their shoes. Never would I have believed that my darling Blake could betray me."

"Wow."

"Oh, yes. I was *his,* completely—and proud to be so."

"You met him here, in the Flat?"

"Yes, I did. Right here, at the Sierra Star. This place belonged to my parents then." Chastity screwed the two pieces of the tea ball together, hung it in the pot and carried the pot, her cup and the cozy back to the table. "To this day, I don't know why he came to town." She set down the tea stuff and claimed her chair again. "He never told me. And you know what? I really didn't care.

"Oh, he was so handsome." She folded her hands on the tabletop and sent a glance across at B.J. Her eyes were shining. "Very dangerous, oh yes, with those exciting pale eyes of his. I was in love from the first moment I saw him. It took me years to start suspecting that he might actually be *the* Blake Bravo, the bad seed of the Los Angeles Bravos—a person who had beaten another man to death with his bare hands and was supposed to have died in an apartment fire."

"How did you find out the truth?"

"I saw a picture of him—of *the* Blake Bravo—in a magazine article about the L.A. branch of the family. I couldn't believe it. The Blake in the picture was *my* Blake."

"So you confronted him about it?"

"Confronted? Well, I wouldn't use such a strong word. I never confronted Blake about anything. He didn't come to me that often and I was always so thrilled just to see his handsome face, to look in those dangerous eyes…" Chastity shook her head. "Go ahead. Say it."

"You said it for me a few minutes ago. The man took you for a ride."

"Oh, yes he did."

"You did talk with him about it, though, about the picture in the magazine?"

"I did. Even I, blinded by love as I was, couldn't help but be more than a little suspicious. The next time he came to me, I gently asked him about who he really was. I showed him the article. I said how much the Blake Bravo in the photograph looked like him, how he never had told me who his people were, or where he came from."

"And?"

"He was so…tender. So sweet and understanding. He pointed out how the picture wasn't all that clear. He said no, of course not. He wasn't that terrible man in the article. Didn't the article say that the man in the picture had been dead for years? I couldn't meet those pale eyes of his. I remember I nodded. He said, 'Look at me, Chas'—that was what he always called me, Chas—he said, 'Chas, I'm not dead. I'm very, very much alive.' He kissed me and…oh, whenever he kissed me, I was a goner. As long as he kissed me, he could say anything and I would believe it."

"Incredible."

"Isn't it, though? I've heard from Marsh, Blake's son in Oklahoma, that Blake could be violent. He never was violent with me. Far from it. With me, he was always a gentleman, though he had that lovely air of risk and danger. Maybe that's why it took me so long to doubt him. Every time he came back to me, it was like falling in love all over again, so tender, so romantic, so absolutely beautiful."

B.J. didn't really get it. She'd never have fallen for a psycho like Blake. But Chastity had been sheltered and innocent, a perfect target for an unscrupulous lover. "So. Though the evidence to the contrary was right there in front of you, he still managed to convince you he wasn't *that* Blake…"

"Yes. That's what he did."

"And then?"

"He left. And I never saw him again."

She remembered what Buck had told her. "He left you pregnant with Bowie…."

"He did."

"What a bastard."

"Yes. He was. And yet…" Chastity's voice trailed off on a sigh.

B.J. got the picture. It wasn't pretty. "EEEuu. You *still* love him."

Chastity shrugged. "I suppose I do, though I know it's not who he really was that I love. God help me, I could never love a man like that. But…my *idea* of him, the way he was with me. That haunts me still."

They sat quietly for a moment. B.J. pondered the things Chastity had told her. The kettle whistled. Chastity rose to pour the boiling water into her flowered china pot.

When she sat again, B.J. decided she'd waited long enough to get back to the subject of Chastity's current love life. "So…you mentioned a romantic problem."

Chastity slid the quilted cozy over the steeping pot. "Mr. Pano—er, Alyosha…he asked me to dinner at the Nugget Saturday night. And then to the Harvest Ball afterward."

Of course. The handyman. B.J. should have guessed. "You're crying because a nice man asked you out?"

"That never happens to me."

"Nice men don't ask you out?"

"Men don't ask me out, period."

"Seriously? None? Ever?"

"Blake was the only guy for me, the only man I've ever known in an…intimate way—and is that so strange? Even in New York City, there have to be *some* women who find their man early and stay true to him their whole lives through."

"Well, I'm sure that there are." Though B.J., personally, had never met one.

But then, how would she have? Though her father

had supposedly been true to her mother—or so he claimed—he'd been with countless women since, sometimes several at once. B.J. had spent her childhood getting to know L.T.'s girlfriends. As soon as she got used to one, the next one came along.

And in her extensive network of acquaintances, B.J. couldn't think of a single woman who'd met and married the love of her life right up front. In her circle, women wanted to test the waters for a while before getting in up to their necks. B.J. thought they were smart, to want a little life experience before making a huge decision like whom to marry.

Buck's image floated through her mind—Buck by starlight, sleeping so peacefully up there in his room.

She smiled, feeling sappy and silly and utterly dewy-eyed. Buck had been her first. After a childhood surrounded by her father's seductive, willing women, she'd been careful on the sexual front. Careful verging on wary. She'd waited for someone special—and she'd known instantly that Buck was the one.

And if it had worked out between them, he would have been the only one...

So, well, okay. Maybe it wasn't so totally unbelievable, now she gave it a little serious thought, to imagine a woman having only one man for her entire life.

"B.J.?"

She blinked and realized she'd been staring all dreamy-eyed into the middle distance, half an Oreo in her hand. "Oh. Sorry." She popped the cookie in her mouth, drank the rest of her milk and plunked the empty glass back down. "Now. Where was I? Ah. I remember. The point is, whatever the notorious Blake Bravo was *really* like, he's *not* anymore. He's been dead for, what?"

"Four years."

"And you haven't seen him in…?"

Chastity fiddled with the cozy, tugging it down more firmly over her pot of tea. "It's been twenty-six years since he left me that final time."

"You're not serious."

"Oh, yes I am."

"Well, alrighty."

"What does *that* mean?"

"Alrighty? That's what you say when you can't think of anything else to say."

"Ah."

"Let's come at this from another angle. Tell me. What advice did Caitlin have for you?"

"She said I should go out with Alyosha."

"And to that I would have to say, listen to Caitlin. Please."

Chastity leaned across the table. "There's more."

"What else?"

"Caitlin said—" Buck's mother lowered her voice to a whisper "—that maybe I'd get lucky and get *laid*."

B.J. faked a gasp. "No."

"Oh, yeah." Chastity wiggled her eyebrows.

Which struck B.J. as just hilariously funny. She clapped a hand over her mouth to keep from laughing out loud—and *that* struck Chastity as funny.

They burst, simultaneously, into twin fits of giggling—fits that, for some insane reason, they both found impossible to control. Chastity hit the table several times in succession with the palm of her hand, as if that could make the giggles stop, while B.J. grabbed her milk glass and held on for dear life, as if an empty glass could help her quit laughing so hard.

They were finally getting control of themselves when the kitchen door swung open.

But it was only Glory, in fluffy pink slippers and a long, zip-up micro-fleece robe. "What's going on in here?"

B.J. and Chastity looked at each other and started giggling all over again.

Glory shut the door and waited, looking irritated. "Oreos?" she asked hopefully, when they finally settled down a little. B.J. pushed the plate toward her. Glory got herself a glass of milk and joined them at the table. "So. If something's funny, I should be told. You know I don't get nearly enough laughs in my life these days."

So Chastity poured herself some tea and told Glory about Alyosha asking her out on a date for Saturday night.

"What's funny about that?" Glory demanded, and added, "You should go," before Chastity could answer.

"You think so?" Chastity's cheeks had flushed a delicate pink. Her dark eyes shone. She looked younger, suddenly—a decade younger, at least.

Glory nodded. "Oh, yeah. It could be great. And you never know." She leaned across the table, dimples flashing and mischief in her eyes. "You might even get laid."

It was well after two when B.J. said goodnight to Glory and Chastity and climbed the stairs again.

She hesitated at the door to Buck's room, a warm yearning moving through her—to tiptoe on in there, shuck off her clothes and get back in bed with him, to cuddle in close to him for the rest of the night.

She reminded herself that if she weakened now and

went to him, he'd be bound to catch her being sick in the morning.

And she just wasn't up for explaining about that. Not yet.

With a reluctant sigh, she moved on—to her bathroom first, where she had a quick shower and brushed her teeth. In her own room, she threw yesterday's clothes on a chair, took off her robe and put on a satin sleep shirt. She crawled under the cold covers of her bed and lay there shivering, wishing she could be with Buck.

Gradually, her body heat warmed the chilly sheets. She closed her eyes and snuggled down.

She woke to morning light—and to Buck, nibbling her earlobe. "I missed you," he whispered. "You never came back to my bed…" He was under the covers with her, all warm and hairy-legged, cradling her spoon-fashion, his big body curled around her back.

Or maybe she was only dreaming….

She made a sleepy sound and eased her hand behind her. Yep. No doubt about it. Buck. In the flesh.

He chuckled in her ear.

And terror shot through her. Her stomach rolled, lurched and—wait.

She lay perfectly still.

Was it possible?

She swallowed. With great care, she drew in a slow breath through her nose…

Yes. Definitely.

The rolling feeling had faded.

A real, true bona-fide miracle had just occurred.

For the first time in weeks, it was morning and B.J.

didn't have to throw up. She caught Buck's hand and tucked it under her chin and dozed off again with a happy sigh.

They got an early-afternoon flight to Las Vegas, where Buck led her on a tour of the two casinos owned and run by his uncle and his half-brothers.

He showed her High Sierra first. They took the famous whitewater rafting ride that wound its way through the casino. And they visited the Gold Exchange, a series of exclusive shops in a central court between the casino and the three-thousand-room High Sierra Hotel.

Next, they crossed the glittering glass skyway that connected High Sierra to her newer sister casino/resort, Impresario.

Impresario had a Moulin Rouge theme. Lots of red velvet and gold leaf, very lush and excitingly decadent. At Impresario's elegant casino, B.J. lost a lot at spin poker and won—though not a lot—at blackjack.

They had dinner at High Sierra's most exclusive restaurant, the Placer Room, with Aaron and Fletcher Bravo and Aaron's very pregnant wife, Celia.

"This is our second baby," Celia said, laying a protective hand over her big stomach. "Our first, Davey, is almost three." Celia was an attractive woman with the prettiest rose petal-pink skin and cupid-bow lips. She confided that she'd worked for Aaron as his personal assistant for three years before she fell in love with him. "We were going along just great. All business, no funny stuff, if you know what I mean. And then one morning—it happened to be Valentine's Day, believe it or not—we were doing just what we did every morning, going over his schedule. I looked up and—bam—I knew. I loved my boss. It was awful."

B.J. grabbed a dinner roll and set to work slathering it with an entire floret of whipped butter. "But it all turned out perfectly in the end, right?"

"Yes, it did." Celia beamed her cupid-bow smile at her husband. Aaron winked back. "And there's more. His brothers, Will and Cade, eventually married my two best friends, Jillian and Jane. We're hometown girls, all three of us. We grew up in New Venice, were friends all through school. We never guessed that someday we'd each be happily married to one of those wild and crazy Bravo boys...."

"So Aaron's got Celia," B.J. said later that night, as she and Buck stood on the balcony of their luxury suite at Impresario with the bright lights of Las Vegas glittering all around them. "And Cade and Will are married to Celia's best friends. What about Fletcher? A bachelor through and through?" That other Bravo half-brother had been mostly silent through dinner.

Fletcher had inherited his father's striking pale eyes. He was also big and handsome, like all the Bravo men. B.J.'s sense of him was of a man under strictest control, a man who could be dangerous—but then, on second thought, she had noticed that sense of potential danger in every Bravo man she'd met so far. Even Brett and Brand had a certain edge about them, though they both worked hard to come off as friendly and harmless.

Buck took her hand and pulled her back inside. He slid the glass door shut. "Fletcher was married."

"He's divorced?"

"Yeah. And since the divorce, his ex-wife died." Buck held her loosely, his arms around her waist. Her little black dress had no back to speak of. He ran a teasing finger over the bare skin of her lower spine.

She rested her arms on his shoulders and twined her hands behind his neck. "Sad. About Fletcher's ex-wife."

"Yeah. But he does have a daughter, Ashlyn. Ashlyn is four, a big-eyed, serious little thing. Very bright, from what I understand. Fletcher took custody after the mother died." Buck pulled her closer. "Shall we dance?" They softly swayed together.

She laid her head on his shoulder and let him lead her. "Um. Nice. I wish…"

He brushed a kiss at her temple. "What?"

"That it could always be like this—the two of us, holding each other, dancing…" She sighed. "Dancing without music…"

"I hear music. When I'm with you, there's always music."

"Hah," she said. But much more softly than usual.

They arrived in Reno at noon the next day, picked up the SUV and drove to the Flat. Chastity met them at the front door to tell B.J. she'd had a call from her father early that morning. "He said for you to call back as soon as you got in."

B.J. felt equal parts concerned—and irritated. Maybe there *was* some kind of problem. More likely, though, L.T. had decided he couldn't go another day without B.J. to order around. "Did he say what the call was about?"

"No. Only that he wanted you to call him immediately."

"He could have called me on my cell," she grumbled. The phone had been working while they were in Vegas.

Buck slipped his hand in hers and gave a squeeze.

"Didn't you tell him he'd have to use the land line to reach you here?"

"So? That shouldn't have stopped him. He never takes instructions. You know how he is."

Buck released her hand and hefted their suitcases. "Come on. Let's go up. You can give him a call and find out what's going on."

She followed him up the stairs—and caught his arm once he'd set her suitcase down at the door to her room. "Repeat after me. 'B.J., remember our deal. You stay here with me until next Friday, or forget the story.'"

He ran his hand down her arm, a lovely, reassuring caress. "And I should say this because?"

"Well, if I *have* to stay here for the sake of the story, that's that, isn't it? L.T. will accept that I'm not going anywhere until the week is up—though he may demand to speak to you. He'll want to see if he can browbeat you into letting me come home."

Slowly, he shook his head. "Uh-uh."

She asked hopefully, "You won't let him browbeat you?"

"There's no reason he would. I'm not telling him you have to stay here."

"Why not?"

He suggested, gently, "Well, because…it's a lie?"

"Only a little one." She held up her thumb and fore-finger, with a tiny space between them.

He wasn't going for it. "Uh-uh. You *don't* have to stay here. You're here because you want to be—and that's the only reason."

She scowled at him. "All of sudden, you're just dripping with integrity."

He moved in closer. She tipped her head up to meet

his eyes and he kissed her on the tip of her nose. "You're tough as nails."

"That's right. I am, but—"

"You can handle L.T. all on your own."

"But I don't *want* to handle him. I don't even want to talk to him. He makes me nuts sometimes, he truly does."

Buck bent his head close again and whispered, so softly, "You're feeling guilty, aren't you?"

"I am not." The denial sounded forced, and she knew it.

He went right on, so softly—so tenderly, "For once in your life, you're having what is known as a vacation. You're doing nothing earth-shattering, just hanging with me. You're here because it's what *you* want to do. And you're enjoying every minute of it."

"Okay. So?"

"So, you're afraid your father will try to take this vacation away from you." She might have argued. If he hadn't been right. He brushed a kiss into the hollow beneath her temple. "Just remember this…"

She wrinkled her nose at him. "What?"

"At this point in your life, when L. T. Carlyle says jump, you can simply say no."

"Yeah. And then pay the price."

"There's a price, either way."

"That's not very reassuring."

"No. But it does happen to be the truth."

Sixteen

The minute she got to the phone, L.T. started in on her. "B.J. About damn time. That woman, Buck's mother, said you and Buck had flown off to Vegas. What for?"

"Buck has two half-brothers there. We went to visit them."

L.T. grunted, a disbelieving sound. "He needed to get with his brothers, for the story?"

"I wouldn't know. I suppose so."

"You *suppose* so?"

"It's Buck's story, L.T. I don't intend to edit it until *after* he turns it in."

There were blustery noises and then, "Fine, fine. But I've been thinking. You've been there a week now. We could use you back here. I want you to talk to Buck, tell him that the deal he made with you, the one about you staying there, or he won't write the story? Tell him that's unreasonable. Tell him I said I need you in New York."

"You need me…."

"Didn't I just say that?"

"For?"

"Well. I don't *need* you, exactly. But you've got your job to do and you should get back to it."

"Is there a problem at *Alpha?* Is that what you're saying?"

"What the hell does it matter if there's a problem? What matters is that you've got a job and you should be doing it. It's called a damn work ethic, and I brought you up to have one."

"So Giles does have a handle on everything? No snags? No major crises?"

L.T. made a low, snorting sound. "Look, B.J. Just tell Buck you've got to return right away."

"No."

There was a pause. Not a pleasant one. Then L.T. said, "What?"

"I said, no. I'm not telling Buck I have to return, because I *don't* have to return. And even more important, I don't *want* to return. I'm having a great time." Oh, it felt just terrific to say that. So she said it again. "A *great* time. I'll be back in a week, as we agreed."

"What the hell's this?" L.T. snorted some more, an old bull pawing the ground, getting ready to charge. "You sound like you're on a goddamn vacation all of a sudden."

"As a matter of fact, that's exactly what I am. On vacation."

"What are you talking about? Nobody gave you a vacation."

"That's right. Nobody did. I haven't had a vacation in years. So I'm taking one now. I'm on vacation. And I'm staying on vacation until a week from today."

"Wait. Hold on. What about the story?"

"Buck's said he would write it. He will. He has a contract, for crying out loud. Don't worry about it. It's a done deal."

There was a silence on the line. An ominous one. And the strange thing was, it didn't spook B.J. in the least. She waited. For once in her life, she decided, L.T. was just going to have to be the one to break the silence.

At last, he muttered, "You're giving me serious heartburn here, you know that? My chest is on fire."

"Take a Rolaids."

"I don't need people on my payroll who crap out on the job."

She had a scary, sinking feeling. But she didn't let him know it. "Are you firing me?"

Another threatening silence—and then, "I'm tempted, believe me."

"But you're *not* firing me."

He wouldn't say he wasn't. Not in so many words. Instead, he settled on a cryptic ultimatum. "One week. Not a day more. Or else."

The line went dead.

B.J. hung up softly, ignoring the urge to slam the phone hard into the cradle. For a moment or two, she just stood there, her fingers white-knuckled on the handset. Then, carefully, she let go. Shaking her head, she went to the bed and sank down on the edge of it.

She was still sitting in the same spot a few minutes later when Buck tapped on the French doors. She signaled him in with a tight toss of her head.

She watched him come toward her. He stopped a foot from her knees. "Well?"

She tipped her head back and looked at him. "I think I hate my own father."

"Bad?"

"Awful."

He sat down beside her, wrapped an arm around her and drew her close. "Tell me…"

She rested her head on of his shoulder. "Oh, he's suddenly decided I've been here too long. Since he had no real reason why I *have* to race back to New York right this minute, he tried to bully me into it."

"He failed, right?"

"Yeah. Then he threatened to fire me."

"But he didn't fire you."

"Not quite."

He stroked her shoulder. "You want to go?"

"Where?"

"Back to New York."

"Hell, no. Not till next Friday. It's one more measly week. He can get along without me until then. He can get along without me, period. Or so he's always telling me. So fine. It's a week. He can wait till then."

He squeezed her arm. "You're shaking."

"I am not—and if I am, do me a favor and *pretend* that I'm not."

"Yes, ma'am." He guided her down to the bed and canted up on an elbow beside her. "What can I do to cheer you up?"

"Have someone go and kill my father?"

He ran a brushing finger along the curve of her jaw. In spite of her fury and frustration at L.T., Buck's touch left an echo of pleasure in its wake. He teased, "You're feeling bloodthirsty today…"

"How can you be so…disgustingly lighthearted about this?"

"Your father is who he is. He's not going to change."

She narrowed her eyes at him. "He never liked you,

when you and I were together. But I suppose you've forgotten what a jerk he was to you, now you're a world-famous author and whenever he sees you, he kisses your ass."

Buck almost smiled—she saw the corners of his mouth twitch. "I haven't forgotten."

"Remember that dinner, at the Castle, after we'd been together, oh, maybe two months? Remember how he put you down through the soup and halfway into the rack of lamb?"

"I remember."

"He used to do that to every guy I ever went out with. He'd want to know who I was dating and then he'd insist I bring them over for dinner. And then he'd humiliate them. You were the last one I ever let him do that to."

"Should I be flattered?"

"Before you, when he did that, I'm ashamed to say, I'd think less of whatever poor guy he'd eviscerated. I'd see them as less of a man, somehow. And within a week or two, I'd stop going out with them. But you…"

"As I recall, he wasn't content to simply stab a guy to the heart. He had to turn the knife, as well."

"Yeah. He really got on you. He said you had no connections and no background. That you didn't even have any training to speak of in your chosen profession, so your dream of being a writer was bound to remain just that—a dream. He said you had no education. And he'd seen no sign that you had any talent."

"Plus, he reminded me, I could barely pay my rent at my fleabag apartment." Buck chuckled low and tenderly stroked her hair back from her forehead. "As I recall, he added that a man without talent or background should always have money, at the very least."

"My father is, was and always has been a true SOB."

"But as I remember, you did defend me."

"Fat lot of good it did."

"You told him to shut the, er, heck up."

"But he didn't."

"Then you jumped up and told me how sorry you were that you had brought me there. You threw your napkin on the table. It was very dramatic. You said, 'Buck. Come on. We're out of here.'"

"But you wouldn't go."

"I knew if I let him run me off then, he'd never forget it. And neither would you."

"Oh, Buck. That's not so...."

He brushed a light kiss across her mouth. "Yeah. It is."

She admitted, "Well. It did impress me. That you held your own with him. You told me to sit back down and finish my dinner and then you turned to L.T. and told him he was right on all counts—and would he please pass the bread basket. I couldn't believe it when you did that, so cool and calm and above it all. You actually shut L.T. up. Knocked the wind right out of him."

"For about three seconds."

"Three seconds is impressive when it comes to my father. One way or another, whether he's holding court or employing his infamous silent treatment, L.T. Carlyle dominates the conversation."

Buck bent close again. "You've stopped shaking."

"Um. Yes. It seems that I have."

His lips touched hers. She wrapped her arms around his neck and enjoyed the moment, which progressed the way such moments often did between the two of them.

One kiss led to another, the top button to the next button down....

And so on.

Until she was naked beneath him, sighing his name, crying out for him never, ever to stop.

He didn't. Not for a very long time.

Much later, they got under the covers for a totally decadent afternoon nap.

"I should take a vacation more often," she whispered, on the verge of dropping off to sleep. "I don't think it gets any better than this."

"It does," he vowed. "Tonight, as a matter of fact."

"What happens tonight?"

"The Annual New Bethlehem Flat Methodist Ladies Auxiliary Potluck, that's what."

When they got to the hall that night, Buck led her through the serving line, leaning close to advise her as they approached each new dish.

"Betty Haven's artichoke and chicken casserole. Oh, yeah." He dished a spoonful onto his plate and she did the same. "Cherie Salinger's cheese pineapple surprise salad. Uh. Maybe not... And will you look at that? Tuna cashew casserole. That's Tina Wurtzburger's and it's the best."

She craned toward him to whisper in his ear, "I don't see any names on these, Buck. How do you know who made them?"

"Before I left town, I never missed a potluck." He caught her wrist as she started to dish herself up some kind of Jell-O concoction. "I wouldn't go there if I were you. That's Magda Lily's mystery Jell-O mold. You never know the kinds of weird things she might put in there. I know, it's hard to believe anyone could mess up Jell-O. But Mrs. Lily manages it every single time."

She took his advice and gave the Jell-O mold a pass. "But it's been more than ten years since you left. You'd think all the dishes would be different by now."

"Uh-uh. The women in my hometown know that when you've got yourself a good potluck recipe, you don't mess with success."

They finished loading their plates and went to sit with Chastity at a table near the center of the room. Alyosha Panopopoulis appeared a few minutes after they sat down.

"Is there maybe room for me?"

"Alyosha! Welcome." Chastity blushed and tapped the empty chair at her side.

The handyman took it. "So. How's life, eh?"

"Oh, just lovely," said Chastity. "Just absolutely fine."

Buck sent B.J. a look with *What's* this *about?* written all over it.

B.J. only shrugged and smiled.

He held her gaze for a moment, looking thoroughly flummoxed, and then he shrugged right back at her. After that, he got very absorbed in his plateful of potluck. B.J. followed his lead—but took care to eat slowly.

Now her morning sickness seemed to have faded, she had no trouble getting food down and keeping it there. She knew she had to start watching her diet or she'd be big as a house in no time at all.

Brett showed up and then Brand after him, each with a full plate. They took seats and dug in.

Glances shot back and forth among the Bravo boys as they saw that their mother actually seemed to be welcoming the attentions of a man. But it was all very friendly and easy.

Alyosha talked about his children. There were five of them—three girls and two boys. The girls all lived in the Bay Area. One son made his home in the San Fernando Valley. The other had lived in Texas for the past eight years. Alyosha explained that when his wife had died five years before, he'd decided to live his dream and move to the mountains.

"And so you see," he said. "Here I am." He beamed at Chastity and she beamed right back at him.

Then Bowie appeared.

Chastity's youngest son stomped up to their table and plunked his plate down hard. The food on it actually bounced. He yanked back a free chair, and sat down with a muttered curse.

His brothers shared another three-way look. "Okay," said Brett at last. "I'll bite. Bowie. Why the attitude?"

"None of your damn business." Bowie picked up his fork and stabbed himself a big hunk of herb-dotted red potato. He shoved the potato in his mouth and chewed with a furious scowl on his face.

A real conversation stopper, that Bowie. They all ate in uncomfortable silence for a minute or two.

Finally, Brand set down his fork. "You're no fun, Bowie. No fun at all. What's your problem now? Glory turn you down again?"

Bowie let out a string of swear words.

Alyosha gasped. "Bowie. Shame on you. In front of your beautiful mother…"

Bowie shoved back his chair. "That's it. I don't need the damn handyman getting on my ass." He glared at his mother. "What's he doing at our table, anyway?"

Buck spoke up then. "That's enough, Bowie."

Bowie turned on him. "Don't you start on me, Mr. Big Shot Famous Author. Who the hell cares what you have to say? You don't even live here anymore."

Chastity put up a hand. "Bowie." Bowie whipped his head around to face his mother. Before he could get out a single rude word, she said, "Leave this table. Now."

"Fine." With another raw curse, he shoved back his chair. It crashed to the floor behind him. He stomped off toward the door. Tossing his plate in a trash can as he went by, Bowie left the hall.

Into the deafening silence that followed, Chastity turned to Alyosha. "I apologize for my son's behavior."

Alyosha laid his hand on hers.

Every eye in the room was on them—and neither Alyosha nor Chastity seemed to care in the least.

Buck was the one who finally took things in hand. He got up and righted Bowie's overturned chair. Then he laughed and cast a sweeping glance around the quiet room. "Show's over, folks."

Within seconds, the room was abuzz with a hundred conversations. Buck took his seat again.

B.J. leaned close to him. "Nicely done."

He whispered back, "You have to know they're all talking about Bowie—and the budding romance between Ma and the handyman."

"Let 'em talk."

"That's the right attitude to have—because believe me. They will."

The next night, upstairs in the hall, B.J. and Buck attended the Harvest Ball. The Ladies Auxiliary, assisted by the New Bethlehem Flat Elementary

School student body, had worked half the afternoon, hanging fall-colored crepe-paper streamers from the ceiling and plastering the walls with construction-paper autumn leaves.

Chastity and Alyosha were there, together, looking like a pair of infatuated teenagers. Buck and B.J. shared a glass of punch with them.

B.J. danced every dance in Buck's arms—except for two: one with Brett and another with Brand.

Brett teased her. "I think you've gone and stolen my big brother's heart—again."

Such talk made her nervous. She redirected Brett's remark. "So what about you, Brett? Who's your special girl?"

The second Bravo brother was distinctly evasive. He would only say that the last thing he needed was a grand passion in his life. "Besides, I just got through my internship and started my practice. I want to get myself established before I start thinking about love and marriage and all the challenges that go with it."

"Love waits for no man," she teased.

"Eventually, I'll find myself a nice, steady, both-feet-on-the-ground kind of woman. I want two kids and a comfortable life."

B.J. faked a snoring sound.

"Wake up," Brett kidded her, "watch out for my toes."

Brand claimed the next dance. The third Bravo brother talked of the big house he was building on a hill a few miles east of town. "You should see the view. Incredible. It's my dream house, or it will be. If I ever find a decent contractor—and I'm not asking for the moon here, believe me. Just show me a man who'll stick with the job." He'd had three contractors so far.

"One couldn't keep a crew to save his soul. Another had a serious alcohol problem. I'd find empty beer bottles all over the site. The third one made zero progress in an entire summer working for me…."

B.J. smiled up at him, thinking that Buck had a couple of great guys for brothers.

Too bad there was also Bowie—who appeared just as the dance B.J. shared with Brand was ending. Buck's baby brother was so drunk, he swayed on his feet. Luckily for everyone, he didn't stay long. He spotted Glory sharing an innocent dance with another guy and stomped right back out again.

By then, B.J. and Brand had joined Buck and Brett at the punch table.

"Someone should have an up-close and personal talk with that boy," Brett remarked quietly.

"Soon," added Brand.

Buck only nodded, his expression grim.

Seventeen

Monday, early, Lupe returned.

The photographer had taken the red-eye and she had a message from L.T. "He said to tell you that the piece Buck is writing had better be, and I quote, 'the best damn Christmas feature yet.'"

Buck made a show of wiping his brow. "Whew. Let me just tell you, I'm really scared now."

Silver bangles jangling, Lupe flipped a swatch of night-black hair back over her shoulder. "The man was seriously hostile. What is *that* about?"

B.J. felt a stab of anxiety. Damn L.T., anyway. He liked keeping her anxious and he always had. "You know L.T." She was proud of how cool and offhand she sounded. "If he's not calling every shot, he's not happy. And if he's not happy, he makes sure everyone knows it."

"Well, the story's not my problem," Lupe said. "The

pictures are. And as I told you before, we need some shots that communicate Christmas, loud and clear."

B.J. led the way into the drawing room, where the morning sun streamed in the windows—and outside it looked about as far from a white Christmas as you could get.

"There's snow predicted for tomorrow," Lupe said wistfully.

Buck shrugged. "We can hope."

They took seats and set to work brainstorming ideas for Christmassy shots.

B.J. came up with the winner. She asked Buck, "Didn't you tell me your mom is big on Christmas?"

"That's right."

"So she's got decorations?"

"When I was a kid, she had an attic full of them."

"You think she still has them?"

"I'd bet a big chunk of change on it."

"Well, okay then. Here's my plan…"

They needed a tree. Buck's mother, it turned out, always sent the boys out to cut a fresh one.

And that gave B.J. another idea. "There's snow higher up, isn't there? We could go up there and cut one down. Lupe could get some shots of that. That way, even if it doesn't snow tomorrow, we'll have some pictures with snow in them."

Buck was shaking his head. "We can't just go out and cut down a tree. Not on Forest Service land, not without a permit." He grinned. "Though there are those who make it a point of pride to get their tree without a permit."

B.J. looked at him blankly. "And they do this because?"

"It's a mountain-man thing."

"Let's stay on the right side of the law, okay?"

"Yeah. Right. Ruin all my fun." But then he remembered. "Hey. My uncle Clovis has some property above the snow line…."

"Complete with trees?" B.J. asked hopefully.

"Lots of them."

"Do you think he'd mind if we took one?"

"We'll never know if we don't ask."

So Buck called his uncle and B.J. went to Chastity to find out if she'd mind putting up a tree for the sake of the story Buck was writing.

Chastity got all dewy-eyed over the idea. "Decorate a tree? Oh, I'd just love to…."

So that was settled. Lupe thought a few shots of Buck and his mother in the snow might work for the article, so Chastity agreed to go with them to choose the tree. They all four—Buck, B.J., Lupe and Chastity—put on their snow gear and piled into the SUV.

At Clovis's property, they found a foot of snow on the ground and lots of gorgeous fir trees to choose from.

Lupe got shots of Buck and Chastity making the choice, arguing over which was the thickest, the prettiest, the one without a bad side. Chastity explained that the best Christmas trees were the ones that grew in the open, with no other trees shading or crowding them.

"I prefer a silver-tip fir," Chastity announced in the lofty tone of a Christmas-tree connoisseur. "The branches are so pretty and even, the needles silvery and curving up. A silver-tip decorates beautifully."

When they finally agreed on the perfect tree, Chastity said it was a pity it wouldn't last until it really was Christmas. Then she brightened. "We'll have to put up a second one. Two trees in one year. Does life get any better than this?"

Lupe got pictures of Buck cutting down the tree, hauling it to the SUV, and tying it on top. They were ready to go when Buck scooped up a handful of snow, molded it into a ball—and hurled it at B.J.

Splat. Right in the face. She wiped snow off her nose and threatened, "Oh, you will pay!" She grabbed a handful of snow and threw it. Hit her mark, too.

Splat. Buck took it square in the chest.

That did it. The battle commenced. Lupe followed them around with her camera, getting shot after shot of the fight as it unfolded.

Chastity got into it, too. Screeching in glee, she hit Buck twice between the shoulder blades as he chased after B.J. In the end, Buck cheated and grabbed B.J.'s jacket. He dragged her down and sat on her.

Luckily, she still had a snowball in her glove. Laughing, she fired it right at his head. Chastity threw hers at the same moment. Two direct hits—from the front and the back simultaneously.

"Double-whammy," B.J. crowed. "Oh, you are so finished."

"Excuse me, but aren't you the one who's pinned to the ground?"

"Yeah—and now you mention it, let me up."

"I don't think so…" He bent closer. The look in his eyes promised a kiss. His lips were an inch from hers when Chastity let fire with another big ball of snow. It hit him in the back of the head. "Hey!"

"Cut that out, you two," said Chastity. "It's time we started back."

"Okay, okay." Then he whispered to B.J. "Wait till we get home…"

She did like the sound of that. "I hope that's a threat you plan to make good on."

"You'd better believe it."

"We won't have time, and you know it. When we get home, we've got to decorate the tree."

"You can put me off. But you can't escape me indefinitely."

As if she wanted to. She would have taunted him further, but Chastity demanded, "Come on, you two. Now."

Buck levered himself off B.J., rose and held a hand down to her. She was tempted to try a trick or two of her own—like yanking him off his feet when he wasn't expecting it.

But they did have a tree to decorate. And it was a long ride back down the mountain to town.

Once they reached the Sierra Star again and got out of their heavy winter gear, Chastity produced a tree stand. They moved the furniture around so they could set up the tree in front of the big window that looked out on the porch. Buck brought in the tree and stood it upright. He and B.J. knelt to screw in the bolts. Chastity directed the procedure, until they had the fir standing straight.

About then, Glory appeared. "A tree!" She sucked in a deep breath through her nose. "Um. Smells like Christmas." Then a crease formed between her smooth brows. "It's a little early though, isn't it?"

Chastity explained that this was a special tree they were decorating for the sake of the Christmas article Buck was writing. "Lupe needs pictures," she said.

Glory got right into the festive mood. "There should be hot cider, shouldn't there?"

"Absolutely," Chastity agreed.

"We've got cider. Leave it to me." Glory headed for the kitchen and Chastity led Buck, B.J. and Lupe upstairs.

They carried box after box down from the attic. Glory appeared with the cider and they all took a mugful.

Glory sipped. "Wait a minute. Where's the Christmas music?"

Chastity gestured toward the ancient-looking stereo cabinet in the corner. "Go for it."

So Glory put a Bing Crosby LP on the turntable. They all grinned at each other as Bing crooned "White Christmas."

"Perfect," said B.J. She was feeling very merry. A girl could easily get into the Christmas spirit around the Sierra Star.

In New York, B.J. rarely had time to enjoy the holidays. Somehow, during the season, B.J. always felt rushed, too busy for a stroll down the Avenue to take in the glittering shop windows, or a visit to the ninety-foot Rockefeller Center tree.

This year, she vowed to herself, she'd make time to appreciate the Christmas wonders her city had to offer.

Buck took it upon himself to comb through each and every one of the endless boxes of decorations. It was just like it had been at Halloween with him: "Look at this one," and "I can't believe you've *still* got this one...."

Lupe took a series of shots of him holding up various handmade decorations and exclaiming over them.

Glory disappeared for a few minutes and returned with a tray of sandwiches. They drank more cider and ate lunch and then they got down to the main event of decorating the tree.

It took an hour just to get the lights on to Chastity's satisfaction. She used the big lights for old-time's sake, she said, but she liked about a thousand tiny twinkling ones laced in and out through all the branches. The work was hell on B.J.'s manicure, which had already taken a number of hits since she'd arrived in the Flat. But she never once complained. Why would she? She was having far too much fun.

At last, Chastity declared the tree effectively lit. They moved on to the job of hanging the decorations. That went much more quickly.

They had maybe three-quarters of the decorations on the tree and Burl Ives was sweetly crooning "The Little Drummer Boy" from the stereo, when Glory spotted Bowie through the front window. He was coming in the gate.

"Oh, no…" She shoved the ornament she'd been about to hang toward Chastity. "Take this. I'm out of here."

Chastity put up both hands. "Listen. Whatever goes on between the two of you, you can't let him scare you off. This is where you live."

"But every time I meet up with him lately, there's trouble. I'd rather just—"

"Chastity's right." B.J. couldn't resist tossing in her two cents' worth. "Don't go." Even Buck gave a grunt of agreement.

Glory bit her lower lip. "I just don't want any more hassle…."

"Stay," Chastity commanded softly, as outside, heavy boots mounted the front steps. "I'll see that he behaves."

A doubtful light in her big brown eyes, Glory turned to hang her ornament on a branch.

The front door opened and slammed shut.

Bowie appeared in the doorway to the central hall. "What's going on?"

Chastity sent him a tight little smile and stated the obvious. "We're decorating a tree."

"What the hell for? It's barely November."

Buck said, "We need pictures for the Christmas article I'm writing."

"Join us," Chastity suggested with teeth-gritting good cheer. "Have some cider."

Bowie tossed back his thick head of blond hair. His eyes were on Glory, who studiously did *not* look at him. "Well," he said grudgingly. "Okay. I just might…"

He came in and poured himself a cup of cider from the pot Glory had left on a serving cart in the corner. He even wandered over, chose an ornament from one of the boxes and hung it on the tree.

Burl Ives launched into the next Christmas song. For several minutes everything went along peacefully enough. Bowie worked on the tree with the rest of them and Lupe continued taking pictures, pausing to change lenses, and to move her flashes and umbrellas into position to get the next series of shots.

When Chastity's orange-colored tabby cat strutted in from the dining room, Buck's mom called a greeting, "Hello, Mr. Lucky." The cat meowed in response—and headed straight for B.J. Surprised, she watched it approach.

B.J. had never been an animal person. People's pets tended to avoid her, which suited her just fine. Not Mr. Lucky, though. Apparently, he saw her in a whole new light. The cat coiled in and out around her ankles, purring.

Ordinarily, she would have ignored it, or shooed it away. But all the good times with Buck lately and today's heavy dose of pre-Christmas cheer must have gotten to her. She had a crazy urge to pick up the animal and pet it, even if it did shed orange hair all over her pricey chocolate-brown lace-insert cashmere sweater—or worse, use its claws and cause a nasty pull.

She had an ornament in her hand. She set it on a marble-topped side table, bent and scooped up the cat.

The ornament, a shiny glass ball with a Santa face painted on it, started rolling. B.J. hoisted Mr. Lucky to her shoulder and reached over to stop the ball from falling. Too late. The bright ornament rolled to the floor and shattered.

B.J. winced. "Oh. I'm sorry." Mr. Lucky purred in her ear.

"No big deal," said Chastity.

"I'll get a broom." Glory headed for the kitchen.

Bowie, who stood near the door to the dining room refilling his cider mug, set down the mug and stepped directly into Glory's path.

Glory glared up at him. "Move."

"Bowie," Chastity said in a warning tone.

"I mean it," said Glory. "Move. Now."

Bowie didn't budge. "You don't have to wait on her," he sneered, with a disdainful toss of his head in B.J.'s direction. "Let her get her own damn broom."

That mobilized Buck. Muttering something unpleasant under his breath, he started forward. B.J. caught his arm before he could take a step.

"Let go," he said softly.

"Please…"

Buck shook off her hand, but at least he stayed where he was.

Chastity spoke again. "Bowie. Stop this."

"Stop what?" Bowie taunted, still squarely in Glory's path. "I don't know what you're talkin' about, Ma." On the stereo, Burl Ives had reached the final chorus of "Winter Wonderland."

"This is pure meanness." Glory drew herself up to her full five-foot-one. "Meanness, that's all this is. Since I said I won't marry you, you have become the meanest guy in town."

For a moment, Bowie almost looked ashamed of himself. "Glory, honey…"

"Just get out of my way."

Bowie's jaw went granite-hard. He braced his legs wide apart, planting himself even more firmly in her path. "What are you gonna do, Glory? If you don't marry me, what kind of life do you think you're gonna have?"

"I don't want to talk about this. I'm *through* talking about this."

Bowie clearly wasn't. "Who's gonna take care of you, huh?"

Glory let out a hard huff of air. "I'll take care of myself, thank you very much. Me and my baby will get along just fine."

"It's my baby, too."

"Then get a job. Help support *your* baby."

"I will, damn it. I said that I would. Glory. Look…" He reached for her.

She slapped his hand away. "Keep your paws to yourself."

"Bowie," Chastity tried again. "I've had it. Stop this. Now."

His mother's command had zero effect. Burl Ives launched into "Silver Bells," and Bowie kept right on talking. "Look at you, Glory. You graduated high school with a big, fat C average. You've never been anywhere and you're *goin'* nowhere. You're a motel maid, for crying out loud. You need me. You and me, we could have a life together, if you would only—"

Glory put her hands over her ears and announced in a sing-song voice, "I'm not listening to you...."

In B.J.'s arms, Mr. Lucky started squirming, sharp claws digging in. She unhooked the animal from her sweater, bent and let it down. It zipped out the door into the hallway and vanished. A very smart cat.

"You *never* listen," Bowie grumbled. "That's half our problem and that's the damn truth."

"Shut up, shut up. I can't hear you...."

Bowie pumped up the volume. "Well, I know who you *have* been listening to." He was shouting now, all but drowning out the holiday tune on the stereo. He pointed an accusing finger in B.J.'s direction. "You've been listening to Ms. New York City over there, now, haven't you? That bitch has been filling your head with crazy ideas."

Beside B.J., Buck swore. "Bowie. You're done."

"The hell I am. I'm just getting warmed up here."

"Buck..." B.J. tried to hold Buck back again, but he only shoved her stalling hand away. Three long strides and he stood beside Glory.

Out of the corner of her eye, B.J. saw that Lupe had begun dismantling her equipment. Did the photographer sense big trouble coming?

B.J. certainly did.

Buck said, "B.J.'s never done a thing to you. You apologize to her and you do it now."

Bowie grunted. "Stay outta this. It's got nothing to do with you."

"You talk trash about B.J., you bet it's got to do with me. Apologize."

B.J. cleared her throat. "Buck, I really don't—" It was as far as she got. Buck chopped the air with a furious hand.

He spoke to his brother again. "Apologize."

"The hell I will." Bowie went into a crouch.

Buck scoffed. "Oh, what? Now you want to start a fight? I'm sad to say, it figures."

"You want a piece of this, big brother?" Bowie wiggled his fingers, waving Buck forward. "You want a piece of me? Come on. Come on and get it."

"Buck!" cried Chastity. "Bowie!" Neither of them so much as glanced her way.

Buck advised, "Glory, step back." With a tiny cry, Glory spun and ran to B.J. B.J. caught her and held on tight as Buck asked Bowie, "What the hell is wrong with you?"

Bowie remained in his crouch, ready for action. "What do you mean, what's wrong with me? I'm a man and that's my woman over there. I love her. She's havin' my baby. And if you'd keep your own woman out of it, you can bet Glory and me would work things out between us just fine."

The Burl Ives album ended, the final festive notes lingering in the air.

Buck spoke to his brother again. "I hate to say it. But you're an idiot, Bowie. A mean, bitter guy who beats up on women to try to convince himself he's something vaguely resembling a man. How the hell did you let that happen to you?"

Bowie's response was a guttural, "Son of a bitch." He

launched himself at Buck. Glory let out a scream and buried her head in B.J.'s shoulder as the brothers went down, landing on an empty decoration box, crushing it flat.

"Buck, Bowie, stop!" Chastity shouted.

Her sons weren't listening. Buck gained the top position. He levered back on his knees and landed a punch square in Bowie's face. Blood exploded from Bowie's nose. He let out a sound that could only be called a battle cry. With a mighty heave, he shoved Buck off him, gathered his legs under him and jumped to his feet. Buck rolled and got upright, too.

They traded more blows. Blood was flying everywhere. A lamp went over and Chastity swore. "That does it," she said. She took off through the hall doorway, just as Bowie leapt on Buck again.

For the second time, the brothers went down, breaking Chastity's coffee table in the process. The sounds of splintering wood joined with the heavy male grunts and the sickening thuds of fists on flesh.

"Holy Mary, the tree!" cried Glory.

"Grab it," said B.J. In unison, they turned to the tree and grabbed the trunk from either side.

"Get back," Glory shouted. She held the tree steady and kicked out at Bowie as he rolled too close. "You get back from this tree, Bowie Bravo, or I will kick you silly."

"Oof! Ow!" Bowie grunted and groaned as Glory kicked him from behind and Buck hit him, a rapid-fire series of punches to the midsection.

"Get away from the tree!" Glory shouted again.

"Okay, okay." Buck got Bowie by the leg, dragged him clear of the tree and then sat on him. "Had enough?"

"Get offa me, you—"

Buck hit him again as Chastity reentered the room. Nobody noticed she had a revolver in her hand until she aimed at the ceiling and fired.

Eighteen

The shot echoed and plaster rained down. Glory cried out.

And then there was silence, except for Bowie's groans.

Buck armed blood off his face, dragged himself off Bowie and staggered to his feet. Bowie just lay there, clutching his stomach and groaning some more.

"Look at this mess," muttered Chastity, shaking her head at her ruined coffee table, her broken lamp, the flattened boxes of decorations and the glittering shards of shattered ornaments littering the floor.

Buck pressed a cut on his lip. Blood seeped through his fingers. "I'll pay for all this, Ma, don't worry. We'll get everything back good as new." He stood over his vanquished brother. "Bowie?" he growled.

Bowie groaned some more.

"Now," said Buck.

"Awright, awright. B.J., I'm sorry I called you a bitch."

"Apology accepted." B.J. spoke up loud and clear.

"Good, then." Buck held down a hand.

But Bowie wouldn't take it. Moaning low, he rolled to his side, gathered his legs close to his chest, and rolled again, groaning sharply as he got his knees beneath him. He dragged himself upright, still clutching his ribs, blood dripping from his nose. "Damn," he muttered, glancing around at the damage. "Sorry, Ma…"

Chastity only shook her head some more.

Bowie turned his bloody face to Glory then.

"Oh, Bowie…" Her frustrated love for him was clear to see in her shining brown eyes.

They shared a long, aching glance. He whispered, "Glory…" as if her name held all his hurt and angry confusion—and his one slim chance for redemption, as well.

She gave a cry and took a step toward him.

But he put up a hand. "Don't." And then he turned and staggered out, disappearing through the doorway that led to the dining room.

Several seconds later, they heard the back door slam shut.

Chastity surveyed the devastation. "Well. The good news is, right at the moment, none of my guests are in the house."

Glory's longing gaze was locked on the dining-room doorway through which Bowie had vanished. She spoke to the man who was already gone. "Oh, Bowie…" The words faded off into a heart-heavy sigh.

"Go on, then." Chastity made a shooing motion with both hands. "Go after him. See if he'll let you patch him up a little."

With a tiny cry, Glory rushed off the way Bowie had gone.

Chastity scooped up a fallen box of tissues from the floor and shoved it at Buck. "Stop bleeding all over my parlor."

He yanked out several and dabbed at a cut on his temple and another one on his cheek. Since his lip was still dripping, he ended up pressing the wad of bloody tissues to that.

"B.J." Chastity was all business now. "Take Buck upstairs, will you? Bandage him up. There's a first aid kit in his bathroom—check the cabinet under the sink." She dropped the tissue box on the marble-topped side table and sent a glance Lupe's way. "I'll need a little help here."

Lupe dared for the first time to step away from the corner where she'd piled her equipment. "No problem," she said. "Whatever I can do…"

Upstairs in Buck's bathroom, a tiny cubicle containing a commode, a sink and a narrow shower stall, B.J. flipped down the yawning toilet seat. "Sit."

Still pressing the bloody tissues to his cut lip, Buck dropped to the seat. B.J. turned for the sink and the cabinet beneath it. The first aid kit—a white plastic box with a red cross on the lid—was right where Chastity had said it would be.

B.J. set the kit on the back of the toilet. She ran water in the sink and wet a few washcloths. Armed with a wet, wrung-out cloth, she turned to her patient.

He studied her face. "You mad at me?"

She didn't answer, only took the wad of tissue from him and tossed it in the wastebasket that was tucked into the tight space between the commode and the wall.

Carefully, she set to work cleaning up his poor, battered face.

The cuts on his temple and his cheek had pretty much stopped bleeding. They were both turning a deep purple-black. She gave him her cloth. "Press this to your lip for the moment, will you?"

He did as instructed, seeking eye contact—which she carefully avoided. She turned again to the sink and wrung out a second cloth. When she faced him once more and began dabbing at the cut on his temple, he nudged her leg with his knee.

She paused to tap the offending knee. "Stop that."

"You *are* mad at me."

She grimaced as she dabbed and swabbed, thinking it had to hurt him.

Buck seemed oblivious to the pain. "B.J.? Come on…" He turned his head enough to brush the uninjured half of his mouth across the inside of her wrist.

She resolutely ignored the way her skin heated at his touch. "Will you sit still?"

He grabbed her wrist. "Think about it. What was I supposed to do? He called you a bitch."

She jerked free of his grip. "Oh, let's see. You might have just…let it alone, maybe?"

"Stand there and do nothing while he called you an insulting name? Uh-uh. I don't think so."

"Believe me, I've been called worse."

"Not while I was around."

"Buck. Listen carefully. I don't need my honor defended—and if I do, I'll defend it for myself."

"But you weren't defending yourself. You were letting it happen."

"So what? That was my choice—the wisest choice, by the way. Look at you. All cut up and bruised and bleeding. And think of the mess downstairs. If you'd left it alone, I wouldn't be patching you up right now. Your mother wouldn't be down there cleaning up the disaster that used to be her front parlor."

His hand dropped to his thigh and a heavy sigh escaped him. He looked beyond her, toward the open door to the hallway.

Fine, she thought, *don't look at me, then.* She finished cleaning the cut at his temple, spread some healing salve on it, and bandaged it up. The injury high on his cheek came next. She cleaned it, too, and put on the salve.

"Your right eye is swelling up." She applied a butterfly bandage to the cut on his cheek.

He squinted at her through the eye in question. "Well, yeah. So?" He lifted one shoulder in an eloquent shrug, one that said he'd had black eyes before and was not impressed that he had another one.

"I'd better get some ice for it." She straightened and turned for the door.

He caught her hand. She stopped in midstride, but refused to turn back to him—not even when he raised her fingers to his battered mouth.

His lips touched her skin in a light kiss that sang through every nerve in her body. "Somebody had to call Bowie on the way he's been acting. He needed taking down a notch."

"I don't think brawling solves anything." She remained resolutely facing the door.

He lowered her hand and gave it a squeeze. "As a rule, I would agree with you. But with Bowie, we've pretty much run out of alternatives. Sometimes, when a man gets too far out of control, the only thing that will bring him up short is a hard right to the jaw—and besides…" He let the word trail off.

Reluctantly, she turned to him. "Besides, what?"

He tugged on her fingers. "C'mere." When she finally gave in and stepped between his spread knees, he let go of her hand and tipped his head back. Those gorgeous dark eyes gleamed at her, one of them soon to be no more than a swollen purple slit. "I didn't start it. You were there. You know I didn't."

Her fingers itched to soothe the bruise on his jaw. "You challenged him."

"Somebody had to."

She realized he was probably right—much as it went against the grain to have to admit that she'd let Buck get in a fight for her sake and done hardly anything to stop it. "Okay. I understand. I guess…" She allowed herself the touch she'd been longing for. Lightly, she stroked the sore spot at his jaw.

He prompted, "But?"

"Oh, I don't know. Right there at the end, I realized…"

"That?"

"Oh Buck, he really loves her. It's more than… animal attraction. More than just possessiveness because she's having his baby. He loves her truly and deeply, I think. And she really loves him."

"That's right." His tone said he knew already—he'd always known.

And she supposed that he had. "He's not very good at loving, is he?" Buck shook his head and she added, "It's just so sad, that's all."

"So you're not mad…you're sad?"

"Life can be so cruel, you know?"

"It's always possible that they'll work it out, eventually."

"How? Like we did?"

He captured her hand again. Gently, he twined his fingers with hers. It felt good—right—to have her hand in his, their fingers woven together. "Hey, come on. It may be six years later, but look at us. Right here. In this dinky bathroom. Together."

But for how long? she thought.

She didn't say it, though. It didn't matter for how long. For now, she was sticking with this moment, and this moment only.

She felt the tender smile as it trembled across her mouth.

He said, "There you go. A smile. Much better."

"Your eye is looking more swollen and purple by the second. Mind if I get the ice now?"

"Only if you hurry back."

"Won't be a minute. I promise." He allowed her fingers to slip free of his. "Keep that cloth against your mouth," she chided. "That gash worries me. You could need stitches there."

"Get the ice, B.J. I'm going to be fine."

Nineteen

"**B.J.**...." It was Buck's voice, soft and tempting in her ear.

She sighed and snuggled deeper under the covers.

"Wake up, you sleepyhead."

Reluctantly, she rolled to her back and opened an eye. Buck's battered face loomed above her. She frowned up at him. "You look truly terrible."

He grinned—or at least, he tried. With his cut lip, it was a lopsided attempt. "I may be ugly, but I feel great. Incredible sex will do that for a guy." Last night, he'd followed through on the threat he'd made after their snowball fight. It had been a most delicious revenge. For both of them.

She suggested, "I'd stay away from young children for a few days, though. One look at you and they'll run away screaming, damaged for life."

"Heh-heh-heh."

"Excuse me?"

"That was the evil laugh of a sex-crazed monster."

"Oh. Well. Consider me terrified." She stretched and yawned. "What time is it?"

"Seven-o-two."

"Ugh. Too early. Wake me up in an hour." She tried to roll back over onto her side.

But he caught her shoulder. "I've got something to show you."

"Can't it wait?" She yawned again, a big, wide one.

"Uh-uh." He threw back the covers.

"Eek. It's freezing." She looked down at her naked body. "I've got goosebumps on my goosebumps. Give me those covers…"

He shook his head and pointed toward the French doors. "Look."

Beyond the glass, the sky was silvery gray, the clouds thick enough to obscure the rising sun. And that wasn't all.

She let out a cry of delight. "Hey. It's snowing." Fat, white flakes drifted softly down. Goosebumps forgotten, she scooted up to her knees. "Oh, Buck. Just what we needed…"

He nodded. He looked extremely pleased with himself, as if he'd been personally responsible for creating the Christmas weather the *Alpha* feature required. "If it keeps up, Lupe can get a bunch of great exterior shots, right here in town."

"Yeah. With the snow on the rooftops, and piling up along the front walk. That would be perfect."

"It would, wouldn't it?" He caught her shoulder again and neatly rolled her beneath him.

"Hey!"

Nudging her legs apart, he settled between them. "There. Now, *that's* perfect."

And he was right. She raised her hips to him, rocking, teasing him. His response was immediate and gratifying. She felt him tucked against her, growing longer. Thicker…

She whispered, "The sex-crazed monster rises again."

He lowered his head and nipped a line of kisses up over the slope of her shoulder and across her collar bones. She moaned and tossed her head on the pillow— and he lifted up and away from her, going to his knees.

"Get back here," she commanded, and tried to pull him close again.

But he resisted. "Always so impatient…" He looked down at her, his gaze burning a path along her naked body. Below, she felt herself growing wet already, felt the softening, the silky liquid slide between her thighs. He bent his head close enough to whisper in her ear, "I do love the taste of you…"

Had she really been chilly just a moment ago?

He nibbled her neck, then licked his way down her body in a zig-zagging path, pausing briefly to tease each nipple between his teeth, to dip his tongue into her navel and give the platinum ring there a tug. She moaned as he ran his wet tongue over the inward curve of her waist.

At last, he reached the neatly trimmed curls that covered her increasing arousal. She clutched his silky dark head as he parted her.

Within seconds, she was writhing and moaning. He caught the tight bud of her pleasure lightly in his teeth and he worked it with his tongue.

She went over the edge, just like that—a quick, hot ride to the peak and a swift, shimmery slide down.

He levered up over her body again and kissed her

on the mouth—a half kiss, really, as he was careful to use only the uninjured side of his mouth. She tasted her own wetness and excitement, and marveled how, even when he had only half a mouth to kiss with, he still managed to do a better job of it than any other man she'd ever known. She reached down between them to clasp him, but he moved his hips out of reach.

"Later," he vowed, pressing a kiss to her throat.

She sighed. She loved to please him—and there was nothing like the feel of him inside her. "Wouldn't take a minute," she coaxed.

He laughed then, a wonderful, rough, sexy sound. "A little anticipation only makes it all the sweeter when the moment finally comes." He sat and swung his legs over the edge of the bed. "And I have somewhere I want to take you. I'm afraid if we don't get going, the snow could be a problem."

"Going, where?"

"Today, I want to show you the family gold mine."

"Gold mine?"

"You're gonna love it."

"Er, just one tiny question."

"Ask."

"If the snow could cause problems getting there, what about coming back?"

"We'll manage."

"You say that with such confidence."

"B.J. Trust me."

"No sensible woman trusts a man who says 'trust me.'"

"Make an exception, in my case."

"Hah."

"Listen. We'll be fine. The road's pretty good most

of the way, a lot of it unpaved, but well-maintained. It only gets iffy the last few miles."

"Oh. Good to know."

"I swear it to you. Not a problem. Brand told me he had extensive work done on the roughest part of the road just last summer. And we've got four-wheel drive. Plus, I happen to know that Ma has a set of chains to fit the SUV."

"Why do I find myself nodding my head? I have to be crazy...."

He winked at her with his good eye. "Sometimes crazy is the best way to be. You're going to love this."

Buck told her that the mine was called the Red Robin. The mineral rights to the Red Robin had come down from Chastity's side of the family. Brett, Brand and Bowie took turns doing the yearly work necessary to hold on to the rights. And there was a cabin—a cabin kept in good repair, stocked with canned goods and plenty of wood for the stove.

"I'm thinking," Buck told her, after they'd both showered and dressed, "that we could stay overnight. Picture it. Just you and me, in a cozy cabin, with a double bed and a blazing fire..."

It was probably a sign of how far gone she was on him by then, that the idea actually appealed to her.

She asked, "What about Lupe?"

"Uh-uh. Not part of my plan—and she doesn't need to go, anyway. She can stay here, get some snowy location shots around town. And fly back to New York tomorrow."

"But we might be able to use some pictures of the mine and the cabin—I mean, the mine is part of your history, right?"

"Ma has piles of old pictures of the Red Robin. We'll go through them before we leave on Friday. You can take your pick."

Well, now, what could she say to that? After all, it would be a lot more romantic with just the two of them.

She could see Buck now, naked in the firelight....

Yes. Oh, definitely.

They packed a duffel bag with the clothes they'd need and Chastity let them raid her pantry for supplies. Buck's mom also provided muffins, fruit and two thermoses: one with coffee for Buck and the other filled with the hot, spicy herb tea that B.J. had recently taken a liking to.

By eight, they were on the road. They sped east on the highway, the big, fluffy flakes of snow coming down thick and steady, slanting at the windshield, gathering in the corners as the wipers shoved them out of the way.

About five miles from town, they turned off onto another road and began climbing in a series of switchbacks, snow coming down thick and steady, and also dropping in globs from the trees that hung over the road, making wet, plopping sounds as it hit the windshield.

After a half hour or so, Buck turned onto yet another road—still paved, but only wide enough for a single vehicle to travel at a time. Not that the lack of room to pass mattered. They saw no other cars. The trees grew closer, inching in nearer the road. They drove in shadow, the lacing of thick pine branches overhead providing a certain amount of cover from the thickly falling snow.

The pavement gave out. For a while, the dirt road

was reasonably smooth. But eventually, the going got pretty rough.

Buck said, sounding pleased, "Now, we're getting somewhere."

They bounced along. He steered the SUV clear of the gullies and potholes as best he could, but there were too many to miss them all.

And it got worse as the road got steeper.

"Almost there," he told her, as the engine revved high, carrying them up a last, nearly perpendicular stretch of chuckholes and boulders.

The engine labored scarily the final twenty yards or so from the crest, but ultimately, with a final lugging surge, the wheels hit the top and the vehicle leveled out onto a flat space, an area still pocked with potholes, but wide enough that Buck could turn around. He backed, and rolled forward, passing the steep road they'd just climbed and driving along what amounted to a wide ledge, with the face of the mountain on one side and a steep drop-off on the other.

The ledge got wider—and then she saw it, through the driving snow: a shadow in the shape of a building, with a high-pitched roof and a chimney pipe. A simple structure of weather-silvered wood.

Rustic. Oh, yes. That would be the word.

He stopped the SUV, turned off the engine and leaned his battered face across the console toward her.

She kissed the uninjured side of his mouth, smiling against his lips. "I take it we're here."

"Yes, we are. Let's get everything inside and get the fire going."

An hour later, they sat at the pine table in the cabin on a pair of roughhewn ladderback chairs. A cheery fire burned in the stove. They were warm and dry and filling their empty stomachs with the muffins Chastity had packed for them.

Buck watched B.J. as she nibbled a pumpkin muffin and sipped that spicy tea she liked. She looked happy. And completely relaxed.

He drank the coffee he'd brought. "See?" He gestured with his thermos cup. "Didn't I tell you? Paradise, plain and simple."

She set down her cup and gave him one of those looks.

He asked, innocently, "What?"

"You really should have mentioned the outhouse when you were telling me about how great this place is."

Buck poured himself a second cup of coffee before explaining, "It's not an outhouse, not technically."

"Oh, no? Looks like an outhouse to me."

"And see, that's where you're wrong. By definition, an outhouse is *out*—meaning away from the main building. If it were an outhouse, you'd have to slog through the snow to get to it. The facilities here are much more convenient than that."

"Because the toilet's in a lean-to beside the back door?"

"That's right. A cinch to get in and get out."

She let out a distinctly indelicate snort. "Buck. It's still an outhouse. A hole in the ground. A slivery slab of cold wood to sit on…"

He leaned across the table toward her and teased, "Whine, whine, whine…"

She pointed at the tub full of melting snow in the corner and then at the big pot of water on the stove. "And there was that other little detail you failed to mention. You know, the one about how there's no running water…"

He sipped his coffee. "There's running water. Cold running water, anyway. In the summer." He indicated the sink and the faucet arching over it. "But Brand shuts it down in early October so the pipes won't freeze."

"And it's too cold out to try to turn it on again, just for overnight, right?"

"You got it." He toasted her with his thermos cup.

"No running water," she groused. "And an outhouse…"

"I thought I just explained—"

"I don't care what you like to call it, it's an outhouse as far as I'm concerned."

She pointed at the Coleman lantern on the table between them. "Oh, and did I mention, no electricity?"

"Everything looks better by lantern-light."

"You think so, huh?" She glanced around them, at the unfinished plank walls and floor, at the old stove and the iron-framed bed and the single battered bureau in the corner. "Believe me, I've been here before." His puzzlement must have shown on his face, because she amended, "Well, not here, specifically, but other places so much like here, it's definitely déjà vu all over again."

He understood then. "Roughing it with L.T.?" She nodded and he reassured her. "This will be much better."

"Oh, yeah?"

"I plan to make it up to you for the lack of plumbing, the absence of electricity and the slivers on the toilet seat."

"You do?"

"Absolutely."

"How?"

"Guess."

A smile broke across that kissable mouth of hers and their gazes caught and held. He knew she felt what he felt—that warmth and anticipation low in the belly. She fiddled with the fuel valve on the lantern between them. "You may be right about looking better by lantern-light. You certainly do. It lends a certain…glow to all those cuts and bruises."

For that, he gave her the best grin he could manage—crooked, maybe. Puffy and black-and-blue on one side. But clearly enthusiastic. And then he reached across the rough surface of the table and rested his hand on her arm. Beneath her heavy sweater, he felt her warmth. He brushed his hand downward, then eased his fingers up under the cuff of the sweater, so he could rub her silky bare skin.

Her breath caught. She leaned closer, mouth soft, eyes shining. "What are you thinking?"

"That I can't wait to get you naked…"

"Oh, really?"

"Really."

"Well, then." She slid her arm free of his grasp, grabbed the hem of her sweater and whipped it off over her head. "How's this?"

Heat flooded his groin. "I'd say it's a damn good start."

"That bed?"

"What about it?"

"Single-spring?"

"That's right."

"Those are squeaky."

"'Fraid so. And you should take off your bra now. Please."

She reached behind her and the bit of blue lace and black satin went loose. "Oops." She caught it before it slipped off.

"B.J."

"What?"

"Let it go."

And, very slowly, she did.

Twenty

The ancient bed did squeak. But neither of them really noticed.

And the old stove kept the cabin toasty-warm. Once they had their clothes off, they saw no reason to put them on again—except for the occasional trip out to the lean-to.

Outside, the snow continued to fall. They made love, and they got up and stoked the fire. And then they made love some more.

Around four in the afternoon, as they lay in bed, Buck asked lazily, "You hungry?"

"I could eat."

He hid his smile. Lately, she could always eat. But since she'd gotten past the frantic dashes to the bathroom every morning, she no longer seemed driven to gobble everything in sight later on in the day.

She threw back the covers and swung those long,

satiny legs over the edge of the squeaky old bed. Her back was to him, slender and shapely. Very fine. She sent him a teasing smile over the gorgeous curve of her shoulder. "Come on. Let's get ourselves a late lunch."

So they got up and heated a can of soup. They split the soup between them and set out apple sections, cheese and some wheat crackers. They even dressed for the occasion—B.J. in one of Buck's sweaters and Buck in an old pair of sweatpants.

After they sat down and dug in, she asked, "Did your father ever come up here?"

He paused with his spoon halfway to his mouth. "Not that I know of. But it's possible, I suppose. Pretty much anything's possible where Blake Bravo's concerned."

She spooned up more soup. "I hear that."

Buck ate a cracker and an apple section, cut himself a slice of cheese—and admired the view.

He liked looking at B.J. Liked the shine to her hair and the strong shape of her nose, the luster to her skin. B.J. wasn't beautiful, not in the classic sense. But she radiated such a fine self-confidence, a sure sense of command. She made a man wonder which way it would go with her—maybe he'd get to be on top.

And maybe she'd do the dominating.

Either way, it would be one hell of a ride.

And, as Buck was fortunate to have discovered, it always was.

In spite of his impatience with what she still hadn't told him, he found himself grinning, thinking, *I'm a lucky man.* And then he frowned.

She swallowed a spoonful of soup. "Okay. You're frowning. What?"

"It just occurred to me. I still don't know what your initials stand for."

"That's right." She reached for a cracker. "And you don't need to know."

"Would you tell me if I guessed it?"

"What part of 'You don't need to know' requires clarifying?"

"Let's see. Bianca Justine?"

She crunched her cracker. "Don't even go there."

"Bessie Jo."

"You are so asking for it."

"Blythe Juliette?"

"Cut it the hell out."

He tried to look pouty—in a very masculine way, of course. It was a challenge, with one eye swollen shut and half of his lip twice its usual size. "Come on. I've waited years to know what B.J. stands for. You always used to promise that someday you'd tell me."

"That was only to get you off my back about it."

He went for devastated. It was kind of a stretch. "Now I am truly crushed." He looked at her sideways. "You never meant to tell me? Not ever?"

She fiddled with her paper napkin. "Buck. Come on. Cut the wounded act. I've never told anyone. Even L.T., who should have done something about preventing the problem in the first place, has the sense never to mention it."

"Your name is that bad?"

"This is so stupid. We don't need to talk about it."

"For some reason, you're ashamed of your name?"

"I didn't say that."

"Consider this. I have my sources. I *could* have found out anytime, if I'd wanted to. But I never have."

"Is that supposed to reassure me?"

"If you tell me, I'll never tell anyone. Plus, I'll let you tie me to the bed and have your way with me." He leaned closer to her, in order to better gauge her expression, then modified his offer. "Or I'll tie *you* up. Whichever. Your choice. Hell. Both. I could go for both."

She was almost smiling. "You are impossible."

"Beverly Jan?"

"Buck…"

"Bobbie June?"

"How long are you going to keep this up?"

"Brenda Jane?"

She set down her spoon, folded her arms across the front of his sweater and tipped her head to the side, studying him. He waited. He couldn't believe it. After six long years, he was actually getting close to learning B. J. Carlyle's given name.

Finally, she spoke. "I'd have to know I could trust you. You'd have to swear never, under any circumstances, to reveal the truth to anyone else."

"Damn. Is it that bad?"

"My middle name? Not so much."

"But your first name?"

She nodded, a slow, severe dip of her head.

He put up a hand, like a witness at a swearing-in. "I do solemnly swear that I will never, under any circumstances, for any reason, reveal your given name to another soul."

"And about my tying you to the bed…"

He tried to look noble, though, under the table, beneath the sweats, his cock gave a hungry twitch. "I'm willing to make the sacrifice."

"I want more."

"Name your price."

"I want *you*. Out in the SUV. First, *before* I tie you to the bed."

He winced, though beneath the table there was now more than twitching going on. "Did you notice there's a blizzard out there? It'll be freezing."

"We'll turn on the heater."

He pretended to have to consider, but not for long. It was just an act and they both knew it. "All right. In the SUV—and then you tie me to the bed. Hard to believe the sacrifices I have to make just to get you to tell me your name."

She shifted in her chair. And he felt her foot between his legs. Her toes touched him—rubbing. He held back a groan and braced his elbows on the table.

He also spread his thighs wider apart.

She said, "Keep this in mind—are you listening?"

"Uh. You bet."

"My name is B.J. What it stands for is not my fault."

Her clever toes kept working their naughty magic down there. He sucked in a slow breath through his nose. "I'll remember that."

"My mother chose the name. It was *her* mother's name. And my grandmother had died a couple of months before I was born…" Buck couldn't help it. A low groan escaped him. He shifted in his chair. "Keep your hands on the table," she commanded in husky whisper.

"Whatever you say…continue. Please."

"L.T. swears he tried to talk my mother out of it. But she wouldn't give in. And she named me…"

He couldn't take it. Before she could order him not to again, he whipped his hand beneath the table and caught her ankle in a firm grip. Her chair scraped the old floorboards as he pulled her closer. He held her foot, tight and warm, against his raging erection. "Okay." He sucked in another breath. She wiggled those toes of hers. "Stop that. And tell me."

She sat up a little straighter and she captured her lower lip between her teeth.

He squeezed her ankle tighter. "Now."

And she whispered, "It's Bitsy. Bitsy Janine."

"No," B.J. said from behind the wheel. "Leave the rest on. That's the thrill, you just undo enough to, er, get the job done…"

At her command, he let his hand fall from the top button of his shirt. They'd already peeled off their heavy jackets, their wool hats and their down gloves and thrown them in the back. She'd taken off her boots and pants. She was naked from the waist down—well, except for those heavy wool socks of hers.

The SUV's heater blasted on high. He felt the warmth flowing out, against the front of him, and up from the floor vent.

In a very short time, she'd be sitting on his lap. He couldn't wait, though a part of the turn-on lay in trying not to look too eager.

She leaned across the console toward him. "Oh, for the days of bench seats." She laid her hand on his fly.

He put serious effort into *not* moaning out loud, and reminded her, "We have to make the best of what we've got."

"An excellent attitude." She took his zipper down. It made a soft, snicking sound that sent a hot thrill of need bursting through him. He shut his eyes, threw back his head—and banged it on the seat rest.

"Careful," she said. She slid those knowing fingers into the opening at the front of his boxers and her hand closed around him—cool. Firm. And tight.

He gasped. He couldn't help it. He opened his eyes and looked down as she guided him out of the nest of his clothing. She bent her golden head. He felt the warmth of her sweet breath. And then she took him—slowly—into her soft, wet mouth.

He thought he would lose it.

But somehow, he didn't. He dug his hands into her hair and surged up toward her.

She took him all the way in, mouth sliding down. He moaned as he bumped the back of her throat—and then she lifted, so slowly, her suction strong, her tongue working, around the crown, against the sensitive slit....

He hit his head against the headrest again. Not that it mattered: the headrest was padded—and he couldn't feel anything but her mouth on him, anyway, working with such slow, sensual deliberation.

He bore the sweet agony as long as he could. Then he took her head in both his hands and made her look up at him. "You," he said. "All of you. Now…"

She touched his face, a breath of a touch against the cut on his cheekbone. He turned his head and brushed his bruised lips against her fingers, at the same time lifting his right hip enough to slide the condom from his pocket, thinking how stupid it was to go on with the charade that they needed protection.

But he went on with it anyway. He fumbled with the wrapper. She took it from him, swiftly got it free and smoothly rolled it down on him.

Then she rose up, all softness and sweet-scented woman. *His* woman, whether she admitted it or not. She slid over the console, one bare, glorious leg flung across him, shifting into place, rising up on her knees, reaching down to position him....

All logical thought flew away as she wrapped those soft, strong fingers around him and she lowered herself slowly, in a delicious agony of tiny degrees. When she had all of him, she began to rock, back and forth—and then up and down.

He threw his head back, groaning, again and again, beating against the headrest in time to her sure, knowing strokes.

"Good," he whispered, "so good…"

"Yes. Oh, Buck. Yes…"

She slowed and she kissed him. A long, deep, wet play of sliding tongues and nipping teeth. He insinuated a hand between them. She cried out as she felt his fingers, parting her, touching the swollen bud at the top of her cleft.

She lost control then and she rode him wildly. He stroked her with his finger as she shattered. Her contractions sent him over, too. He wrapped both arms hard around her and he buried his head in her fragrant hair as his own climax ripped him wide open and turned him inside out.

Back in the cabin, they bathed. Sponge baths. It took a while.

He found some cord in a drawer, cut four lengths of it, and handed it over. She met his eyes and they shared a smile.

"Later," she said. The word was both a promise—and an erotic threat.

She set the lengths of cord on the empty explosives box that served as a nightstand and they got under the covers together.

She snuggled in close and whispered, "Tomorrow, before we go…"

"*If* we go," he corrected her.

She clucked her tongue. "Are you saying we could be snowed in?"

Outside, the snow was still coming down. "If it keeps up like this, it's possible."

"For how long?"

"Probably not more than a day or two."

She stiffened a little in his embrace. "Probably? Buck, I do have to go back to New York on Friday. I promised L.T. As much as he makes me crazy, I always try to keep my promises."

He smoothed her hair back from her brow and pressed a kiss to the crown of her head. "Don't worry. The snow is supposed to stop tomorrow. And then, after that, there's a warming trend predicted. One way or another, we'll get down off this mountain by Thursday."

"You sound certain."

"I am." He spoke with more assurance than he felt.

In the earthen basement/pantry beneath the floor, his brothers had enough food stored up to last them a week, maybe two. And they'd brought plenty with them. They had two full cords of wood neatly stacked in a shed about ten feet from the back door.

They'd be okay, whatever tricks the weather pulled on them. Maybe she wouldn't be able to keep her promise to L.T.

If not, so be it.

There was a hell of a lot more at stake here than her word to L.T. Life would go on, even if she didn't hustle back to Manhattan Friday in order to press her pretty nose to the grindstone known as *Alpha*.

She would get back eventually. And before they left this cabin, she would tell him about his baby—and he would have her promise that she would be his wife.

"Buck?"

"Yeah?"

"Will I get to see the gold mine?"

Her hand rested on his chest. He took it, raised her fingers to his lips and kissed them, one by one. "Ah, Bitsy. Anything for you."

She yanked her hand away. "If you *ever* tell another soul about that name…"

"I won't. I swear. Not ever." He caught her hand again. "But let me call you Bitsy, now and then, okay? Just, you know, between us."

"I hate that name."

He laid her hand on his chest again and petted her fingers, until she loosened her fist and laid it flat against his heart. "I kind of like it," he dared to whisper. Her hand snapped tight again. He stroked it, slow and steady, until she let it relax once more. Then he suggested, "And it *is* your name."

"No, it's not."

"Yeah. It is. It's part of you. Maybe not a big part, but it's the name your mother gave you."

She lifted her head to look at him. Whatever she saw in his beat-up face must have soothed her, because she laid her head back down and snuggled in against his shoulder. "I don't even remember her…."

"Not at all?"

"Uh-uh. Not really. I have some old photos. And the stories L.T. tells, about what a wonderful woman she was. I think that she was…loving, you know? I have a sense of her, I guess you could say. A sense of being held in gentle arms, of her voice, singing me a lullaby. And then…" The words trailed off.

He nuzzled her hair. "And then, what?"

She sighed. "Oh, I don't know. A huge emptiness. A gaping hole of loss, right in the center of my toddler self…"

He wrapped his other arm around her and gathered her in, pressing his lips to her temple, against her cheek, in her hair. "But you came through okay, now, didn't you? You came through just fine."

"Sometimes I wonder…"

"Don't wonder. Ever. You're one damn fine woman. Take it from the man who knows."

She laughed, then, an easy laugh. "Okay. Bitsy. Now and then, but just between us."

They lit a second lantern when they sat down to share a late dinner. And then it was time for him to finish paying for the privilege of knowing her given name.

They stripped the bed, except for the bottom sheet, and Buck stretched out on it, naked as the day he was born, arms and legs spread wide. She tied his wrists to the wrought-iron headboard and his ankles to the legs of the bed.

"You're pretty good with those knots, you know that, Bits?"

"I'm a woman of many talents."

"No argument there."

Having secured the final knot, she began nibbling her way up his right shinbone. It was good—the feel of her teeth, nipping, the sexy swipe of her clever tongue.

But still, he found himself thinking of a certain Stephen King novel. He lifted his head off the mattress and asked, "You ever read *Gerald's Game?*"

She looked up from licking his kneecap. "Stephen King, am I right?"

He nodded. "Husband—Gerald, get it?—ties his wife to the bed for a little edgy love-play."

She sat back on her excellent haunches with a sigh. "Why do I get the feeling you're about to ruin the mood?"

He put on his most innocent expression—no mean feat, spread-eagled and butt naked as he happened to be. "Okay. Never mind."

"Tell me."

"Well, if you insist. After all, there is the fact that your every wish is my command…"

"Just get it over with."

"Okay, okay. Gerald's wife is tied to the bed. Did I mention they're in an isolated cabin?"

"I think you might require a spanking."

"Uh-uh. Not part of the deal. You'll have to tell me more than your real name to get me to agree to any slapping or paddling. Got any more secrets to share?" He almost dared to hope that she'd give it up about the baby.

No such luck. "You're tied up. I can do what I want with you."

"That wouldn't be nice—not to mention, fair."

She scowled at him. "Continue."

"With the story?"

"What else?"

"Well, it's right at the crucial moment…and Gerald has a heart attack. Dies right there, on the floor of the cabin."

"And?"

"Isn't that enough? Gerald's dead and our heroine is tied up and can't get free. No one to help her. I think there's a starving dog in there somewhere, and the dog eats Gerald's—"

"Stop."

"Let me just say, it's a grisly little story."

"I'll bet. Thank you so much for sharing."

"Hey. Anytime."

She shook a finger at him. "You never did care much for bondage or restraint."

"Oops. Nailed me."

She raked that silky hair back from her face, plowing her fingers through the thick strands. He watched her breasts rise with the movement. His gaze wandered lower, to the gorgeous curves of her belly, the glint of her navel ring—and lower still, to the soft, sleekly trimmed hair between her firm thighs...

He never had been able to resist the sight of her naked.

She grinned. "Now we're getting somewhere." And she got up on her hands and knees, bent over his growing erection—and licked it.

That did it. He couldn't hold back a groan.

She looked up his body and into his eyes. "Oh, Buck..." Her voice was sweet and slow as molasses.

"You know, Bits, on second thought, maybe I can get into this scene after all."

It snowed all the next day, which was Wednesday. Buck loved every minute of being locked in a one-room cabin with B.J. In the evening, over dinner, they talked about how they might not get out tomorrow, either.

B.J. said she wondered if Buck had planned things this way.

He admitted, "I wanted this time with you. And when I saw my chance, I took it."

She seemed to have grown surprisingly philosophical about their dilemma. "What can I do? If we're stuck here, we're stuck."

"I promise to make being stranded with me as bearable as possible."

She grinned then. "So far, you're doing a bang-up job."

Late that night, in bed, she confessed that she'd always tried to be the son L.T. never had. It wasn't working. It never had. "Lately, I find myself thinking that the only thing for me to do is quit the magazine. L.T.'s always stepping in and I think he always will. He never lets me take complete charge of my own job."

He said, "I understand your frustration. After all, I know L. T. Carlyle. But I also know that you're the best at what you do, that L.T. counts on you more than he realizes."

She made a low, scoffing sound. "Or wants to admit."

"So then, maybe you *should* quit. Give the old tyrant a chance to learn the hard way how much *Alpha* needs you…"

She never said right out that she *would* quit. He found himself wondering if she *could* quit. *Alpha,* after all, was the center of the world as she'd always known it.

Thursday dawned. The snow had stopped falling, but it lay, white and sparkling, two feet deep, outside the cabin door. The day was cloudy, but noticeably warmer. The slow melt began in a steady, drip-drip-dripping off the eaves.

They shoveled a path to the mine entrance and Buck took her inside the main tunnel. She admired the rusted ore cart a few feet beyond the cave's mouth, and he gave her a quick rundown on the concept of hard-rock mining, and on the various milling procedures for separating veins of gold from quartz rock.

All day, he waited for her to tell him about the baby. She never did.

They went to sleep that night to the sound of water dripping from the cabin's tin roof. When they woke in the morning, a glance out the single window over the sink showed the two feet of snow had melted down to patches on the ground.

They ate a quick breakfast, got dressed and went outside to check things out. It was an easy stroll across the clearing to where the steep road cut down the mountain. The road was muddy, but clear. In the trees around them, birds trilled out giddy tunes, as if in sheer delight at the sight of a sunny day.

Buck turned to her. "Well. I'd say we're free to head out of here."

B.J. looked in his eyes and thought of the magical time they'd just shared.

She didn't want to go. She could have stayed there forever, just the two of them, hanging out in the cabin, making love, talking all night…

And really, what could it hurt to stay a day or two more?

L.T. would be furious. But so what? He'd get over it. And so far, Giles had been managing just fine without her. He could manage a little longer.

"Buck, I was thinking…" It was as far as she got.

They both heard the sound at the same time. A vehicle was laboring toward them up the hill. It turned the corner on the last switchback below and came into view: a battered blue pickup.

Buck said, "That's Ma's pickup…"

They waited as the old truck toiled upward, spraying mud, bouncing over rocks and potholes. As it neared, B.J. could see Chastity in the passenger seat, a grim expression on her lived-in face. Bowie, his face as battered as Buck's, had the wheel.

At last, the pickup crested the hill, gears grinding for that final push. It was still rolling to a stop when Chastity shoved open her door and jumped down. She came straight for B.J.

"What?" B.J. didn't like the look on Chastity's face.

Chastity took her hand. "Come here. Come with me...."

Buck demanded, "Ma. What's up?"

But Chastity ignored him. She led B.J. into the cabin and over to the rough pine table. "Here," she said. "Sit down."

B.J., bewildered, watched as Buck and Bowie entered. Bowie looked bleak.

Buck said, "All right, Ma. Out with it. What the hell's going on?"

Chastity, who had never let go of B.J.'s hand, knelt right there in front of her.

A shiver slid down B.J.'s spine. "Chastity. You're scaring me..."

"It's your father—" Chastity said, and hastily added "—he's alive, don't worry."

B.J. couldn't breathe. Her stomach rolled. Somehow, she managed to ask, "What happened?"

And at last, Chastity told her, "He's had a heart attack."

Twenty-One

They raced down the mountain behind the old blue pickup, bumping over ruts and potholes with no concern at all for the undercarriage of the SUV. At the Sierra Star, B.J. only had time to throw her clothes in her suitcases and hug Chastity and Glory goodbye, promising both of them that she wouldn't lose touch.

She scribbled her home address and phone number onto a business card and pressed it into Glory's hand. "Any time you need me, I'm there."

Glory gave her a brave smile. "And I'm here for you. Always...."

Even the surly Bowie shook B.J.'s hand and said he hoped her dad would be okay.

The jet was waiting for them in Reno. While it was being cleared for takeoff, B.J. called the Castle. She got a first-hand report from Roderick. In his dry, matter-of-fact way, L.T.'s ever-loyal retainer assured her that her father had received the best care available, including the new, less-invasive non-bypass surgery, which meant a smaller incision in his chest and a series of high-tech clamps to keep certain areas of his heart still while the surgeon grafted on veins L.T.'s calf and chest.

Roderick admitted that it had been a close call. Wednesday, L.T. had complained of acid indigestion—as he'd been doing on and off of late. The supposed indigestion had grown worse.

B.J. asked bleakly, "Heartburn, you mean?"

"Yes, Ms. B.J. Heartburn. That's right."

She heard her father's rough voice in her head, last week, on the phone: *You're giving me serious heartburn here, you know that? My chest is on fire.*

She'd told him to take a Rolaids. Never for a second had she imagined there might be something to his complaint....

"Ms. B.J.? Are you still there?"

"Yes, Roderick. Go on."

"There's not much more to tell. Your father retreated to his study, where Ms. Jessica found him—on the floor, clutching his chest. We had him raced to Mount Sinai. They have a top cardiac unit there. And now he is doing well, recovering more rapidly than he would have after traditional surgery. His surgeon has said he may be allowed to come home tomorrow, or perhaps Sunday."

B.J. felt numb. L. T. Carlyle: mortal, after all? It couldn't be....

Roderick added, "Ms. Jessica says he's been asking for you."

B.J. doubted that *asking* was the right word, as L.T. never *asked* for anything or anyone. He blustered and commanded.

And she had little doubt he was nothing short of livid that she'd been unreachable on the day he'd come so close to meeting his maker.

She felt pretty bad about that, herself. Beneath the shock and numbness, she recognized a definite and distinctly unpleasant sensation: guilt. She *should* have been at the Sierra Star when Jessica called to tell her what had happened.

If she hadn't been snowbound with Buck, having the best time of her life, she'd be at her father's side right now....

They left the ground at a little past two in the afternoon. The flight took five hours and fifteen minutes, but they lost three hours to changes in time zones. It was after ten at night when they landed at Teterboro.

Roderick had seen to it that one of L.T.'s limousines was waiting when they touched down. The driver loaded their bags in the back, and they headed for Manhattan and Mount Sinai Hospital.

When they arrived at the hospital, Buck insisted on going in with her. She tried to tell him that it wasn't necessary.

But he shook his head and took firm hold of her hand. "Yeah. I think it is."

"He'll probably be sleeping. They might not even let me in to see him...."

"So let's find out."

Inside, they were directed to the Guggenheim Pavilion, where an aide, a redheaded woman with a pleasant smile, took them in tow and explained regretfully that L.T. was sleeping and visiting hours had ended at nine. The aide made reassuring noises. "Your father is doing very well, Ms. Carlyle. Chances are he'll be released in the next couple of days."

"I just…I've been away," B.J. said, as if that explained anything. "If I could just *see* him. I promise not to wake him up…."

The aide agreed, finally, with the stipulation that she do her best not to disturb the patient. "Your father's friend, Jessica, is already in the room with him." The woman turned her pleasant smile on Buck. "Family and household members only. Are you a relative?"

B.J., not really wanting Buck to go in with her, opened her mouth to say no.

But Buck was quicker. "Just call me Cousin Buck."

The aide shrugged. "Well, then. This way…"

They turned for the wide doors that led to the patient area. The doors whooshed open and shut behind them and all at once, B.J. realized that she was glad, after all, for the warmth and strength of Buck's hand in hers.

The aide stopped at the door to one of the rooms. "Here we are." She signaled them in ahead.

B.J. cautiously pushed open the door. The sweet, humid scent of too many flowers enveloped her. Even in the dim light, B.J. could see that every available surface had a flower arrangement on it.

For a moment, the shadowy sight of all those flowers baffled her. But then again…

Of course. People would have sent flowers.

L.T. was widely admired as a man to be emulated: a great hunter, a lover of beautiful women, a success in the truest sense of that very American word. Flowers might not be L.T.'s thing—far from it. But news of his heart attack had made *The Times,* a column on the fifth page. B.J. had read it for herself during the plane ride home. Millions of others would have read it by now, as well. Flowers would definitely have been sent—a lot of them.

Jessica, in an armchair at L.T.'s side, jumped lightly to her feet and came straight to B.J., holding out her slender arms. "I'm so glad you're here," her father's girlfriend whispered in her ear.

For the first time, as she hugged Jessica, B.J. felt what might be called affection for L.T.'s latest *Alpha* Girl. The past few days must have been hell, but Jessica had stuck by her man—was still sticking by him, though it seemed the worst danger was past and no one would have faulted her if she'd chosen to spend tonight at the Castle in L.T.'s luxurious king-sized bed.

The aide had already gone. Jessica pantomimed drinking coffee and mouthed, "I'll be right back." B.J. gave her a nod. With a bright smile for Buck, who had moved back near the room's wide picture window, Jessica left them, bracing the door halfway open on her way out, so they'd have enough light to see by.

B.J. turned to her father. L.T., snoring steadily, lay face-up on the bed. They had him hooked to an IV drip and also to a couple of monitors that made slow beeping sounds.

B.J. approached the bed. Up close, she could see the bruises of stress and pain beneath her father's eyes. His skin had a grayish pallor and seemed loose on the bones of his face.

Smaller, she thought. He looked smaller, somehow— less vital. As if he'd somehow shrunk inside his skin.

His left arm, the one with the IV in it and the monitors attached, lay along his side. His right was bent, the hand resting on his chest. B.J. looked at that hand and considered laying her own on top of it.

She didn't do it. Partly because she didn't want to wake him—and partly because there'd never been a lot of touching between them, not since she was six, when he'd told her that she couldn't sit on his lap anymore. He wasn't raising any daddy's girl, he'd growled at her. He wanted her to grow up to be strong and self-sufficient, a woman who stood proudly on her own two feet....

And what to do now? Okay, she'd seen him. He was alive. Should she sink into the chair Jessica had vacated?

Or was it better that she and Buck just go ahead and leave. She could return in the morning, maybe....

She ought to be better at this, she really should.

But all she kept thinking was that she wished he were wide awake and mean as ever. She wished he would open his eyes and yell at her.

And right then, as her wish took form, he granted it—more or less.

His snoring snorted to a stop. His eyes drifted open, unfocused at first. But then he spotted her. He actually managed a scowl.

"It's about damn time you showed up." His voice was raspy. He couldn't quite deliver his usual ear-grating shout.

"Hi, L.T."

"Where in hell have you been?"

"It's a long story."

He grunted. "Fine. Spare me the details. I want you at work first thing tomorrow."

"Tomorrow's Saturday."

"So? That never stopped you from working before."

"You're right. I'll check in at the office in the morning."

"Harumph. Good." His scowl deepened. "Where's Jessica?"

"She went to get coffee, I think. She said she'd be right back."

"It stinks to high heaven in here. Smells like a damn greenhouse. Tell her I want all these flowers out. *I* told her. But since I've been in a weakened condition, she had them all brought in anyway."

"I'll tell her, L.T."

"And get me a cigar."

"To that I would have to say…ask the nurse."

"The nurse?" he sneered. "What's the nurse going to say but no?"

"'No' works for me. You've had a heart attack, remember?"

"As if I could forget."

"I'm guessing—though I'm no expert—that you'll be giving up cigars."

"Who asked you?—and you're guessing wrong."

She decided not to argue the point. There had never been much of a percentage in arguing with L.T.

He lifted his head off the pillow and squinted toward the window, where Buck's shadowed shape was visible. "Who's that? Buck?"

Buck spoke up. "L.T. Good to see you."

"No, it's not. I look like holy hell—and let me make this perfectly clear. Whatever's up between you and B.J., keep it in Manhattan from now on."

"However you want it, L.T."

A rattling laugh escaped her father. He groaned and pressed his hand to his chest. "Uh. Hurts. They cut me open, sliced me right down the center. Me. L. T. Carlyle. Never thought I'd see the day." L.T. narrowed his eyes at B.J. again. "And you. I ought to fire your ass."

First rule of dealing with her father: never let him see he's hit the mark. "Go for it."

He let his head drop back to the pillow. "You watch yourself from here on in—or I just might."

Twenty-Two

Buck went home to B.J.'s apartment with her.

They were barely in the door, their suitcases piled all around them, when he took her in his arms. He kissed her. Gently, with no heat—at first. A reassuring, I'm-here-don't-worry kind of kiss.

Nice. Comforting…

At first.

But no kiss the two of them shared could stay merely *nice* for long. Heat bloomed, a night flower of longing and hunger, between them.

It was good, so good. To forget the rushed trip home from their mountain retreat, and her father, so weak and old-looking…

She backed up against the door, dragging Buck with her, kicking off her Jimmy Choos, unzipping her favorite curve-hugging Chloé jeans and shimmying them down. She lifted one leg, got it free of the jeans, then bounced to the other, kicking, sending the jeans flying, along with her blue satin thong.

Buck unzipped his fly.

And then he lifted her and settled her onto him. She wrapped her legs around his hard waist and locked her arms around his neck and felt him pressed all the way inside her, so deep and so good…

So good…

She rode him until they both cried out with sweet, mind-shattering release.

Once it was over they sagged against the door. He pressed his forehead to hers, whispered the name she let only *him* say, "Bits…" And then he straightened, gathering her drooping, tired body against him. "Bedroom?"

She whispered the way.

He carried her in there and set her, so carefully, down on her bed. Then he undressed her. She lay there, letting him do everything, too drained to argue that she could undress herself.

He took off his own clothes and pulled back the covers. "Scoot over." With a sigh, she rolled onto the cool, clean sheet. He slid in beside her and settled the covers over them both.

"Sleep," he whispered. "It will be all right…"

She cuddled in close to him, sighing, vaguely aware that, once again, they hadn't thought to use a condom—as they hadn't that time at the Sierra Star, and several times more during their stay at the cabin.

He never mentioned the lapses.

Then again, neither did she.

B.J. was up at six the next morning. She kissed Buck goodbye and headed for the hospital to check on her father.

L.T. was awake and ornerier than ever. She stayed with him for half an hour or so, listening to him complain about everything from how bad his incision itched to how much he wanted a cigar to how she had let him down big-time by disappearing out there in the sticks, making herself unavailable in the event of a crisis—like, for instance a heart attack or worse.

At eight, she escaped him, leaving him in Jessica's patient, tender care. She went to the office, which was empty—no full-lipped Melanie to greet her; no Giles, no Arnie. She spent six hours tackling her twin in-boxes: the one on her desk, where a mile-high pile of papers had magically formed during her absence, and the cyber-one; over a thousand e-mails waited for her attention. She also had a raft of messages in voice mail—Monday, for those.

She stopped in again at the hospital before going home. L.T. was madder than he'd been in the morning. They'd unhooked him from the IV and the beeping monitors. But they were keeping him until tomorrow, just to be on the safe side.

L.T. didn't want to wait until tomorrow to go home. He told everyone that. Loudly and repeatedly.

For an hour or so, B.J. joined Jessica—a saint, that Jessica—in a pointless and thoroughly frustrating effort to soothe him. Then B.J. gave up and went home.

Buck wasn't there. Not that she'd expected him to be. He'd told her that morning he would go back to his place, to get things together there after the trip.

B.J. unpacked her suitcases, put half the stuff away and the other half in a pile for the cleaners. She sorted her mail and paid a few bills. She glanced guiltily at her Stairmaster in the corner of her bedroom, but didn't have the energy to put it to use.

At about six, she stretched out on the couch and wished Buck was there and thought about what she would do for dinner. She must have fallen asleep.

Because she woke to the wonderful feel of soft lips against hers.

"Umm." She opened her eyes. Not a dream. The real thing: Buck. She kissed him some more. When he lifted his head, she said, "I'm so glad I thought to give you a key—and I could almost swear I smell pizza."

"Maybe because you do." He pointed at the pizza box on the coffee table beside them.

"I think you're my ideal man."

"Can I get that in writing?"

"Just hand me a pen."

On Sunday, they let L.T. go home. Both B.J. and Jessica hoped that getting out of the hospital and back to his own private castle would improve his attitude.

It didn't.

Langly Titus Carlyle was good at many things. Convalescing wasn't one of them.

He bristled at the very mention of how he had to change his lifestyle—stop smoking cigars, cut down on the cocktails and the red meat—or he'd be headed straight for another coronary. He hated the fact that he had to be taken care of, hated that he wasn't well enough to keep up with things at *Alpha*. He despised having to take medication. He said the drugs they had him on messed with his brain.

Every day, B.J. felt more grateful for Jessica, who bore the brunt of L.T.'s fits and rages. Serene and uncomplaining, Jessica treated him with tenderness and honest concern.

"How do you do it?" B.J. asked the sweet-natured

blonde one evening in mid-week, when she and Jessica were alone in the front hall as B.J. was leaving.

"I love him with all of my heart," Jessica said in that small, breathy voice of hers.

"So…what's to love?"

Jessica fluttered her long eyelashes. "Aside from being brilliant and funny and handsome and bigger than life? Not much, I guess."

"You forgot to mention that he's also a massive pain in the—"

Jessica giggled. "Yes. There's that, too." Her gorgeous smile faded. "He needs someone like me. And you know what? I've never been so happy as since I've been with him."

B.J. figured that maybe Jessica did love L.T. She found that truly astonishing. B.J. herself kept fantasizing about walking out the Castle's front door and never coming back.

L.T. just refused to let up on her. She visited or spoke on the phone with him daily. He would demand to know everything that was going on at *Alpha*—and then he'd yell at her for wasting his time with minutiae.

Her days were truly packed just keeping up with the magazine *and* her ill-behaved convalescing father. By the end of that week, she was ready to kill someone. Preferably L.T. But he was a sick old man and she didn't feel right about yelling back at him when he started in on her.

And yes, maybe she was a little afraid that if she got into it with him, something bad would happen. He'd get more worked up than usual. He'd have another heart attack and it would be all her fault. She'd have to live the rest of her life with the knowledge that, not only had she *not* been there for his first heart attack, she'd *caused* the second one.

As the days ground slowly by, B.J. grew more fragmented and distracted. The morning sickness she'd thought she'd left behind put in a reappearance. More than once, she had to race to the bathroom down the hall from her office. Her coworkers gave her strange looks. She pretended not to notice.

Giles suggested that maybe she ought to see a doctor for that stomach problem of hers.

She told him to mind his own business.

He shook his head, gorgeous golden hair flying out. "See, that's what I like about you. So tough, so mean. Such a rotten attitude. That's a lot to admire."

Personal time was at a minimum. She rarely saw Buck. They did make a date on Wednesday for Thursday night.

Thursday, things went late at the office and she was stuck in a meeting with Arnie until after seven. It completely slipped her mind that she was supposed to join Buck at that new Italian restaurant in Tribeca at seven-thirty—and she'd turned off her cell for the meeting, so she missed his call when he tried to reach her.

She was in the cab on the way to her place when she remembered their date. Appalled at herself—B. J. Carlyle never broke a date or missed an appointment. Ever—she gave the cabbie a new destination, called Buck with gushing apologies and went to the restaurant.

Buck was understanding about the mix-up, but when they got back to her place for coffee, he said he was worried about her.

"You're pushing yourself too hard, wearing yourself out."

She admitted, "Yeah. Okay. I'm tired. L.T. is on me constantly. And my job is as stressful as it's ever been—and by the way, Arnie wants to know where the Christmas feature is." They'd been back from California almost a week and Buck had yet to turn in the story.

"You'll get it. Soon. And the story isn't the point."

"Buck. Come on. The December issue goes to press in six days. I have to have it."

"Forget the story for a minute."

"Buck—"

He cornered her against the jut of counter that marked off her kitchen from the dining alcove, one hand to either side of her, holding her in place. "The real problem isn't your job, is it?"

"Buck. Listen…"

"No. You listen. I think if L.T. would cut you a little slack you'd be fine. He's causing you a world of stress, ragging on you constantly. He's pissed because you escaped his sphere of influence for a couple of weeks—and had a terrific time doing it. He's possessive, pure and simple, and he needs to get over that and let you have your own damn life. Tell him to back off."

And that *did* irritate her. "He's a sick man. I can't just—"

"He's out of hand and out of line. You know he is. Back him off. Or I'll do it for you."

She put her hands on his chest and pushed—steadily, not a shove, exactly, but a clear indication that she wanted him out of her personal space. "*You* back off."

He did, but then he turned on her. "Damn it. You can't go on like this. It's not good for…" The sentence died unfinished. He swallowed, tried again. "It's not good for you."

Why the hesitation before the word, *you?* she

wondered. But only in passing. Right then, she was too caught up in her frustration at him to put much attention on an odd quirk of phrasing.

She drew herself up. "Don't tell me what's good for me. And don't you dare intervene with my father. Just stay the hell out of what doesn't concern you, okay?"

He answered, so quietly, "No. It's not okay. Not okay in the least." He snagged his jacket off the back of the chair where he'd left it when they came in. "Good night, B.J."

"Buck—"

He put up a hand. "Look. If I stay, I'll say some things you don't want to hear."

So she let him go, figuring that was better than an ugly argument—she let him go and she missed him like hell. She wanted him; she *cared* for him. A lot. But her doubts about the two of them did nag at her.

Here they were, back in the real world. And the easy closeness they'd shared in California had all but evaporated.

B.J. knew the new distance between them was her fault. She had a problem and she'd always had it. She was just one of those women who didn't do well with a man on any kind of long-term basis.

Around midnight, unable to sleep for thinking of him, she called him. They made up, more or less, and set another date for the next night at a restaurant they both liked in SoHo.

Friday was a madhouse at *Alpha.* Arnie called her in at five to rag on her about the Christmas feature. She vowed she'd get it out of Buck by Monday.

Then Arnie broke the big news.

"Your father's decided he's not up to handling the heavy load of his publishing and editorial duties. From now on, I'll be taking a lot of the burden off him at the publishing end. He's going to keep the title of publisher, but I'll be associate publisher."

"Meaning you'll be doing all the work."

A slight smile tipped the corners of Arnie's mouth. "And getting a hefty raise and a huge bump in stock options for my efforts."

B.J. felt vaguely hurt that L.T. hadn't told her his plans. But the decision seemed perfectly reasonable. The truth was, for the past year or two, Arnie had been handling the bulk of L.T.'s duties on the publishing side, anyway—and he'd assumed *all* of them since the heart attack.

She gave Arnie a nod. "Well. I guess congratulations are in order."

"Thanks—and there's more."

"Oh?"

"L.T. also plans to resign as editor-in-chief."

Her heart bounced into her throat. At last. L.T. had promised she'd be the one stepping up when he decided he was ready to step down as editor-in-chief. Strange that L.T. hadn't told her himself. But whatever. It was a big promotion for her and she was so ready for it, a huge step toward her eventual goal of fully filling her father's big shoes, of being editor-in-chief *and* publisher of *Alpha*.

"Arnie, this is…well, I have to say, it's about time."

Arnie wasn't smiling now. "We've hired Bob Alvera for the job."

She blinked. Surely she'd misunderstood. "Bob Alvera? Features editor at *TopMale?*"

"That's right. He'll be coming on board the first of December."

B.J. rose from the chair in front of Arnie's desk. She

did it slowly. Her legs felt kind of numb. Her stomach churned. She swallowed. Hard. No way she would give in to morning sickness right now. She would get out of this office with her head high—and *without* vomiting—if it killed her to do it.

"Thanks for the update. I really appreciate it."

"L.T. wanted you to know."

So he had you *tell me.* "And now I do."

"Get me that cover story. ASAP."

"You'll have it by Monday." She walked out of Arnie's office and down the hall to her own office, where she collected her briefcase, laptop, coat and bag, turned off the light and got the hell out of there.

Out on Broadway, she hailed a cab. It took an extra hundred beyond the round-trip fare and a giant tip on top of that, but she managed to convince the cabbie that a ride upstate would be a great idea.

L.T. was out of bed for the first time.

She found him in his study, playing some game on his great big computer with its giant-sized flat screen. When she walked in and shut the door, he glanced over with a grunt and then went right on click-click-clicking that remote mouse of his.

She waited in front of the door.

Eventually, he took his hand off the mouse and sat back in his chair. "So. Stole a minute out of your busy day to drop in on your old dad."

She longed to lunge at him, grab him by his saggy-skinned neck and spit in his eye. But she kept her cool. "I talked to Arnie. He told me you're hiring Bob Alvera as editor-in-chief."

L.T. grunted again. A mean gleam came into his eyes. "We can use some new blood around the magazine."

Sometime during the drive upstate, as her cold rage had increased, her stomach had stopped rolling. Now it felt like an icy ball of lead. She stood tall. "That was *my* job. You gave me your word."

"You're not ready yet. Give it time."

"I'm ready. More than ready. And you damn well know it, too."

"Right now, *Alpha* needs a man's steady hand at the helm."

The icy ball of lead in B.J.'s stomach went molten. "I do not believe you said that—you, who always told me I could be and *was* as good as any man."

"Yeah. Well. Maybe I was wrong."

"You weren't. And you know you weren't. I'm the best that there is. You know the work I've done. I deliver a quality product and I do it on time, every time. I have a vision for *Alpha* and it's an exciting one."

"What about the Christmas feature? You should make your damn boyfriend get off his ass and deliver on the contract he has with us."

"The feature will be ready on time—and it will be fabulous, for your information."

"Well, we'll see about that, now, won't we?"

She just looked at him. At that moment, she almost wished he'd have another heart attack. She wished he'd fall off that big red leather swivel chair of his with its nifty nail-head trim, fall off and roll around on the floor moaning in agony. He could die right there on his Persian rug and she wouldn't lift a finger to save him.

He said, "You let me down, B.J. Let me down big-time."

"How? By taking a vacation for the first time in my life?" Everything on her body felt too tight—her skin, her hair, her fingernails. She felt as if the top of her head just might pop off and explode right there under the soulful gaze of the enormous moose head on the far wall.

L.T. sat back in his chair. "I don't think there's any more to say at the moment. If you'll excuse me, I'd like to get back to my game."

Oh, he was wrong, wrong, wrong. There was a lot more to say. But B.J. didn't dare get into it. If she did, there would be yelling—a lot of it.

And in spite of her fuming fantasies of him moaning in pain on the rug beneath her Manolos, she didn't really want him dead.

No. Better not to get into it. At this point in time, with him still recovering, a shouting match was simply not a good idea.

"Good night, L.T." She turned to go.

He hurled the last salvo at her retreating back. "Get that feature out of Buck. Now. Or start polishing your résumé."

She returned to *Alpha*. She always had plenty on her plate there and she couldn't face going home to her apartment where there was nothing important to do. Not now, when her professional life seemed to be falling apart. Not now, when she felt such pure fury toward L.T., her rage made a taste like dirty metal in her mouth.

In her office, she flicked on the light, shut the door, hung up her coat and sat down at her desk. She booted up her computer.

And after that…

What?

Nothing, really. In the end, she was just too angry to get any work done. She felt trapped and lost and small…and betrayed.

The phone on her desk rang now and then. From her bag, she heard her cell beep. She ignored the sounds. She brought up her résumé and worked it over a little and wondered if she'd actually have the guts to do what cried out to be done: To say goodbye to *Alpha* and strike out on her own.

To walk away from the life she'd chosen for herself, the life she'd always known, the life that had always seemed the perfect life for her: the life of L. T. Carlyle's only child and heir, the woman who took what her father had created and made it bigger and better and more profitable than ever.

How long did she sit there, staring at her computer screen, wondering where she was going to go next?

Hours.

Around nine, the line to the security desk downstairs started beeping. She tried to ignore it, but it didn't stop. Maybe the building was on fire.

She picked up.

"Ms. Carlyle?"

"What is it?"

"Mr. Bravo's down here. He insists on coming up."

Omigod. Buck. She'd completely forgotten that they had a date. She clutched the phone and stared at her office door and could not believe she had done that. Again.

"Ms. Carlyle, should I send him up?"

Oh, this was bad. How could she have—?

"Ms. Carlyle? Are you there?"

"Yes. Yes, I am. Please. Send him right up." She set down the phone and hurried out to meet him at the elevator. Oh, how could she have done that? How could she have blown off a date with him for the second time in as many days?

She stood in front of Melanie's empty desk in the dimmed after-business-hours light and waited anxiously for the elevator doors to slide open.

When they did, she didn't know what to say. She looked in his dear, handsome face, and her throat just locked up tight on her. She made an odd, squeaking sound and then somehow, she got out, "Oh, Buck. I am so sorry…"

He stepped out of the elevator and took her by the shoulders, strong hands warm and steady, his gaze seeking hers. "Okay. What's happened?"

And that did it. That opened the floodgates, somehow. It all came pouring out in a furious rush. She told him everything. How Arnie had told her what L.T. had done, hiring Bob Alvera from *TopMale* to take *her* job. How she'd gone to the Castle and confronted her father and L.T. had said that she'd let him down, that *Alpha* needed a man at the helm.

When she was finished, Buck took her hand and led her behind Melanie's wide black desk. "Here." He spoke gently. "Sit down."

She sagged into the receptionist's chair. "Oh, Buck. I'm so sorry I stood you up—again. I can't believe I did that. It's so not like me. But, well, my mind's been on other things and I just—"

"More important things, you mean."

She couldn't read his expression. "I didn't say that."

"You didn't have to."

"You're mad at me, aren't you? Oh, I don't blame you. I just—"

He was shaking his head. "I'm not mad."

She frowned up at him. "You're not?"

"No."

"You're sure?"

"Positive."

She stared up at him for a long moment, trying to read him, trying to tell if he really meant what he said. And then L.T.'s betrayal overwhelmed her again. "I just… Oh, Buck. I don't know what to do."

He dropped to the edge of the desk, hitching a leg up, bracing an arm on his thigh. "Yeah, you do."

"No, I—"

"Tell L.T. to keep his word to you, or you quit." He folded his hands between his spread knees. "And then, if he doesn't give you the job he promised you…"

She swallowed. "Actually do it, right? Leave *Alpha*…" He nodded. "Oh, Buck. It's just not that simple."

"You're wrong. It *is* that simple. I know your father. You not only have to draw the line with him, you've got to hold that line, or he'll steamroll right over it."

"You don't understand."

"Yeah. I do. Your father rules your life."

"No…"

He wore a sad smile. "Yeah. L.T. demands all your energy and all your attention. The truth is, B.J., you don't have room in your life for another man."

"No. That's ridiculous. I—"

"You said it yourself, remember, back at the cabin? You've spent your whole life trying to be the son L.T. never had. You're still trying to be that guy. And B.J., you're not a guy. I think it's about time you started being the smart, beautiful, savvy daughter L.T. *does* have—and while you're at it, you could also try and remember to keep your dinner dates."

She let out a cry. "See? I knew it. You *are* mad at me."

He rose from the edge of the desk and he put out

his hand to her. Warily, she laid her fingers in his. He pulled her up to him. "You're the woman I want, B.J. You're the woman I've *always* wanted. I've been as patient as a guy like me can ever be, but this, I can't take. To watch you driving yourself to the limit like this, to see how unhappy you are, and to know there's not a damn thing I can do about it."

"Oh, Buck, I—"

He put a finger to her lips. "Wait." She swallowed, nodded. "It's just not working, this thing with us. Right now, in your mind and heart, you're back at Castle Carlyle, yelling at your father, saying all the things you're afraid to say to him in reality, because he's working you and he's doing a damn fine job of it. He's got you convinced that you can't say what's on your mind, because if you do, he'll keel over dead."

Though she knew he was right, she opened her mouth to argue, anyway. He didn't even let her get started. "Don't deny it. We both know it's true. L.T. is running you ragged, and since we got back to the city, this thing between us is going nowhere. For a while there, in California, I dared to hope…" He didn't finish. He didn't seem to have the heart to. He only said, "We've got to face it. It's just not working."

What could she say? She looked up at him and couldn't believe this was happening to them all over again—and at the same time, she saw that there was really no other way it could go.

He waited. When she didn't speak, he advised again, "Draw the line on your father. And once you've drawn that line, maybe you ought to put a little effort into trying to figure out what the hell happened to Bitsy."

She frowned at him. "Bitsy? I don't understand…"

"Give it some thought."

"But I don't—"

He put up a hand. "One more thing. You might as well know that *I* know about the baby."

B.J.'s heart stopped dead—and then started pounding so hard she feared it would punch its way right out of her chest. "I...what?"

"I heard you telling Glory that morning at the Sierra Star. I've been waiting for you to tell *me*."

"Buck, I..." There had to be something she could say. She just couldn't imagine what it might be.

"When *were* you planning to tell me?"

How could she answer him? She was still stuck back there with the fact that he knew. That he *had* known. For more than two weeks now.

He knew. It explained a lot, really. The way he never mentioned it when they forgot to use a condom, the way now and then he said things that didn't quite add up...

"Oh, Buck...you haven't said a word, in all this time. That's just not like you."

He looked at her steadily. "I had some crazy idea I ought to be patient, to let you get around to it in your own way. But I'm tired of waiting. I can see now that waiting isn't going to do me any good." He asked again, "When were you planning to tell me?"

"I, um..."

"When?"

"Well, I don't know, exactly. A couple of months, I guess..."

"Wrong answer."

"Buck, I'm sorry. So sorry, I—"

"Goodbye, B.J." He turned for the elevator.

"Buck. Wait..." He paused, turned back. Her throat

clutched as if it had some huge foreign object lodged in it. She coughed and managed to clear it. "Aren't you going to, um, do that Bravo thing?"

He seemed puzzled. "That Bravo thing?"

"You know, *demand* that I marry you?"

He gave her another of those wry, sad smiles. "Will it do any good?"

This was so insane. He was breaking her heart all over again—and how did he understand her so well? "No. I guess it won't."

"I didn't think so—and I almost forgot. Check your e-mail. I sent you the story a few hours ago."

She hadn't the faintest idea what he was talking about. "The what?"

"The story. Your precious Christmas feature."

"Oh. The story…" She wished it mattered now.

"Goodbye, Bitsy." He turned and punched the button. The elevator doors slid wide.

And she knew she couldn't bear it—couldn't stand to see him go.

But she also knew she had no right to stop him.

She shut her eyes, tight, to block out the sight of Buck walking away. A moment later, she heard the soft rumble of the doors shutting. She felt for the chair behind her and sank into it.

And then she did the one thing she never, ever let herself do.

Bitsy Janine Carlyle broke down and cried.

Twenty-Three

The next day, Saturday, bright and early, B.J. headed for the Castle.

She found her father and Jessica enjoying breakfast in bed. Jessica gasped when B.J. banged back the massive, heavily carved bedroom door. "Pardon me. I told Roderick you wouldn't mind if I just busted right in here."

"What the hell?" L.T. threw down his spoon. It clattered against his tray as he grabbed a napkin and mopped up the dribble of yolk on his chin.

"I have news." B.J. crossed the threshold and marched to the foot of the huge mahogany bed.

The ever-thoughtful Jessica picked up her tray and started to slide from the bed. "I'll just—"

"Stay right where you are, Jessica," B.J. commanded. "This won't take a minute."

Her father huffed. "This is beyond it. Have you lost your mind?"

B.J. folded her arms over her chest and considered. "Hmm. It's an interesting question…."

"Get out."

"I will. Shortly."

"What is wrong with you? Can't you even let a sick man enjoy his breakfast in peace? I didn't raise you to—"

"I quit," she said pleasantly.

"Huh?" said her father. It was a dazzling moment. L. T. Carlyle, speechless at last.

"I said, I quit. I'm leaving *Alpha*."

"What? You can't—"

"Oh, yeah. I can. And I am. I'm quitting *Alpha*. I'll be glad to stay on for a couple of weeks if you need me. But the truth is, it's time I rearranged my priorities. I'll need a job with a little more flexibility. And since you've set me up with such a nice, fat trust fund, I can take as long as I like to find just the right place for me."

"Flexibility? All of a sudden you're talking flexibility?"

"That's right. I can't drive myself until I drop anymore. I have someone else to consider."

Her father snorted. "Who? Buck? Buck can't deal with you having a damn job?"

Buck. Just the mention of his name caused a tightness in her chest. She pressed her lips together and shook her head. "No. Not Buck."

"Well who, then?"

"My baby."

Her father sucked air like a landed fish. "Your… what?"

"You heard me."

He blinked. "No."

"Yeah."

L.T. slumped back against the pillows. "A baby? *You*, B.J.? You're having a baby?"

"Isn't that what I just said?"

Her father's face flushed flaming red. B.J. thought, *This is it. It's happening. He's having another heart attack. Any second now, he'll be grabbing his chest and groaning in agony....*

L.T. shook his head as if to clear it. He snorted. "I don't believe it..." He snorted some more. But he didn't groan. He didn't clutch his chest or start to turn blue. He only went on blustering in the usual way. "What the hell are you gaping at?"

"Uh, nothing." Amazing. Wonderful. The dreaded second heart attack was simply not happening. He was fine. *Fine*. The sweetest sensation of relief flowed through her. "Whether you believe it or not, it's true. I'm pregnant. I'm keeping my baby. And I quit."

Jessica spoke—softly, as usual. "Congratulations, B.J."

"Thank you, Jessica." B.J. nodded at L.T. "See you later, Dad." And she got the heck out of there.

She went straight from the Castle to the office.

After finally facing down her father, she was ready to deal with Buck's cover story. In the empty, silent break room, she made herself a cup of herb tea.

She'd always liked working Saturdays, liked the silence of the deserted hallways, liked how much she could accomplish without the usual weekday interruptions. And then there was the bustle and excitement, the day-to-day challenges of the regular workweek. She'd adored all that, too.

B.J. smiled to herself as she sipped her tea. Yeah. She'd liked this job. A lot. She was going to miss *Alpha*.

But there were other jobs. Monday, she'd start making calls. She had connections and she was damn good at what she did and everyone in New York publishing knew it.

Her smile widened as it occurred to her that *TopMale* would soon be needing a new features editor.

In her office, she booted her computer. Her silly hand was shaking as she checked her e-mail and found the one from Buck.

Two attachments: a scan and a document.

She opened the scan first and found an old black-and-white photo of the cabin at the Red Robin. A very young woman and a man ten or fifteen years older stood in the foreground, the cabin B.J. remembered so well behind them.

The woman was Chastity, when she was barely more than a girl, smiling shyly at the camera. The man beside her had his head turned toward her, so B.J. couldn't really make out his features. But she knew who he was: the notorious Blake Bravo.

Who else could it be?

She moved the picture to the side of the screen and read Buck's e-mail note.

Here's the story. I've been working it over, trying to get it right. I think it's fine now—or I hope it is.

Got the photo from Ma. Thought you'd get a kick out of it.

As you can see, dear old Dad did visit the Red Robin, after all. It was a month or two after they married. Ma told me Uncle Clovis took the picture.

Ma and Blake stayed on at the mine after Uncle Clovis went on down the mountain. Ma says I was conceived there, in the cabin. She says it was one of their most beautiful times together.

Just like you and me, Bits. Pretty crazy, huh?

Bits...

B.J. reached up and touched the word on the screen—and it hit her like a physical blow, tightening her stomach, bringing out a grunt of pain.

He would probably never call her that again...

Her hand a little clammy on the mouse, she closed up the scan and opened the document. She couldn't help fearing that she just might be in for man-eater revisited, though she knew that Buck wouldn't—*couldn't*—be that cruel.

She read quickly.

Halfway through, all her stupid, small-minded fears vanished. It was beautiful. Perfect. And truly Buck's story: where he came from, the boy he'd been, and the man he had become. He'd left her out of it, completely—or at least, he'd left out B.J.

There were, however, mentions of a tender reunion in a miner's shack with a long-lost love named Bitsy.

Who would ever know?

More important, B.J. realized, as she picked up her cooling tea and drank the rest, she didn't care if they did know.

Now, if she only had the guts to go to Buck, to beg him to take a chance on her just one more time...

B.J. spent Thanksgiving with her father and Jessica.

L.T. gave her the silent treatment. Fine. Two could play that game. And she had Jessica to talk to. The big-eyed blonde was all atwitter at the news that a baby was on the way. She asked when the baby was due and if B.J. had seen a doctor yet.

Yes, B.J. said, she'd seen a doctor Monday. She was due in June.

L.T. sat at the head of the table and glowered through the meal. Every once in a while, Jessica would reach over and tenderly pat his hand. B.J. mused that there had been a time—a time not all that long ago— when her father's furious silences would have cut her to the bone.

She would always pretend he couldn't affect her, insisting to him, and to herself, that he couldn't push her around. It was a good front she put up, so good she'd almost had herself convinced it was real. But deep inside, she would be terrified of losing his love and approval.

And she would always, somehow, end up doing exactly what L.T. told her to do.

Not anymore.

She hoped someday that the rift between them would heal. She would do her best to make that happen—but never again would she appease L.T. at the expense of her true self.

If only Buck could see her now.

If only she had the nerve to go to him...

The day after Thanksgiving, she did the Avenue. She took her time about it, ambling along, admiring each and every one of the gorgeously decorated Christmas windows.

Starting at her apartment, between Ninth and Tenth streets, she went first to Macy's on Herald Square, then detoured back to Fifth. From Lord & Taylor, she headed up the Avenue to Saks, where the line went around the block just to view the displays. She got in line and she waited her turn.

After Saks, she bought a bag of roasted chestnuts from a street vendor and made a special stop at Rockefeller Center to admire the giant tree. It wasn't lit yet, but it was up and it was beautiful.

The stroll took hours. She savored every step. Her city did Christmas like no other city in the world.

Her final day at *Alpha,* Arnie threw a surprise going-away party for her, right there in the office. He hired a top caterer and he had the big table taken out of the main conference room, had a piano rolled in there, complete with piano player.

Bob, the new editor-in-chief, gave a speech about how much he hated to see her go. Giles, who was stepping into her job starting Monday, sang a Billy Joel medley in her honor. After a rousing chorus of "Only the Good Die Young," he dropped to his knees in front of her and begged her not to leave.

B.J. grinned and said she had to go—and then she reached down a hand to him. Everyone applauded as Giles jumped up, grabbed his former boss, and danced her around the piano.

She was gathering up the last of her things from her office, when Arnie came in to say a private goodbye.

"Great party, Arnie. Thanks."

"You've got a job here any time you want it," he said, and she knew that he meant it—and not only because the day would come when she would own the place.

The office closed early and B.J. headed home to her apartment.

When she got there, she had a surprise waiting for her in the lobby.

"B.J.! Finally. I thought you'd never come."

B.J. barely had time to put down the box of stuff from her desk and open her arms before Glory flung herself into them.

Their rounded stomachs bumped. They jerked apart, laughed, and then grabbed each other close again.

"You okay?" B.J. whispered in Glory's ear.

"Same ol', same ol'. My family won't get off me to say yes to Bowie. Bowie's been trying not to be such a big butthole as before, but… Oh, Beej, I just had to get away, you know?"

"It's okay." B.J. hugged her tighter. "I'm glad you're here."

Glory pulled back a little. Her huge dark eyes were moist with tears. "You think you could put me up for a few days?"

"You've got a place here for as long as you want one."

"You mean it?"

"You bet."

They stayed up late that night. They had a lot of catching up to do.

Glory reported that Chastity and Alyosha were together constantly.

"He's always out of there early in the morning, way before the sun comes up, but I know he stays the night sometimes. They are so gone on each other. It's really cute. And you should see Chastity. I'm not kidding. She looks twenty years younger. She sings now, around the Sierra Star, just crooning away while she mixes up her muffins. She's not what I'd call a great singer, you know? But she sure gives it a lot of feeling."

B.J. chuckled. "I'm glad for her—for both of them."

"Yeah. Yeah, me too…"

Glory asked about Buck.

B.J. told her everything.

And Glory told B.J. what she already knew.

"You have to go after him. You have to tell him that you've finally stood up to that father of yours. That you love him and you want to be with him. That you're *ready* to be with him. B.J., I think that's all he's waiting for. Up till now, he's had to do all the chasing. It's time you showed him you know how to go out and get your man."

"Maybe…"

"What's that, *maybe?* No *maybe* about it. Go get 'im, and you'll see."

"I don't know…" B.J. told her what had happened six years ago. She admitted, "I guess, well, I'm pretty terrified that I'll find him in bed with someone else. And worse than that, I'm scared it's just simply…too late. That when he walked away from me two weeks ago, it was finally for good."

Glory said what she'd said more than once before. "You're nuts. Buck is crazy for you. And he's too smart to make the same mistake twice. There'll be no other woman in his bed. I guarantee it. If you go after him, he'll be there. Ready and waiting for you and only you."

B.J. still doubted that Buck would take her back. But she did know she was going to have to go find out for sure.

Soon…

By the next morning, at the breakfast table, Glory was having second thoughts about her own situation.

"I didn't sleep at all," she said. "I'm kind of seeing that maybe I shouldn't have run off like that. I guess I'd better make some calls…"

B.J. handed her the phone. Glory called Bowie first. He didn't answer, so she tried the Sierra Star. Chastity told her that Bowie was frantic—the whole town was worried. Bowie was out looking for her.

"Tell him I'm fine," Glory said. "And yes…I know. Running away doesn't solve anything… Yeah. Okay. I'll be home as soon as I can get a flight. Call my mom for me?…. Oh, Mrs. B., you are the best…" She paused to grin at B.J. "B.J. says hi… Uh-huh. I'll tell her. Bye." Glory hung up. "Mrs. B. says hi—and I need to get myself a flight home."

"Consider it handled." B.J. called Jessica, who said she'd make all the arrangements. The jet would be ready at Teterboro within the hour. Once that was taken care of, B.J. called Glory a cab.

When Glory's ride arrived, B.J. went down to the street with her to say goodbye. A light snow was falling. It gleamed in Glory's dark hair and dusted her shoulders as B.J. gave her one last hug.

Glory ducked into the cab. B.J. stood at the curb, waving, until the cab disappeared into traffic on the way up the Avenue.

Back in the apartment, B.J. took off her coat, her wool cap and her mittens. Her place seemed too quiet and just a little bit empty, now her friend was gone.

The day stretched ahead of her. She had nothing pressing to do.

Or did she?

There *was* one thing….

B.J. bundled up warmly again and went back downstairs. Melvin held the door for her.

"Merry Christmas, Melvin."

The old sweetie tipped his hat to her. "Happy holidays, Ms. Carlyle."

"Oh, Melvin. I so hope you're right about that."

He helped her into a cab.

"Where to?" asked the cabbie. She gave him Buck's address.

All the way uptown, B.J. stewed. Was she doing the right thing? What if he already had someone else? What if she walked in on him and it was the same as six years ago?

What if he wasn't even there? Or what if he *was* there, all alone—and he told her it was too late, he didn't want to try again...

The snowfall increased. It was coming down thick and heavy as the cab reached Buck's block. B.J. told the cabbie where to pull in. The cab slid up to the curb and she handed the money over the seat.

She got out. The cab pulled away. And she just stood there on the sidewalk, the snow a thick white curtain all around her, not knowing what to do with herself now she'd come this far.

Finally, with snow caked on her shoulders and clumping in her eyelashes, she turned to face the big brick building where Buck lived.

There was no doorman. Just a vestibule lined with mailboxes and an inner door. B.J. still had the key that Buck had given her. She used it and took the elevator to the fifteenth floor.

When she reached his door, she hesitated again. The minutes ticked by as she tried to drum up the guts to ring the bell.

Twice, she started to walk away. But after a few steps, she would realize that if she didn't go the distance with this now, she might never gather the courage to try again.

And then how would she ever forgive herself?

At last, she made herself do it. She lifted her red-mittened hand and she pushed his doorbell.

After several seconds that seemed like centuries, the door swung inward.

And there he was.

He looked her up and down and then, at last, he said, "It's about damn time."

Twenty-Four

"You're home," B.J. said, as if stating the obvious might make it more true.

"Got back yesterday."

"From?"

"A two-week assignment. In Mexico. For *National Geographic.*"

"Oh. Well. I guess I'm lucky I caught you." *Lucky.* Perfect word. She felt, at that moment, like the luckiest woman in Manhattan—and it got better. He wore khakis, a coffee-colored sweater that matched his eyes and a pair of tan mocs. "You're…fully dressed."

He almost smiled. "That I am."

"Are you…" She had to gulp before she could say the rest. "Alone?"

He did smile then. "Yes, I am. I'm decorating my tree. I have popcorn. And hot cocoa."

"Hot cocoa? No kidding?"

"If you'll come in, I'll be happy to pour you a cup."

"Well, you know, cocoa sounds lovely." She stepped inside and he shut the door behind her.

"Let me take your coat." He helped her out of it, causing those wonderful, zinging little thrills of sensation every time his fingers happened to brush against her shoulders or her arms or, just once, so lightly, the side of her neck. He hung the coat on the rack by the door. "Your gloves and your hat?" She handed them over and he shook the snow from them and hung them with the coat. She gave him her scarf and he hung that up, too.

Then he led her out of the small foyer and into his living room, which faced the park. Beyond the picture window, the snow came down in thick, white swirls.

And in front of the window, on a card table, stood the most pitiful-looking tree B.J. had ever seen. Most of the needles were missing.

"What happened to your poor tree?"

He shoved a box of ornaments aside to clear a place for her on the sofa. "Ma sends me one every year—fresh-cut, from home. Some years it gets here in great shape. This year, not so much…" His voice trailed off. "Here. Have a seat."

She stayed on her feet. They stared at each other. Finally, she managed huskily, "I've quit *Alpha.*"

"I heard."

"You did?"

"The world of publishing is a pretty small one."

"Oh. Yeah. I guess it is…."

He regarded her steadily. "Are you sorry you quit?"

She answered without having to even think twice. "No. I'm not. I took your advice to heart, Buck. I truly did. I quit, and I'm glad I did. I've drawn the line on my father, the way you suggested, and it feels really good."

"How did L.T. take it?"

"We're not exactly speaking now, L.T. and me."

"He'll get over it."

"Yeah. I think that he will. Eventually. And I… Oh, Buck. I've really messed up, and I know it. For all my life, I had this idea that love wasn't for me. But I'm getting past that, I honestly am. And I've been kind of hoping…" She hesitated, but then she forced herself to stumble on. "Oh, Buck, I…"

"Yeah?"

And she went for it, went right, straight to the heart of the matter. "Buck. I love you. I love you so. I think I always have."

That did it for Buck. He held out his arms to her. She moved into them.

They shared a kiss—a long, deep, hungry one. When he lifted his head, he muttered, "Damn, you had me worried there. I was starting to think maybe you'd never come and get me."

"I'm here."

"I can hardly believe it."

"Consider yourself taken."

"I love you, Bits. Marry me." It was a command—but a tender one.

"Oh, yes. I will," she answered proudly.

And after that, there was no more need for words.

The next day, they visited Castle Carlyle to tell L.T. and Jessica the news. Jessica, who loved Christmas almost as much as Chastity Bravo did, had decked the Castle out in true holiday style. She was just thrilled for them.

"Oh," she said breathlessly. "You're getting married. Isn't that great?"

L.T. surprised them. He was happy, too. "I'm having a grandchild," he said, "and the more I think about that, the more I like it. B.J. Buck. Feel free to thank me now."

"Excuse me," said B.J. "We should thank you for what?"

"For getting the two of you together, that's what. If it wasn't for my stepping in and talking Buck into writing the Christmas feature, the two of you wouldn't even be on speaking terms."

B.J. couldn't let that go without calling him on it. "As I recall, you had *me* writing it."

"Harumph. Well. And that didn't last, now, did it? Buck wrote it and it is brilliant. Very possibly, that issue will be our bestselling ever."

"Dad. Why is it that whenever there's credit to be taken, you're always the first one to claim it?"

"You think I got where I am today by being shy? So what about it? Thanks *are* in order and I'm ready to accept them."

Buck spoke up then, graciously. "Thanks, L.T."

"Ahem. All right, then. You're welcome, both of you."

Next, L.T. admitted that he wanted B.J. back at *Alpha.*

"I've had my ear to the ground on this," he announced. "I happen to know you turned down the offer from *TopMale.* I'm guessing you want your job back and I'm willing to give it to you—in fact, I'm willing, after serious thought and weighty consideration, to move you on to the next level, after all. Editor-in-chief, B.J. Take it. It's yours."

"I thought I told you, with the baby coming, I'm not going to be working eighty-hour weeks anymore."

"I know that. We'll deal with it."

"What about Bob Alvera?"

"I have other plans for Bob."

"Scary," B.J. said under her breath.

"What was that?" L.T. growled.

She twined her fingers with Buck's. "We'll talk shop later, Dad. Right now, let's break out the sparkling fruit juice and share a toast."

Jessica rang the service bell and Roderick came in bearing a sterling silver tray: champagne for Buck and Jessica, fruit juice for B.J. and L.T.

"Roderick," said her father. "You'll have a little bubbly with us, I trust?"

The faithful retainer allowed that just this once, he might.

B.J. took it upon herself to propose the toast.

"To the season," she declared. "To hope. To keeping the faith—and to real men everywhere." Her father preened. B.J. granted him a fond and tolerant smile and then turned to Buck. She raised her glass high. "Men who are strong enough to be tender, smart enough to know what they want, shrewd enough to get out and go after it—and sure enough to stay the course on the rocky road to love."

Everything you love about romance...
and more!

*Please turn the page for Signature Select™
Bonus Features.*

BRAVO
UNWRAPPED

BONUS
FEATURES
INSIDE

Author Interview:
A conversation with
CHRISTINE RIMMER

USA TODAY bestselling author Christine Rimmer has written more than fifty novels for Silhouette Books. Recently she chatted with us as she took a break from writing her latest book.

Please tell us a bit about how you began your writing career.

I always loved to write. Somewhere in my twenties I began to realize that I wanted someone to *pay* me to write so I could do it for a living and not have to work all those draining day jobs. For several years I kind of felt my way along. I have a background in theater; I wrote several plays. I tried my hand at poetry and short stories. I wrote scripts for self-help tapes and a pilot for a TV show. (Never sold. Title: *Pet Patrol*. And I think that's all anyone needs to know. <g>) The whole time I struggled trying to find my place in the writing world, I read romances to decompress, to sweep me away from my daily troubles. Then I just happened to read an article in *Writer's Digest* magazine about a romance boom. I decided to try my hand at romance. I studied hundreds of romances—no hardship, believe me. My first romance went to Harlequin Temptation and I've been a romance writer ever since.

Was there a particular person, place or thing that inspired this story?

I love a strong heroine. I wanted to write how a real powerhouse, go-getter career woman finally finds the love of her life. So I did.

What's your writing routine?

Writing is my job. I work about eight hours a day at least five days a week.

How do you research your stories?

The usual sources. Books on any given subject, sometimes interviews with experts, magazine articles. The children's section of the library is very useful for the basic info on a setting—clear, well-organized information with lots of pictures! Oh, and the Internet. I don't know how I got along without it. But I have it now and that's what matters. <g>

How you do develop your characters?
Tough question. I used to do character charts and "interview" my characters. I used to write long character histories. But over the years it's pretty much become intuitive. I try to keep peeling down to find the deepest truth hidden within any given character's psyche. I'm looking for the secrets they're keeping from themselves....

If you don't mind, could you tell us a bit about your family?
I'm a native Californian. My dad and mom grew up in the same small mountain town, two of a four-person high school class. They're still going strong over sixty years later. I have a loving husband and two sons and two cuddly cats named Tom and Ed.

When you're not writing, what are your favorite activities?
Reading. Playing Trivial Pursuit. Watching Lifetime movies...yum. Oh, and I enjoy gardening. And travel when I can find the time.

What are your favorite kinds of vacations? Where do you like to travel?
Someplace tropical. Blue seas and white beaches...

Do you have a favorite book or film?
Recently, I've been enjoying the Whitley Strieber vampire books: *The Hunger, The Last Vampire* and *Lilith's Dream*. And I loved *The Other Boleyn Girl* by Philippa Gregory.

Marsha Zinberg, Executive Editor, Signature Select program, spoke with Christine Rimmer at her home in Oklahoma.

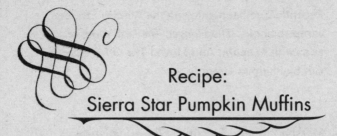

Recipe:
Sierra Star Pumpkin Muffins

Sierra Star Pumpkin Muffins
(with very special thanks to Barbara Ferris)

Prep time: 15 min. Cook time: 25 min. Servings: 12

1 1/2 cups flour

1 tsp baking soda

1/2 tsp baking powder

3/4 tsp salt

1/8 tsp nutmeg

1/2 tsp cinnamon

1 1/2 cups sugar

1/2 cup vegetable oil

2 eggs

1 cup canned pumpkin

1/3 cup water

12 walnut halves

Instructions:
Preheat oven to 350°F. Combine dry ingredients in mixing bowl. Mix in oil, eggs and pumpkin. On low speed, gradually mix in water until well blended. Pour batter into greased (or use paper cups) muffin pan.

Chastity Bravo's Special Hints:
I mix mine by hand. I use a flat whip in a clear bowl so I can see that I've mixed everything thoroughly. A large can of pumpkin is 3 1/2 cups. I triple the recipe and it makes 3 dozen muffins and a small loaf, too (bake the loaf close to 1 hour). There will be a little of the pumpkin left in the can. I do keep the muffins refrigerated after baking. They also freeze well. I use this recipe to make small loaves of bread, too. For bread, bake for 50 minutes to an hour.

The Ballad of Blake Bravo

Note to readers: The notorious and now deceased Blake is the father of several Bravo heroes, including Buck, the hero of Bravo Unwrapped.

Harry and Blake Bravo were the sons of privilege, born to Jonas Bravo, a multimillionaire who made his money in a number of big land deals in Southern California in the 1930s and 1940s. Harry, the oldest, was a good boy, the favored son. And Blake was the troublemaker, a boy born to end up on the wrong side of the law.

By the time Blake was twenty, his father had had enough. Jonas disinherited Blake. For a number of years Harry gave Blake money whenever his ne'er-do-well brother showed up with his hand out. But then Blake ran into their father one day when Blake came to try to talk his softhearted older brother into another "loan." Jonas ordered him out. Blake physically attacked his father, beating him badly. Harry came to his father's aid and won the fight, trouncing Blake soundly.

Blake's attack on their father was the final straw for Harry. He told Blake he never wanted to see his face again—and he never did. Neither did their father, Jonas, who died a couple of years later.

A year after Jonas Sr. died, Blake murdered a man with his bare hands in a barroom brawl. To evade capture and trial and a lengthy imprisonment, Blake faked his own death in an apartment fire. To this day, it is not known whose body was found in the smoldering ruins of the fire—or how Blake managed to falsify dental records so that the body's records matched his own.

But Blake was not finished with the family that had scorned him. Five years after Harry threw Blake out of the Bravo mansion for the last time, Blake heard of the birth of Harry's second son, Russell (later called Dekker Smith and hero of *The Marriage Conspiracy*). Blake hatched a plot to kidnap the baby and hold him for ransom. He talked a gullible girlfriend,

Lorraine, into falling in with his scheme. They broke in to the nursery late at night to snatch the child—running into a problem when the baby's older brother, Jonas (named after his grandfather and six at the time; hero of *The Bravo Billionaire*), woke in the room next door and caught Blake and Lorraine in the act. Blake grabbed the six-year-old and clamped a gloved hand over his mouth. Jonas fought valiantly to get away, while Blake told Lorraine they'd just have to take *both* children.

Lorraine freaked. She started arguing. She never should have agreed to do this. A baby was one thing, but how was she going to keep a six-year-old quiet while they waited for the ransom demands to be met? As the two kidnappers argued, Jonas kept struggling. Finally Blake knocked the child unconscious and he and Lorraine took off with the baby. Jonas suffered a concussion, was comatose for several hours—and ended up with amnesia when it came to the events of the night his brother was taken.

Blake dropped Lorraine and the baby off at a secret location and went about negotiating for the two-million-dollar ransom, which he demanded be paid in diamonds, as they are compact and easy to carry. Harry and his wife, Blythe, paid, as instructed, getting the diamonds from a diamond dealer. Still completely unaware that his own brother had taken his baby son, Jonas had the police in on the whole transaction in hopes of catching the kidnapper if there was a single slipup.

Blake didn't slip up. He got away clean. And once he had the diamonds, Blake decided it would be unwise to return the baby; it would be only another opportunity to get caught. In the meantime, Lorraine, who was unable to have children herself, had developed a powerful attachment to the child.

For a year Blake, Lorraine and the baby lived under a series of aliases, keeping a very low profile, never staying in one place too long. During that year Harry died of a heart attack, leaving Blythe to suffer a mental breakdown and his older son, Jonas, without a father or a brother—or, essentially, a mother for a number of years, until Blythe recovered.

As time passed and Blake became more and more certain he had gotten away with his revenge, Lorraine began making "settling down" noises. She wanted them to get their own little house in a nice town and live like a family. Blake had little interest in spending his life with Lorraine and his dead brother's kidnapped child. He had zero intention of playing the family man.

They were living in Oklahoma City at that point. Since it was obvious Lorraine really cared only about the boy, Blake saw his chance to get rid of both the woman he'd tired of and the child who had, to him, been only a means to an end. Through his various nefarious connections, he sold off a few diamonds and set Lorraine up with a new identity, complete with birth certificate that "proved" the baby was hers. Thus she became the widowed single mother Lorraine Smith, living in Oklahoma City, raising her "son," Dekker, alone.

Blake himself, confident by then that he'd pulled off his revenge and gotten away scot-free, started using his own name again. He took up with a Norman, Oklahoma, woman, whom he married when she became pregnant (with Marsh, hero of *The Marriage Agreement*).

For three decades Blake kept the bulk of the diamonds stashed away, knowing if he ever tried to sell off too many of them, he'd be likely to get caught. Marsh's mother died when Marsh was sixteen, leaving the teenage Marsh at the mercy of the abusive Blake. But Blake was gone a lot. And while he was gone, he took more than one unsuspecting woman as a lover. He even "married" these women, which made him a polygamist on top of all his other crimes.

When Blake Bravo finally died for real, of heart failure, in *The Marriage Agreement,* Marsh found the missing diamonds and, with the help of his long-lost cousin Jonas, uncovered the truth about baby Russell's kidnapper. Since then, more than one illegitimate Bravo has discovered his Bravo family ties.

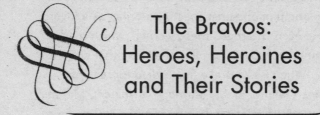

The Bravos:
Heroes, Heroines
and Their Stories

THE BRAVO BILLIONAIRE—Jonas Bravo
and Emma Hewitt

MARRIAGE: OVERBOARD—Gwen Bravo McMillan
and Rafe McMillan
(Online read at www.eHarlequin.com)

THE MARRIAGE CONSPIRACY—
Dekker (Smith) Bravo and Joleen Tilly

HIS EXECUTIVE SWEETHEART—
Aaron Bravo and Celia Tuttle

MERCURY RISING—Cade Bravo and
Jane Elliott

SCROOGE AND THE SINGLE GIRL—
Will Bravo and Jillian Diamond

FIFTY WAYS TO SAY I'M PREGNANT—
Starr Bravo and Beau Tisdale

MARRYING MOLLY—Tate Bravo and
Molly O'Dare

LORI'S LITTLE SECRET—Tucker Bravo and
Lori Lee Billingsworth Taylor

BONUS FEATURE

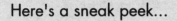

Here's a sneak peek...

BRAVO FAMILY WAY
by
Christine Rimmer

Coming in March 2006 from Silhouette Special Edition

Fletcher put a hand—so lightly—at the small of her back. Cleo went where he guided her, stunningly aware of the press of his palm against the base of her spine.

They took the elevator to the office tower. As they stepped into the car, Cleo eased away from him. She turned and backed against the brass railing that ran along the mirrored elevator walls.

They looked at each other, neither of them speaking. She found herself achingly aware of how small the space was, how, with only a step or two, she would be in his arms.

Crazy. Ridiculous. She was not, under any circumstances, going to end up in Fletcher Bravo's arms.

She shifted her gaze, and she was looking at her own reflection in the mirrored wall behind him. Did she look as guilty as she felt?

BONUS FEATURE

Before she could decide if she did or not, the elevator whooshed to a stop and the doors parted.

Marla had a manila envelope all ready for her. Cleo took it with a smile. "Thanks."

From behind her, Fletcher said, "I'll see you to your car."

No way, she thought as she turned to him. She made a joke of her refusal. "You don't want to do that. You saw the way I pull out of parking spaces. I might actually run over you this time."

"I'll take my chances."

Danny had said it that night last week. *He's after you.*

And he was. He *still* was—his hand on hers at the table, his palm settling so possessively at the small of her back as they left the restaurant…

Subtle, knowing touches. What a man does to draw a woman in. Nothing obvious. Nothing blatant. Making it so very easy to pretend it isn't happening…

But it was happening. And she had to stop denying, stop pretending it wasn't.

Guilt tightened her stomach as she remembered how she'd assured Danny that she wasn't interested.

Liar, she silently accused herself. She was interested. She just didn't want to be—no. Wrong, damn it.

She wasn't going to be. She was stopping this

slow and oh-so-clever seduction, stopping it right here and now.

She drew herself up. "No," she said firmly. "I enjoyed the lunch. Thank you."

He held her gaze for a second too long. She felt the heat, zipping back and forth, arcing between them. And then he said silkily, "No need for thanks. I'm pleased that we're going to be working together."

...NOT THE END...

Look for the continuation of this story in
BRAVO FAMILY WAY by Christine Rimmer,
available in March 2006 from
Silhouette Special Edition.

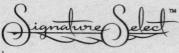

MINISERIES

National bestselling author

Janice Kay Johnson

Patton's Daughters

**Featuring the first two novels in her
bestselling miniseries**

The people of Elk Springs, Oregon, thought
Ed Patton was a good man, a good cop, a good
father. But his daughters knew the truth, and his
brutality drove them apart for years. Now it was
time for Renee and Meg Patton to reconcile…
and to let love back into their lives.

**"Janice Kay Johnson gives readers romance and
intrigue sure to please."—*Romantic Times***

Available in January

Where love comes alive™

If you enjoyed what you just read,
then we've got an offer you can't resist!

Take 2 bestselling love stories FREE!

Plus get a FREE surprise gift!

Clip this page and mail it to Silhouette Reader Service™

IN U.S.A.
3010 Walden Ave.
P.O. Box 1867
Buffalo, N.Y. 14240-1867

IN CANADA
P.O. Box 609
Fort Erie, Ontario
L2A 5X3

YES! Please send me 2 free Silhouette Desire® novels and my free surprise gift. After receiving them, if I don't wish to receive anymore, I can return the shipping statement marked cancel. If I don't cancel, I will receive 6 brand-new novels every month, before they're available in stores! In the U.S.A., bill me at the bargain price of $3.80 plus 25¢ shipping and handling per book and applicable sales tax, if any*. In Canada, bill me at the bargain price of $4.47 plus 25¢ shipping and handling per book and applicable taxes**. That's the complete price and a savings of at least 10% off the cover prices—what a great deal! I understand that accepting the 2 free books and gift places me under no obligation ever to buy any books. I can always return a shipment and cancel at any time. Even if I never buy another book from Silhouette, the 2 free books and gift are mine to keep forever.

225 SDN DZ9F
326 SDN DZ9G

Name	(PLEASE PRINT)	
Address		Apt.#
City	State/Prov.	Zip/Postal Code

Not valid to current Silhouette Desire® subscribers.

Want to try two free books from another series?
Call 1-800-873-8635 or visit www.morefreebooks.com.

 * Terms and prices subject to change without notice. Sales tax applicable in N.Y.
** Canadian residents will be charged applicable provincial taxes and GST.
 . All orders subject to approval. Offer limited to one per household.
 ® are registered trademarks owned and used by the trademark owner and or its licensee.

DES04R   ©2004 Harlequin Enterprises Limited

Signature Select™

COMING NEXT MONTH

Signature Select Spotlight
SUNDAYS ARE FOR MURDER by Marie Ferrarella
FBI agent Charlotte "Charley" Dow is on the hunt for her sister's murderer and finds herself frustrated, yet attracted to agent Nick Brannigan. Working together, Charley and Nick must battle the mind of a psychopath, as well as their own personal demons, to put the serial killer away.

Signature Select Collection
WRITE IT UP! by Elizabeth Bevarly, Tracy Kelleher and Mary Leo
In this collection of three new stories, three reporters for a national magazine are given a unique assignment to write about dating practices for the urban set. And when Julie, Samantha and Abby each get to work, love and mayhem result.

Signature Select Showcase
THE QUIET GENTLEMAN by Georgette Heyer
On becoming the new earl of Stanyon, Gervase Frant returns from abroad to take possession of his inheritance. However, he is greeted with open disdain by his half brother and stepmother. When Gervase becomes prey to a series of staged "accidents," it seems someone is intent on ridding the family of him...permanently.

Signature Select Saga
WEALTH BEYOND RICHES by Gina Wilkins
Brenda Prentiss lived a simple life—until she inherited over a million dollars from a stranger! Now several attempts have been made on her life and her benefactor's son, Ethan Blacklock, is the prime suspect. Ethan must prove to Brenda that he's not out to protect his money...he's protecting *her*.

Signature Select Miniseries
PATTON'S DAUGHTERS by Janice Kay Johnson
The people of Elk Springs, Oregon, thought Ed Patton was a good man, a good cop, a good father. But his daughters know the truth. Both police officers themselves, Renee and Meg have been estranged for years. Now the time has come for the Patton sisters to reconcile... and to let love back into their lives.

The Fortunes of Texas: Reunion
THE LAW OF ATTRACTION by Kristi Gold
Alisha Hart can't believe how arrogant fellow lawyers like Daniel Fortune can be, especially when he offers her a bet she can't refuse. Daniel can't wait long for victory, and soon their playful banter turns into passionate nights in the bedroom. But could this relationship with Alisha cost him the promotion to D.A.?